Show Me How

By Molly McAdams

Show Me How
To the Stars
Trusting Liam
Changing Everything (novella)
Letting Go
Sharing You
Capturing Peace (novella)
Deceiving Lies
Needing Her (novella)
Forgiving Lies
Stealing Harper (novella)
From Ashes
Taking Chances

Coming Soon
I See You

Show Me How

A THATCH NOVEL

MOLLY McADAMS

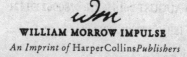

WILLIAM MORROW IMPULSE
An Imprint of HarperCollins*Publishers*

This book is a work of fiction. References to real people, events, establishments, organizations, or locales are intended only to provide a sense of authenticity, and are used fictitiously. All other characters, and all incidents and dialogue, are drawn from the author's imagination and are not to be construed as real.

Excerpt from *I See You* copyright © 2016 by Molly Jester.

EPub Edition AUGUST 2016 ISBN: 9780062391421

Print Edition ISBN: 9780062391438

10 9 8 7 6 5 4 3 2 1

For Amy. Your friendship has been such a beautiful gift to me.

Prologue

Charlie

ONCE UPON A *time* and *happily ever after* . . . words I grew up hearing from Disney and children's stories, and words I'd always believed in. As I grew up and my reading material grew with me, my standards for my Prince Charming morphed, but never lessened. I was so sure I would find my Prince Charming, even if he wasn't as *princely* as I'd dreamed when I was a little girl.

As I said, my reading material had grown with me.

I'd always thought every event in our lives—major or otherwise—was just another part of our story that made us who we were meant to be for our Prince Charming. I knew my story would never be found forever engraved on the pages of a novel, but still I waited for my love story to put all other love stories to shame. For my happily ever after . . .

Only to find out that none of it was real.

Chapter One

Charlie

May 22, 2016

"YOU ONLY GRADUATED three hours ago," my older brother unnecessarily reminded me in that authoritative tone he often used. "Let's just focus on moving you home, and get you settled there for a while. Then when you're ready, you can look into getting your own place. I don't understand why you're trying to rush this."

And I couldn't figure out why he was dismissing the importance of all that I needed to do. "Because I have a court date in a month, Jagger, and I need to have everything done by then. *I* don't understand why you're trying to *stall* this."

"A *month*? Charlie!"

"Jag," his wife began, but didn't continue when Jagger shot her a look.

"She's barely giving herself any time, Grey," he said firmly, then glared at me. "And when were you going to tell us that you set up a court date?"

"You should have known that I would schedule it for as soon as possible."

"It would have been nice to know that you scheduled it at all."

"You knew this was coming!" I said with a frustrated laugh. "This shouldn't be as shocking as you're making it seem."

He blew out a harsh breath. "It's not, and of course we did. I want this to happen for you, but you should've known that you would need time to get everything in order once you got home. A month isn't enough time, Charlie. I would have told you that before today, and you wouldn't have this deadline. We need to push the date back."

"No," I said decisively. "It wouldn't be long enough if I took my time adjusting back to life in Thatch. But I don't need to adjust to life in Thatch, I was only gone for nine months. I've graduated, which was one of the conditions, and as soon as I can, I'm finding a job and I'm moving out."

Jagger groaned and scrubbed his hands over his face. "Do you realize how much easier everything would be for you if you and Keith just stayed with us?"

"Because that will look so great on me. Single mom chooses to live in back room of brother's warehouse with toddler son because it's *easier*." I scoffed. "What would the judge say, Jag?"

Jagger didn't respond, because he already knew.

I dropped my voice so it wouldn't carry into the living room of my off-campus apartment, where my son was playing with Grey's parents and my niece. "Once Keith started talking and saying 'Mama,' I had to spend over a year making sure he wouldn't call *me* his mom until everything finally came out about whose son he really was. Do you have *any* idea how much that killed me?"

Jagger locked his jaw and his eyes darted to the floor, but he didn't respond.

Grey stood a few feet away with both hands covering her mouth, her eyebrows pinched and eyes filled with pain.

I knew they both were imagining having to do the same with their daughter, Aly, who had just started saying "Dada" and "Mama" within the last couple months.

"Then, after all that, he spent the next eight months trying to understand that I *was* his mom, and finally got to the point where he understood it . . . and I left for school. To him, it probably looked like what Mom always did to us, Jagger, just kept leaving. He probably thought I wouldn't come back."

"No, we never let him think that," Grey assured me. "And you were home every other weekend and you Face-Timed every day. He never thought you weren't coming back, Charlie."

I'd already known that, but it never made it easier on me. I waved off her worried look, and waited until I had

Jagger's attention. "You demanded that I *go away* to finish college. I did. I have two more conditions to fulfill from the judge, and nothing will stop me from checking them off as fast as possible so I can get custody of Keith. He's three and a half years old, Jagger. I know you want to help me, but I want my life with him."

One month, I thought to myself. *One month and Keith will finally be my son.* A tremor or fear rolled through me. *Hopefully.*

"Okay," my brother finally said with a deep breath out. "But don't rush into finding somewhere to live just because of this court date. You two have a place with us, and you can stay there as long as you need. That appointment can be pushed back, all right?"

I nodded quickly, though I had no intentions of doing that. I would find the perfect place for us in time. I knew it.

Jagger held my stare for a few more seconds, then took a step away. "I'm gonna start loading up the cars so we can leave soon."

Grey knocked her shoulder into mine once Jagger sauntered away, and whispered, "I'm proud of you for standing your ground."

A soft exhale burst from my chest. "I've never had a problem standing up to him, it's everyone else I have a problem with."

She sent me an amused look. "Charlie, you have a problem even *talking* to other people. But I've never seen you stand up to Jagger like this, I think maybe this time away has helped you come out of your shell just a tiny bit more."

"Wishful thinking. I've been practicing that speech for about a month now." I looked to my front door, and tried to keep the hopeful tone from my voice when I asked, "Speaking of loading up the cars, where's Graham? Are you sure he and Deacon didn't head back to Thatch already?"

Grey's brother, Graham, and his best friends had all been at my graduation, but a couple of them had left directly after in order to get back to work on time. Graham and Deacon, however, had been with us at lunch, and I hadn't seen them since we'd all left to come back to my apartment.

Or, at least, I'd thought we'd all come back here. But we'd been back for close to an hour now, and the guys still hadn't shown.

I wasn't exactly torn up about it, even though having Graham's truck would mean that we would be able to easily fit all of my stuff into the vehicles for one quick trip home.

Grey shook her head and pulled her phone out of her pocket to check the screen. "No, he said they'd meet us back here. Maybe I should call—"

"No, that's okay," I said quickly, happy to prolong my time away from a certain cold, brown-eyed boy.

Just then there was a quick rap on the door before it opened, and Graham and Deacon walked in.

My heart and my stomach betrayed me. Both took off in a dizzying swirl of fluttering wings and too-fast beats that were nearly impossible to ignore until I caught on to what the two guys were talking loudly about . . .

Who had just had the hotter twin.

"That's disgusting," I whispered to myself.

It was also very common for those two.

My arms instinctively wrapped around my waist as I tried to find something or someone to disappear behind. Trying not to draw attention to myself, I stepped slowly back until I was standing behind Grey.

"Wow, moving on to the girls in Walla Walla, huh?" Grey asked. "Must be nice not to have to worry about already having pissed them off."

Graham sent his sister an annoyed look, and Deacon placed both hands on his chest dramatically as he declared, "Grey LaRue, you know you're the only girl for me."

"Easton," Grey and Jagger corrected, at the same time that Graham said, "Dude, she's married and has a baby." Each word was annunciated, as if he'd gotten tired of explaining this over and over again.

Deacon shrugged. "Technicalities. And if I call you Grey Easton, I'm admitting defeat to the guy claiming to be your husband," he said in a teasing tone.

Grey just shook her head as Deacon planted a loud kiss on top of it.

His eyes met mine and turned cold as they dipped down quickly over my body before moving around the apartment.

Irrational, betraying heart.

"Charlie," Deacon mumbled distractedly, irritably. The only word he'd said to me in well over a year.

I was so busy pushing back the anxious and dejected feeling provoked by his cold stare that I didn't bother responding. He probably wouldn't have heard it anyway, or at least pretended not to.

Grey turned to find me behind her. An amused smile joined the sympathetic look in her eyes when she realized what I was doing. One of her eyebrows arched as she stepped away so I was no longer hidden. A challenge to see what I would do.

I didn't move.

"Hey guys," she said, turning her attention back to the newcomers. "I know you just got here, but go help Jagger load up the cars so we can leave."

Deacon nodded as he took slow steps away from us, and pointed toward where the kids were in the living room. "Hey, with the after-lunch special I just had, I'm ready for anything as long as I don't get stuck with one of those things."

"Disgusting," I mumbled again, low enough that it would have been impossible for him to hear me, but his frigid gaze snapped back to me.

Grey made a face at him. "You're gross. And we already know about your aversion to kids, Deacon. We're not going to torture you by making you ride in the car with them."

He looked away from me and clapped loudly, the unexpected sound making me jump. "All right then. Let's do this."

TWO AND A half hours later, the truck and cars were loaded down, we were only a dozen minutes from Thatch, and Keith was talking away . . . to Deacon, who was sitting in my passenger seat.

We could have easily put the last couple boxes in my passenger seat, but Graham had loaded them in his truck instead, and claimed that he didn't have any room for Deacon. Before Deacon could understand the depth of his words, Graham had hopped into his truck and driven away—his booming laugh trailed behind.

Even though Deacon had been around Keith more times than I could count, once Jagger and Grey had *finally* convinced Deacon to get into my car and we had left, he'd spent the first thirty minutes stiff as a board—only moving to look quickly into the backseat to make sure Keith hadn't made a move toward him, even though he was asleep that entire time.

Soon after Keith woke, they'd somehow gotten into a debate about sharks and bears, and which would make a better best friend. Bears would, if you were wondering, because they like honey and Keith thought he liked honey too. And ever since the conversation had started, I hadn't gotten the two to shut up . . .

Not that I'd tried. It kept Deacon's glare from me and took away the uncomfortable silence between us.

" . . . and when the ladybugs land on you, they take your supapowers away."

"What?" Deacon asked loudly, and from the corner of my eye I saw his face drop from where he was turned in his seat to look at my son. "They're going to take my superpowers away? I won't let them. They can't. I have a protective shield."

"They dun care," Keith responded. "They get frew it."

"But they're *my* superpowers."

I glanced into the rearview mirror in time to see Keith shrug, and with a tone that said this disturbing news weighed heavily on his three-and-a-half-year-old self, said, "I dun make the ladybug wules."

A startled laugh burst from my chest before I was able to slap my hand over my mouth.

"This isn't funny, this means war on all ladybugs," Deacon said seriously, but when I glanced at him, the amusement that had been lighting up his face abruptly disappeared.

I looked back at the road and tried to push back the sick feeling twisting through my stomach, weaving through the betraying fluttering that hadn't left since he'd sat next to me.

Deacon turned his head again to face Keith, and jerked back. "Hey, kid. Kid," he called again when he didn't get a response, prompting me to glance at Keith.

"He's asleep," I mumbled.

"But we were just talking."

It took a few moments for me to realize Deacon was watching me, and when I glanced at him, I found his stare expectant. I swallowed past the tightness in my throat, and lifted a shoulder as I attempted to give him the same indifferent tone he always gave me. "Yeah, he has this thing about cars. He always falls asleep as soon as we start driving, and sleeps throughout the drive and for a few minutes after it ends. If the trip is long, he'll sleep through most of it, but I think he wanted to talk to you, so he tried to stay awake once he woke up."

"Huh." There was a brief pause before Deacon said softly, "This kid . . . he's actually really funny. Is he always like this?"

I couldn't contain my next smile. "For the most part. He just talks about the most . . ." I trailed off when I met Deacon's gaze again.

Cold. Unforgiving.

Confusing.

He'd never treated me like this before, and I didn't know what had happened to make him look at me and talk to me the way he did now, seeing as we hardly ever spoke to each other, even when we were in the same room.

Deacon—and Graham and their other best friend, Knox, for that matter—had been in my life for as long as I could remember. Those three boys had been inseparable growing up, which meant all three were often found near Grey, acting as protective older brothers. Where Grey was, Jagger wasn't far behind; and where Jagger went, I went too.

I'd never gotten comfortable enough to talk freely with the boys as I had with Grey, but they'd all been nice. Never hostile. Never like this.

That sickening feeling in my stomach magnified at Deacon's hardened stare, and I didn't understand it. It was as if I deserved this look—but I knew I couldn't. There was nothing I had ever done to him.

"Um, he talks about the most random things. He has a very active imagination." I hurried to finish, each word quieter than the previous one, then stared straight ahead at the road when Deacon's aggravation became too much.

Deacon didn't respond, and after a couple minutes, he straightened in his seat and pulled out his phone for a distraction.

And I was thankful for it. I was able to breathe easier knowing he wouldn't try to talk to me again . . . knowing his eyes were busy.

But then the cemetery that rested just before town came into view, and I thought I might have preferred the sick twisting in my stomach from Deacon to the painful clenching of my heart over a guy who would never see or hold his son.

I TRAILED MY fingers absentmindedly through Keith's hair as he slept sprawled across my lap that evening. We had unloaded everything and gotten my things situated in the warehouse I shared with Jagger and Grey, but I hadn't been able to put off bringing Keith to the cemetery any longer. He'd been begging me ever since he'd woken up that afternoon, and no matter how much my heart rebelled against being here, I knew Keith wanted this . . . *needed* it.

I leaned back, putting my weight on one arm, and let my eyes move from my son to the stone just a foot from where the blanket ended that we were sitting on. The flowers Keith had picked out for him were resting across the base, and something about the look of them bothered me. Like this was all too fresh, too new.

Like I was being sucked back in time four years, to when Ben had been lowered into the ground.

Dozens of beautiful flowers had been on his casket, and even more had been placed on top of the freshly packed dirt. Now whenever we visited his grave with fresh flowers—and Keith demanded we bring new flowers *every* time—all I could think about was that day.

It felt like I'd never get away from it.

Like I'd never get away from the heartbreak and pain I'd gone through before and after he'd died, and then the years of secrets I'd gone through after.

Chapter Two

Charlie

May 25, 2016

"Hammer smash!"

There are those moments when you know something is about to happen; something you should try to prevent. But that feeling is mixed with confusion as you're slowly pulled from your dreams by the yell of your toddler, and it takes a second too long for your muscles to react. And then in a fraction of a second, you're yanked into awareness, and your world is filled with the bright lights of your room . . . and pain.

My eyes cracked open, and I only had a fraction of a second to understand why my son was flying through the air, and to tense my body, before Keith slammed down onto my stomach. I choked out a cough and rolled, sending him sprawling onto the bed.

"Hammer smash! Hammer smash!" he shouted, and jumped for another round of jump-on-Mommy.

Now that I was more alert, I shot my arm out to prevent him from landing on me, and waited until I saw his blue eyes directly in front of my own before I released my hold on his waist.

"Mommy, I see you!"

"Morning," I wheezed out, and rolled onto my back again.

Keith scrambled up until he was sitting on my stomach, and beamed down at me.

Despite the lingering pain in my stomach, my chest swelled with love for the little monster sitting on me. I ran a hand through his dark hair, and asked, "Who are you today?"

His face fell. "Mommy! Hammer!"

I feigned confusion. "Who has a hammer?"

"I do!"

"And who are you?"

"*For*, Mommy." His tone dripped with disappointment that I hadn't guessed.

"Oh . . ." I drew out the word, and nodded slowly. "I thought I might have seen a little Hulk in you this morning, with the 'smash' and all, but I was wrong. You are very clearly Thor."

He sighed. "Mommy . . . Hulk smashes wiff his hands. For smashes wiff his hammer."

I bit back my smile and tapped his nose. "*Hits*. Thor *hits* with his hammer. He also throws it."

Keith took a second to take in my words, and then his eyes lit up. "Hammer frow!" he yelled, but just before he could throw an imaginary hammer at me, I threw my arm up in front of me.

"Captain America shield!"

Keith's hand hit my arm, and grabbed tight. "Mommy!" he whispered in awe, then released my arm to pat it. "Dood shield."

I pulled him close to kiss his forehead, then asked, "What time is it?"

He shrugged against me. "I dunno. But Uncle J is tryin' to make breakfast."

After months away with only weekends to see him, I wanted nothing more than to snuggle up for a few minutes with my son as I had the past mornings; but dangerous, dangerous words had just left his little lips.

Jagger messed up cereal. He'd burn the warehouse down if he actually attempted to cook something.

"Is he?" My voice rose in alarm as I hurried to move *Thor* off my stomach. "Well, I think we should go put a stop to that before we no longer have somewhere to live."

Keith froze, and looked up at me with wide eyes once I was standing. "We can't live here anymore?"

I bit back a curse, and bent so I was at eye level with him. "Of course we can. But Uncle J shouldn't be cooking. Go stop him before . . . just go stop him."

I gave Keith's back a little pat as he turned, and

watched him race from our room. "Uncle J, Uncle J! Mommy said stop! Uncle J! Hammer frow!"

A smile lit up my face as I listened to Keith's voice trailing behind him.

Jagger had been brooding ever since I'd *informed* him that I was moving back to Thatch three days ago. But I would take his moody pouting if it meant I could wake up every day to "hammer smashes," and hear my son's sweet voice echo throughout the warehouse at all hours of the day.

I pulled my long blond hair up into a high ponytail as I emerged from the bathroom minutes later, and padded down the hallways to the front of the warehouse.

This warehouse had been the home of our grandparents' business when Jagger and I were growing up, but had been cleared out and left to Jagger when they passed since they didn't trust our mother to hold on to it.

I didn't blame them.

Our grandparents had left their money equally split among our mother, Jagger, and me. While Jagger used a chunk of his for college and remodeling the warehouse into a place to live, our mom had blown through her third within two years of their passing. For years after, she tried to swindle Jagger out of his, and had even gone after Grey for money when she had spent most of Husband Number Eight's money.

But we hadn't seen or heard from Mom in a year and a half, and as awful as it sounded, our lives were better for it. She had never been a parent, only a person who brought endless heartache, and flitted in and out of our lives for as long as I could remember.

Jagger had raised me. I still had him and Keith. I didn't need anyone else.

My smile from earlier returned when I found Jagger and Keith play-fighting in the living room with Aly crawling after them.

I sniffed dramatically and asked, "Is that burnt water I smell?"

Jagger paused and sent me a sarcastic look. "Ha h-uh! Time out," he wheezed as he slowly fell to his knees, clutching his stomach.

Keith's smirk was victorious. "For *always* beats Loki, Mommy!"

"Of course he does, especially when he takes a cheap shot," I said teasingly, and pulled him into my arms.

"What's that?" Keith asked, excitement dancing in his eyes at the thought of learning something new.

"It's what you just did to Uncle J." I forced back the laugh that was begging to be released when I glanced at Jagger, now lying on his back, still holding his stomach with one hand and attempting to stop Aly from flopping on him with the other. I directed my attention back to my son and whispered, "Can you do something for Mommy?"

Keith nodded vigorously, his blue eyes even brighter. "Yes!" he whisper-yelled back to me.

I squatted down to whisper in his ear, and loved the way he wiggled with anticipation. "Can you go say you're sorry to Uncle J for taking a cheap shot?"

He deflated, and when I pulled back, was giving me a look as though I'd just crushed his dreams. "I guess," he said with a sigh, and trudged slowly over to Jagger. With the same look and sigh, he mumbled, "Uncle J, I'm sorry for taking a cheap shit."

"Oh gosh," I groaned, and dropped my face into my hands as Jagger barked out a laugh. "Stop laughing," I hissed, then looked back up at Keith. "Baby, it's *shot*. Cheap *shot*."

Keith shrugged. "That's what I said!" He looked between Jagger and me, and I could tell he didn't know if he should start laughing as well, but the confusion held out. "Does this mean I didn't beat Loki?"

"Nah, you definitely won this one, bud," Jagger said, his words still laced with amusement.

"Yeah! Hammer frow!" Keith yelled, then tore off out of the main room, back down the hall toward our room.

I walked over to pick Aly up, and lifted an eyebrow as I stared down at my brother. "Did you guys watch anything other than *The Avengers* while I was at school?"

Jagger's eyes widened. "Do you want me to name all the Marvel movies?"

"No need. I get it."

The front door opened, and I turned to see Grey walking in with boxes of food.

I glanced quickly to the kitchen, but didn't see any food out. "I thought you were making breakfast," I said to Jagger, accusation creeping through my tone.

He shrugged impishly as he walked away to help Grey. "Had to get you out of bed somehow."

"Being jumped on by a toddler would have done the

job, you didn't need to make me worry about the safety of the building."

"She's so dramatic in the mornings," he mumbled as he took the boxes from his wife and passed a kiss across her forehead. Jagger's eyes narrowed as they darted over Grey's face, and remained on her as he slowly stepped back toward the kitchen. "And you look extremely happy for someone who barely slept last night."

I made a face. "Ew."

"Not like that!" Grey said quickly.

"*Aly*, Charlie." Jagger shot me an annoyed look. "She was up all night with Aly."

"Anyway!" Grey took Aly from my arms, then swayed away from me. Her eyes were only for her daughter, but her singsong voice floated back to me. "Favor repaid, Charlie. You're welcome!"

"What favor?" When Grey didn't immediately answer because she was busy cooing at Aly, I thought of her excited smile, and wariness crept over me. "Grey . . . what favor?"

Her golden eyes danced when she nodded in Jagger's direction. "You have a job now."

Jagger held up his box-filled hands. "I don't know why she's gesturing to me. I didn't do shit."

Keith's war cry announced his presence before I heard the sound of his slapping feet against the hard floor. "Cheap shit!"

"Well, that's rude and so not appropriate, bud," Grey murmured.

"*Jagger*," I bit out when he laughed loudly. "Keith, baby, it's cheap *shot*."

"That's what I said!" Keith said in exasperation as he slowed to climb up in a chair at the table, where Jagger was now laying out the food.

"People are going to think I cuss around him all the time."

Grey bit down on her bottom lip, but the corners of her mouth still lifted. "We can just blame Jagger."

"Heard that," he called out without lifting his head.

"Again, *anyway*," Grey began, drawing out the word. "I was talking to Mama while I was waiting for our food, and she mentioned needing another person or two at the café. I might have said something about you being back and in need of a job. One thing led to another, and . . . surprise?" she said uneasily when my face fell.

"You got me a job at Mama's Café?"

"Uh . . . yes?" When I didn't respond, she hurried to say, "If you don't want to work there, you don't have to forever. But it's *something* while you try to find a job somewhere in Thatch or around here. Or you don't have to work there at all; I can talk to Mama. I just thought since you pretty much got me the job at The Brew, I would—"

"No! No, it's fine!" I said quickly, and smiled in an attempt to appease her. "I appreciate it, thank you. You're right; I need something and it's always hit or miss with trying to find openings around here. So again, thank you."

Grey still looked worried, like maybe she'd done something she shouldn't have.

"I think working at Mama's will be great!" I said more sincerely. "I'll call down there after breakfast and see when she wants me to come in."

"Um . . . well, she asked if you could come in tomorrow before ten so you don't get slammed with a breakfast or lunch rush right away."

So soon. It felt like I had no time to prepare for being surrounded by people I wasn't used to. Had no time to prepare for what I had been attempting to avoid since I'd moved back to Thatch. For *who* I had been attempting to avoid.

Mama's only grandchild, and someone who frequented Mama's Café: Deacon Carver.

I forced my smile to remain, and nodded in acknowledgment. "Perfect."

Deacon

May 29, 2016

"It's my favorite part of the week!" I boomed as I watched one of my best friends and his fiancée climb out of his truck. "I get to feed Harlow!"

Knox's fiancée shook her head but smiled affectionately. "What do you mean *week*, this is nearly a daily thing," Harlow called out.

"Dude. *I'm* feeding her," Graham said, and shoved at my arm as we walked across the parking lot.

"You both realize by now that she feeds herself, right?" Knox asked once we were closer.

I scoffed. "No. Pretty sure we feed her."

"She isn't a baby."

"*She* also needs to fit into her wedding dress," Harlow butted in, and kissed both Graham's and my cheeks in greeting. "So no more putting extra food on my plate."

"You're no fun," I grumbled.

"Warriors need extra food," Graham added, his tone making it clear that he had no plans to stop.

As if we would no matter what Harlow or Knox said.

Underweight couldn't begin to describe Harlow when she'd come back into our lives nearly a year ago. *At death's door* was a better description.

Beaten, but not broken. Literally skin and bones, but as Graham always said, still a fucking warrior. Bravest and strongest girl I knew, and Graham and I had taken it upon ourselves to get Harlow back to a healthy weight.

Didn't matter that she was nearly there, I doubted either of us would ever stop feeding her. The memory of her bleeding out in our kitchen and barely able to stand after running from her psychotic and abusive husband was burned into my memory, as I knew it was Graham's.

"Let's just eat, I'm starving," Knox said as he pulled Harlow against his side and led her into Mama's Café.

We weren't in there for more than a few seconds before my grandma, Mama, popped around the corner.

"Well if it isn't some of my favorite people!" She hugged us all and then waved us away. "Your booth is there, as always. I gotta get back in the kitchen to make sure all's well."

"The place will still run just fine if you take a break,

Mama," I called out, but knew she wouldn't bother with an answer.

If she wasn't everywhere in her café at all times, she worried it would fall apart. I didn't know why she allowed anyone to work for her since she just tried to do all of their jobs herself anyway.

My eyes caught the back of a slender blonde waiting on a table a few booths away, and dipped down over her subtle curves as I followed my friends to our usual booth.

Then again . . . if it brought in girls who looked like this, I would never complain that Mama hired people.

I slid into the booth, but still had only managed to see the back of the new girl before she was out of my sight.

"New waitress," I mumbled to Graham, and started to lay claim on her in case she looked as good from the front, when he spoke.

"Oh yeah! Wait, you didn't know?"

I leaned away from him, surprised that he knew something about the café that I didn't. "No. And how the hell did you know? You been coming here in the mornings without me?"

Graham's face fell. "First, you sound like a jealous girlfriend. Second, no. Thir—hey!"

Knox and Harlow echoed Graham's greeting, and I turned to see who they were talking to—and immediately regretted it.

My gaze narrowed on the blond girl standing next to our table, just a foot away from me, holding a pad of paper and a pen.

This had to be a fucking joke.

My gaze quickly dipped over her body to confirm that she was in fact the girl I had just been checking out, before slowly sliding up to her face again. She was avoiding looking at me. Not like that was new.

She avoided anyone's eyes if she could.

But this was different. She knew it. I knew it.

And I wanted her gone.

"Charlie," I said through gritted teeth.

Her blue eyes darted to me and away so fast that I would have missed it if I had blinked.

"Uh, hey everyone," she said softly, her discomfort forcing a short huff from my chest.

"Grey said you were working here now. How's your first week been?"

Charlie glanced to Graham, and the corners of her mouth pulled into a shaky smile. "It's only been a few days, but it's been good." She cleared her throat and inched away from me, toward Knox. "What can I get you guys?"

I didn't stop glaring at her the entire time my friends gave their orders, and loved that she looked more and more uncomfortable with each order. When it came time for me, I finally looked away and said, "Mama knows what I want."

I didn't have to be looking at her to know her body had gone still. I could feel it. After a few seconds, she whispered, "Um . . ."

I glanced back up and raised an eyebrow. "This is usually the part where waitresses leave."

"Deacon," Knox rumbled in disapproval.

Graham smacked my arm and said, "Dude, what the hell?"

When I didn't add anything, Knox said, "He wants what Graham's having, Charlie. Thank you." He waited until Charlie was out of the dining area, and in the kitchen before he shoved his foot into my leg. "What Graham said: What the hell?"

"What?"

My friends scoffed, but Harlow just looked around at us as she took in what was happening. She didn't know Charlie well enough to defend her. She didn't know what I knew.

"Don't act like you don't know what we're talking about," Graham hissed. "What'd Charlie ever do to you?"

Of all of us, I was surprised that Graham didn't share my feelings.

Before I could respond, Harlow asked, "Did you try to sleep with her?"

Graham's face fell, and mine twisted in disgust.

"Deacon, you didn't . . ." Graham trailed off. "What'd you do?"

"What did *I* do?" I said with a laugh, and shook my head as I sat back in the booth. "Nothing. And, no, I didn't try to sleep with Charlie." Graham kicked at my leg twice, but I continued. "I wouldn't touch her even if she was in my bed and begging."

The silence that followed my statement felt thick, and I knew before I turned my head that she had come back.

Sure enough, when I looked to my right, Charlie was standing there holding our drinks. She wasn't looking at me, or anyone, just staring at a spot on the table as crimson stained her cheeks.

My stomach dropped and guilt tore through me, but only for a moment before I was able to lock on to my disgust again. She had hurt one of people I loved most in this world. It was about time she hurt too.

She licked nervously at her bottom lip, and had to attempt to speak twice before there was any sound behind the words. "Mama already had your drinks waiting," she explained, but stood still for a few more seconds before she hurried to place the drinks on the table.

"You're an asshole," Knox growled when Charlie left.

Graham was running a hand over his face, and shaking his head slowly. "Get out," he demanded.

"I'm not gonna apologize."

"No shit," he bit back immediately, but he still looked disappointed in my response. "But someone has to for you, and someone needs to make sure she's okay."

"Why?"

Graham's frustration was palpable. "Because it's fucking Charlie, that's why. Now move."

I let him out of the booth, and started to sit back down as he stalked off, but stopped. "Forget it. I'm not hungry." I pulled out my wallet and tossed a ten on the table. "Tell Graham I walked home. See you two later."

I didn't expect a response from them, and didn't wait for one. I just turned and walked out, ignoring my best friend on my way out as he spoke quietly to the girl I never wanted to see again.

Chapter Three

Charlie

May 30, 2016

JAGGER SIGHED FOR the fifth time in as many minutes, and turned his green-eyed stare to me from the driver's seat of my car. He didn't say anything, just gave me "the look." The one I had seen so often growing up with him. The one that meant he was about to switch from my big brother to my parent.

When he didn't say anything, I closed my book and set it down, then relaxed against the side of the warehouse. "Well?"

A dejected laugh fell from his mouth, and he lifted his hands before letting them fall to his lap in defeat. "I don't know what you want me to say. I don't know what's wrong with your car—I know nothing about cars."

My shoulders sagged a little.

"Take it to the mechanic, or better yet—"

"Here we go," I murmured.

"—go buy a new car."

"Jag . . ."

"You can't have a car that doesn't work half the time, Charlie. Especially not now that you're back here and will be driving Keith more. What if you go somewhere with him, and then get stuck?"

"I'll call you?"

His face went void of any emotion. "Charlie. Look, I know I didn't let you touch your money until you turned eighteen, but you've had access to it for four years now—that's plenty of time to get your own car. A *reliable* car."

"It just seems like a waste when I have a car already!"

"Again," he began with a laugh, "a car that only works half the time! This car wasn't exactly new when Grandma left it to you, and then it sat there for years until you were old enough for it." When I started to defend myself and the car again, he cut me off. "You know I wouldn't tell you to spend the money on something like this if I didn't think it was necessary, but it's necessary. It's *been* necessary. You have the money—" He cut off quickly, and his eyebrows drew together. "You do still have your money, right?"

"I'm not Mom," I bit out, and Jagger's face softened.

"I didn't mean it like that. You know I didn't."

I released a weighted breath, my head shook as I tried to push away the initial hurt and anger at his question. "Yeah, I do. Other than school and that apartment in Walla Walla, I've only started a college account for Keith."

He nodded in acknowledgement. What I'd said wasn't news to him. "Then go buy a car. Something Keith can grow into, and you can have for a long time. All right?"

I lifted a shoulder and started to say I'd think about it, but stopped abruptly at Jagger's next demand.

"Until then, take this thing to the mechanic the next time it starts."

That was something I definitely would not be doing. "I'm sure it'll be fine without that." Before he could respond, I grabbed my book and stood, then took a step toward the front door of the warehouse. "I need to go if I'm walking to work."

Jagger looked like he was going to argue about the mechanic, but decided against it. "Take my car today. Keys are on the hook inside."

"Thanks, Jag," I said quickly, and slipped back into the warehouse to grab my purse and his keys before he could find something else to argue with me about—like how I should stop looking for my own place.

It felt like I didn't take a full breath until I was in his car and pulling out of the alleyway. I'd made it through another parental-type lecture from Jagger; now if only I could make it through this shift without Mama's favorite person coming in to pin me with his cold stare.

Deacon

May 30, 2016

My phone began ringing just as I pulled into work. A glance at the screen had me hissing out a curse when I caught sight of the name.

I'd been expecting this call ever since I'd walked out of Mama's the morning before, and was surprised it had taken him this long to ream me. Or maybe I was surprised that she hadn't immediately run home to tell her brother about what I'd said.

I shut off my car, and took a steadying breath as I answered the call. "Yeah, Jagger?"

"You working today?"

My brow pinched when he didn't immediately begin laying into me, and I glanced up at the building in front of me. "Uh, yeah . . . just pulled in. Why?" I asked, drawing out the word.

"When you get a break today, can you do a favor for me?"

My initial surprise deepened when I realized Charlie hadn't mentioned anything about the day before as Jagger went on, but my frustration over her slowly filled my veins once the *favor* was laid out for me.

I opened my mouth to say no, but shut it and sighed through my nose.

Grey would kill me if I said no, and it would unnecessarily bring up a discussion with Jagger right then that I didn't want to have.

After a few seconds, I conceded. "Sure. Yeah, I'll be there."

Charlie

May 30, 2016

Who listened to your ~~stories~~ sad songs
The shoulder that you cried on
Out on that cliff you walked on
When

I rapidly tapped the edge of my pen against the pages of my notebook as all of the words in the world failed me.

"When . . ." I said under my breath. "When you . . . no."

I let my eyes slide shut and imagined a simple melody, and tried to hear my words interwoven with the notes, but each time I stopped on that last word. Something felt off about what I had already written down, and I knew that when I fixed it, I would be able to go on.

My mom had always taken credit for my ability to sing and write poetry, which had turned into writing songs, just as she had taken credit for Jagger's amazing ability to draw—as long as music was blasting nearby. Saying it was all because she'd named us after members from her favorite band, the Rolling Stones, and had had music playing nonstop while we were growing up.

Except she hadn't really been around while we were

growing up, and—as she chose to forget—I spent most of my time reading novels, and would have preferred to have the ability to write them. But I'd never been able to figure out how to expand my dreams into something longer than the poems and songs that filled this notebook when inspiration hit.

And this song . . . these *words* were begging to get free, but my thoughts were scrambled after having locked that night with Ben away for years.

I ran through the words in my mind again and again. Just as I stopped my furious drumming on the paper to write down a few more words that had burst into my mind, the door to Mama's opened, and my break ended as the beginnings of the lunch rush came filing in. I hurried to get out of the booth and smiled timidly at the two groups of people. Grabbing a handful of menus, I led the first to my section at the back of the restaurant as the words I had worked so hard to unscramble slid from my mind.

It wasn't until I reached into the far left pocket of my waist apron for a check holder nearly an hour later that I realized why my apron had felt so odd since the lunch rush had begun.

My notebook wasn't in there.

I spun in a circle to face the front of the restaurant. Fear and embarrassment flooded me as I scanned the filled booths up there.

"Charlie."

My head snapped up at the sound of my name, and

I stared wide-eyed at Wendy, another waitress, as she looked me over, plates of food balanced precariously along her arm.

"You okay?" she asked.

"What?"

Her eyes darted over my face quickly again, her eyebrows pulled together. "Are you okay? You're just staring off with a check in your hand. Did a table run out on you?"

"No! No, nothing like that. I just . . . I just realized that I left my notebook at one of the booths in your section." Before I could tell her that it contained words that were somewhat personal, her eyes lit up with acknowledgement.

"Is it brown, soft leather?"

"Yes!" I said in relief.

"Well, whoever found it left it on the desk up front. I just saw it there when I went to grab menus to seat a couple. I put it in the cabinet up there."

"Thanks, Wendy." My voice still ached with the relief I felt, but the thought that someone had possibly read my words had my cheeks darkening from my embarrassment.

I hurried to take the check to my waiting table, then rushed into the kitchen to grab another's food as I tried to force unwanted thoughts from my mind.

But throughout the rest of my shift, all I could think about was that someone had held my notebook; had seen my words. Even Jagger knew not to touch my notebook or ask to see what I wrote in there. And I wondered what the stranger, or strangers, had thought. Had they mocked my darkest dreams and deepest thoughts? Had they been immature and destroyed them? Had they torn the ink-filled pages out to be hateful?

Each pass to the front desk to seat newcomers left me itching to grab the notebook from the cabinet, but I'd known I wouldn't be able to stop myself from inspecting the pages right then instead of doing my job.

It was a long three hours.

As soon as I clocked out, I nearly ran to the front. Dread filled me and my hands shook as I finally opened the cabinet, and I dropped to my knees to reach in and rip my notebook from its depths.

After wasting only half a second to run my hand over the cover, I opened my notebook and quickly scanned each page. My worry lessened with each piece of paper that slid beneath the tips of my fingers. A soft, nearly inaudible laugh bubbled from my throat when I got to the page I'd been working on during my break, and I started to shut the notebook when I realized what I'd just seen.

A different-colored pen.

More words crossed out. More added.

A note on the side of the page in a messy, masculine scrawl that most definitely did not belong to me.

Who listened~~ed~~S to your ~~stories~~ sad songs
The shoulder that you ~~cried~~ CRY on
Out on that ~~cliff~~ LEDGE you ~~walked~~ walk on
When

The note on the side read:

RIGHT . . . SO I DON'T KNOW YOU, BUT I'M
NOW FUCKING TERRIFIED FOR YOU. IF
I HAD THE TIME, I'D WAIT TO SEE WHO
SHOWED UP LOOKING FOR THIS JOURNAL.
I CHANGED SOME WORDS BECAUSE I WANT
YOU TO KNOW THAT I'M HERE LISTENING
TO YOU. AND "CLIFF" SOUNDED SO FINAL.
DON'T LET WHATEVER YOU'RE FEELING BE
FINAL. I'LL BE BACK. WILL YOU HOLD ON IF
YOU KNOW I'M COMING BACK FOR YOU?

I read the note again . . . and then again. Each time my brow pinched tighter. I glanced up at the few words I'd managed to get out during my break, then let my face fall into the pages of the notebook as a groan escaped me.

I sat down right there, behind the greeter's desk of Mama's Café, and rewrote the small part I already had, and added the words that were now flowing to my fingers because of the smallest change this stranger had made.

> Who listens to your sad songs
> The shoulder that you cry on
> Out on that ledge you walk on
> When you're sinking
> Who ~~knows your~~ keeps your secrets locked up
> When ~~I'm~~ there's no one you can trust
> I know it's much more than just wishful thinking
> Just say the words and I'll be there

The last line I threw in because of the stranger's note, and smiled to myself at the words. Then below their note, I wrote my own response:

> I'm sorry if I scared you, but I'm not suicidal. (I believe that's what you were thinking?) This is actually about a pseudo-relationship with a guy. I appreciate your words, and I believe anyone who had been thinking of ending their life would have loved receiving your note. As much as I want to know who this heroic stranger is, I need to get home. However, I will leave this here in hopes that you find it, and that it gives you peace of mind.

I stood and placed my notebook on top of the desk with a note below asking for the notebook to be left there. Then, despite the way my body rebelled at the action, I forced myself to walk away from my notebook and out of Mama's Café.

Chapter Four

Charlie

May 30, 2016

I PULLED INTO the alleyway beside the warehouse minutes later, my mind still reeling from the stranger who had taken the time to write to someone they didn't know. I brought Jagger's car to an abrupt stop when I saw Keith dart from the warehouse to the front of my car, where it still sat from that morning.

I watched as he disappeared behind the propped-up hood of my car, and my stomach dropped.

I looked around the alleyway, but saw only Grey's car in its usual spot. I tried to think if I'd seen any other cars parked on the street on my way in, but I'd been so consumed in another's words that I hadn't been paying attention.

My fingers danced anxiously on the steering wheel as I contemplated leaving, or finding another way to get into the warehouse—like a window—where I wouldn't have to walk past my car, and eventually I blew out a harsh, determined breath.

For all I knew, Jagger was attempting to figure out the problem with my car again. Doubtful, but not completely improbable.

But no matter how many times I told myself that my brother was there, I knew better. I knew who was standing behind that hood. And just the thought of seeing him made my stomach clench and my body tremble.

I pulled Jagger's car behind mine and shut it off. With another deep breath in, I stepped out and walked toward the sound of my son's animated voice. Each step felt weighed down and harder than the one before it.

When *his* voice wove between Keith's words, I faltered. This was the problem with Thatch. There were no strangers in this town. Everyone knew everyone else's business. And there was nowhere to hide.

Shops closed down if the owners wanted to go spend time on the lake, and businesses made house calls.

Like the auto repair shop: Danny's Garage.

Like the mechanics there.

Especially when the owner's son was Deacon Carver.

Maybe I needed to leave. Take Keith and find a place to live somewhere outside this town. Because attempting to hide from the guy whose family practically owned Thatch was proving to be impossible.

"Aliens came from a spot in the sky."

"Aliens!" Deacon said in a shocked voice. "Where?"

Keith sighed. "They're not here anymore. I'm Iron Man. I made them go back."

Deacon sighed dramatically. "Kid, I don't know what the world would do without you."

"I know," Keith said seriously. "But that's why no one can fix Mommy's car, not even *you*! Because aliens hurted it."

I walked into their view in time to see Deacon fighting a smile, his mouth slightly open to respond. But his large frame tensed when he caught sight of me, and his mouth fell into a sneer.

Irrational, betraying heart.

"Mommy!" Keith shouted as he barreled into my legs.

"Hey, honey," I said softly, and ran a hand through his hair as he began talking a mile a minute.

"Mommy, Deaton's tryin' to fix your car, but I told him he couldn't fix your car. Because the aliens came after it. Right, Mommy? But I'm Iron Man and I made them go away so they can't come after any more cars."

"I heard. I could've sworn I was woken up by Captain America this morning."

He sighed. "That was like, five years ago!"

"Oh, of course," I said as I fought my own smile, and turned us toward the warehouse. "Why don't we go inside so Deacon can work?"

My son's face fell, but it was Deacon who responded.

"*He* isn't bothering me," he said in a gruff voice.

There was an odd pang in my chest as his words from the day before mixed with his implication then. Embarrassed heat crawled up my face, and despite how hard I tried not to, I looked over my shoulder at the angry scowl on his face.

Light brown eyes were narrowed on me, as cold as ever.

Again, the way he looked at me made me feel as though I deserved his anger—and I wanted to hate him for it.

"Keith, go inside."

"But—"

"Go inside," I whispered, but my tone left no room for discussion.

After an exaggerated huff, he trudged into the warehouse.

My embarrassment and hurt and anger snapped with the sound of the door shutting. "What did I ever do to you?" I demanded through clenched teeth, and turned to fully face Deacon as he pushed from my car, and rose to his full height.

"To me? Not a damn thing."

A frustrated laugh burst from my chest, but my eyes pricked as tears gathered in them. "Then why have—why are you—I don't understand . . ." I trailed off, fumbling for the words as he slowly closed the distance between us.

For each step he took toward me, I took two back.

For as long as I could remember, Deacon had called

me "Charlie Girl" and had tried to joke with me in an attempt to bring me out of my shell. But that Deacon had been missing for years. Out of his friends, he had been the fun one and nearly always had a lax smile and booming laugh . . . but that guy was nowhere to be found now.

Grey always referred to Deacon as a teddy bear. The man in front of me was anything but.

He was tall and had a large, intimidating frame, courtesy of his love for the gym. His white shirt stretched tight over his chest and shoulders, and was stained with grease, as was his jaw. His dark hair was wild from running his hands through it over the course of the day. And his honey-colored eyes, darkened with frustration, highlighted the angry set of his mouth, which curled into a taunting smile when I backed into the warehouse wall.

"You gonna try to finish that thought, Charlie?" he asked in a low voice. "Is the shy, sweet girl trying to find a backbone for once? Oh wait, no, you know all about backs, don't you? You were probably on yours when you got pregnant."

My mouth slowly fell open as his words tore through me. "What?" The word was nearly inaudible, but I couldn't find my voice anymore.

"Everyone around here acts like you've done nothing wrong, and I don't fucking get it. Shy, sweet Charlie," he mocked again. "No one would have ever expected you to try to ruin a relationship—and who knows how much longer you would've gotten away without anyone knowing?"

"You know *nothing*," I choked out.

He placed his hands on the wall above me, and leaned

down. "I know you fucked Grey's fiancé . . . that's all I need to know."

"It wasn't—"

"It wasn't *what*?" he asked in a dangerous tone, cutting me off. "Somehow you have everyone around us feeling *sorry* for you because you had to "deal" with Ben's death alone. Had to hide the pregnancy, and then pretend Keith wasn't yours. None of that would have happened if you'd kept your legs closed in the first place."

"You're an asshole."

Deacon barked out a sharp laugh. "Why? Because I'm the only one who would dare be mad at *innocent* Charlie for what she did to a girl who is like my sister? Because I'm not as blind as the rest of them? You somehow twisted the situation around so that everyone was not only mad at, and blaming, Ben for something that *you* had equal part in, and then lied about for years; but you also had them feeling fucking sorry for you! Forgive me for seeing the situation for what it was," he said with a sneer, then pushed away from me and turned back toward my car, but called over his shoulder, "Go on, go tell Grey and Jagger so they can feel sorry for you some more."

I wiped at the few tears that managed to fall, and gritted out, "I don't need or want anyone to feel *sorry* for me. I have never claimed to be innocent, and I will always hate myself more than anyone else could for what I did to Grey. But I will never be able to regret what happened because it gave me Keith, and he is the best thing in my life."

"What?" He glanced over at me from where he was now bent under the hood again. "You mean the kid you pawned off on your brother for a year? Yeah, excuse me if I don't buy your *perfect mother* act, either."

No! A shuddering breath left me as fear and lifelong insecurities clawed at me. *He doesn't know me; I'm not like my mother,* I thought desperately.

As soon as he released me from his cold stare, I turned and slipped inside the warehouse, letting the weight of my body shut the door as I stumbled back against it.

I looked up at the ceiling and blinked quickly, trying to force the tears away, but my chest still heaved with a silent sob.

I wanted to hate him. I wanted to hate him so much . . . but I couldn't. Because Deacon had just said everything I'd been thinking of myself for years.

Ben, Jagger, and Grey had been best friends for most of their lives, and even though Ben had been with Grey for years, I'd loved him for as long as I could remember. He was my Prince Charming, my white knight coming to rescue me from my tower, my everything . . . even if only in secret.

It wasn't until the spring of my senior year of high school that I'd found out my feelings hadn't been one-sided.

"Why do I want you so bad when I love her? And why do I love her when I know she should be with him?" Tortured, whispered words I'd waited years to hear, and words I would never forget.

For two nights, my fairy tale seemed to come true. For two nights, everything seemed to finally be right in the world. I had Ben, and Jagger would finally have Grey. The way it was always meant to be.

Before I could even begin to grasp the high Ben had given me, he yanked it away the night he asked Grey to marry him, and drove the knife a little deeper when he told me that what we'd done was a mistake. As I had told Deacon, a mistake I would never regret, because it gave me my son. But months later, just before their wedding, Ben had died from an undetected, rare heart condition. He'd known about Keith, but only for a short time before he was gone.

Upon my mom's demand, I kept the pregnancy a secret, pretended it was her child, and didn't tell anyone the truth until Keith was two years old.

I've never felt so free as when those words left my lips.

Not because a secret that had been weighing on me was finally out in the open, but because after years, I was finally allowed to grieve for the only love I'd ever had.

And now, four years after his death, and I still hurt. It felt like a weight was pressing on my chest when I thought of him, making it nearly impossible to breathe. It felt like something vital to my body and soul had been ripped from me.

Four years later, and I still wanted to hate him for what he'd done to me, and the way he'd treated me, in those last months. I wanted the chance to yell at him face to face for telling me that he loved me, but wasn't *in* love with me, after taking everything from me and making me believe that we could have it all.

Four years later, and I was still so sure that I was in love with him despite everything. I had a feeling the greatest love I would ever know had been taken from me too soon—and I would never know anything like it again.

Four years later, and guilt still clawed at my chest whenever I thought of how I betrayed Grey, even though she had clearly found her happy ever after with my brother.

And Deacon Carver had taken it, all of my grief and my hatred and my guilt, and thrown it in my face.

Fast, little footsteps sounded down the hallways, headed in my direction.

I quickly swiped at another tear that fell free, and blew out a slow, calming breath before pushing away from the door. I turned just in time to watch Keith fly into the living room—his smile was wide, and his face smudged with black streaks.

"Look, Mommy! Now I'm like Deaton and Uncle J!"

My stomach clenched, but my smile didn't falter as I lifted him into my arms to get a better look at his charcoal-covered face. "Wow, look at you! Is Uncle J drawing?"

He nodded enthusiastically, then began squirming. "I wanna go show Deaton!"

"Uh . . ." I sucked in air through my teeth, and scrunched up my nose. "How about not right now, buddy? He's busy, remember?"

Grey and Aly emerged from the hall, quickly followed by Jagger.

"What do you think?" Jagger asked, beaming at me. Just like Deacon, he had black smudges on his jaw, and his hands were stained the same.

Only difference was Jagger created art to earn those stains, and Deacon was probably destroying my car out of spite.

Before I could answer, Keith repeated, "I wanna go show Deaton!"

I hesitated before letting him down. "Okay . . . but only for a second!" I added on quickly. "He's busy."

"All right!" Keith shouted, and rushed out of the building.

I didn't realize I was staring at the closed door, chewing on my bottom lip until Grey bumped my shoulder with hers.

"You look red, you okay?"

"Huh?" I said quickly, and turned to look at her and a sleepy Aly.

"I said you're red. Are you okay?"

I tilted my face away from Jagger when he came toward me. "Yeah, just a long day." At least it wasn't a lie.

Grey's calculating eyes roamed over me, but Jagger spoke before she could.

"What'd Deacon say?"

My next breath got caught in my throat, and my body stilled as I finally met Jagger's gaze. My voice came out breathy as I fought against the trembling I had only just succeeded in stopping moments before. "What do you mean?"

"About your car?" he responded slowly, drawing out the words.

"Oh." I hoped the relief that washed through me wasn't noticeable. "Um, I'm not sure. Car talk I don't understand." I glanced back at the door and mumbled, "I should get Keith before Deacon freaks out that a child is near him."

Grey laughed. Jagger just shrugged and said, "Deacon said he's funny. Keith's been out there most of the time with him, and Deacon hasn't gone into hiding yet. I'm sure he's fine."

But I'm not.

Not to mention I was terrified that Deacon's hatred for me would eventually bleed over to Keith.

I was walking toward the door before I knew I was moving, and once I had it open and those light brown eyes snapped up to me and hardened, I realized I hadn't thought of a real reason to pull Keith away.

I ignored my racing heart and fluttering stomach, and the embarrassment that still filled my veins, and looked down at Keith with a forced smile on my face. "Come on, buddy."

"Mommy," he said in disappointment.

"I've been gone all day, I want time with you too."

Deacon's disbelieving sneer forced my eyes back up to him, but he didn't say anything.

He doesn't know me; I'm not like my mother. He doesn't know me; I'm not like my mother, I reminded myself, and forced myself not to react. *I refuse to be her.*

"Besides, I'm sure Deacon will be leaving soon," I said through clenched teeth; the hint that I wanted him gone was clear.

He laughed haughtily and nodded as he glanced back into the car. "Yeah. Yeah, kid, I'm done here, just need to clean up."

Keith nodded, as if he'd been waiting for Deacon's dismissal, and walked toward me. "See ya later, Deaton!"

I shut the door before Deacon could respond, and turned to see my brother and his wife watching me with expressions ranging from worried to curious.

Not willing to let them question anything they may have interpreted from Deacon's or my tone, I clapped and turned to my son. "What do you say we watch *Iron Man* while I start making dinner?"

He sent me a cheesy smile. "Watch myself? Mommy . . . you're silly." But he still turned and raced toward the couches. "Last one there's an egg!"

For the first time since I'd arrived home, my smile was genuine. "It's *rotten* egg, buddy!"

"That's what I said!"

But throughout *Iron Man*, dinner, and relaxing with my family . . . I was distracted. Deacon's hateful words had long since slipped from my mind, and been replaced with a messy scrawl I couldn't stop seeing.

Every glance at the clock with the hopes that it would be an acceptable time to go to sleep left me trying to convince myself that my restlessness was simply because I had purposefully left my soul at Mama's in the form of a notebook.

But I knew I was lying to myself.

I knew I was letting my mind run wild with possibilities.

I wanted to get to work the next day to see if the stranger had come back. I wanted to see if I would find out anything more about them—about *him*, I had decided based on the messy scrawl. I wanted to see if he would have anything to add or change about the song. I wanted to know if he would still care at all once he knew I had no plans to take my own life.

The thought that something would be waiting for me the next day had a ridiculous smile creeping across my face, and a giddy excitement coursing through my veins.

Deacon

May 30, 2016

After leaving the warehouse, I stopped by the garage to see if there was anything else my dad needed before the day ended, then hurried to clean up before racing over to Mama's Café. I barely acknowledged the familiar voices and faces when I stepped inside, my attention immediately going to the top of the greeter's desk.

To anyone looking at me, I was calm.

On the inside, it felt like I was dying. It was as if I'd just finished running a race, when instead I'd driven over here and walked inside. My chest felt tight and my stomach was churning. The past hours could have meant something I refused to think of for someone I didn't know. And all I could think of was that if I had stayed in the café, if I had waited for the owner of the journal to come back, I might have changed their mind.

But then my eyes fell on the journal—exactly where I had left it. For a moment, the sight of the brown leather left a sinking feeling in my gut until I noticed the small slip of paper below it, with the words: Please leave here, neatly scrawled across it.

The handwriting looked too familiar not to recognize. I doubt I would ever forget it after having stared at it for so long earlier—after trying to decode the words they'd formed.

I took a second to glance around to see if anyone was watching me—expectantly or not—then snatched the journal and paper from the desk and walked quickly toward the booth I always sat at.

I flipped through the pages until I found the one I was looking for, but only had time to see that there was something written below my note before I had to stash the journal next to me when one of the waitresses walked up.

"Well, well . . . Deacon Carver. What can I do for you tonight?" she asked. Her voice dripped with sex, and her tone held so much meaning. The look she gave me promised a night I knew I needed after the day I'd had.

I couldn't remember her name, I rarely tried to remember their names, but I remembered *her*. If I hadn't already known from personal experience that she was bat-shit crazy, I had no doubt I would have told her to come to the house that night.

Unfortunately for her—and my memories—I didn't forget girls who wrecked houses and screamed like banshees when they found out I didn't want to be tied down, and I also didn't have the patience to deal with her now.

I'd been consumed with stress and guilt all day over finding what I thought was the beginnings of a fucked-up suicide note, had just released a year-and-a-half's worth of pent-up anger on Charlie because I couldn't seem to control myself around her lately—and was hating myself for it—and now this waitress was keeping me from seeing what had been written back to me.

"Absolutely nothing," I responded gruffly. "Whoever is cooking right now, tell them I need the usual for Graham and me. To go."

I stared at her expectantly until she turned with an exaggerated huff, and waited until she was back in the kitchen before pulling the journal back up.

The relief that pounded through my veins as I read the note written back to me was so intense that my hands began shaking.

They hadn't been about to commit suicide—she *hadn't been about to*, I internally amended as I stared at the neat, feminine handwriting.

A harsh, relieving breath forced itself from my lungs, and I had to set the journal on the table when the shaking of my hands made it too hard to read the words again.

And again.

She'd added more to what I had originally thought was the beginning of a suicide note, and now thought might be a poem. If what was in front of me then had been written down earlier that afternoon, I probably wouldn't have spent hours panicking that this girl was going to kill herself.

I wouldn't have said what I had to Charlie.

I ran my hand through my hair, agitation poured from me as I tried to force her face from my mind.

With a rough breath out, I focused on the poem . . . but after reading it again, I still felt depressed as shit for the girl. Because if this was supposedly about her relationship with a guy, then she had no fucking clue that he was using her, or that she was nothing more than the best friend. Because those words pretty much summed up how Graham, Knox, and I all talked to, and thought of, Grey.

Sister. This girl wasn't in a relationship, she was thought of as a sister.

After grabbing a pen from a different waitress as she passed by, I added a couple words to the last line, and wondered why the hell I was smiling over the fact that she'd left my other changes in as I wrote back to her.

YOU'RE ALIVE! CHRIST, YOU HAVE NO
CLUE HOW DAMN SCARED I'VE BEEN ALL
DAY. BUT I THINK WE MIGHT HAVE OTHER
PROBLEMS NOW. THIS RELATIONSHIP . . .
ARE YOU SURE YOU WANT TO BE IN IT?
YOU SAY YOU'RE ALWAYS THERE FOR
THIS GUY, LISTENING TO HIM ABOUT
EVERYTHING APPARENTLY . . . SO WHO'S
THERE FOR YOU? WHO'S LISTENING TO
YOU? I DON'T KNOW YOU, AND YOU DON'T
KNOW ME—OR, HELL, MAYBE WE DO; THIS
IS THATCH—SO YOU DON'T HAVE TO LISTEN
TO ANYTHING I SAY. BUT FROM WHAT
I'M READING, I THINK YOU'RE PUTTING
WAY MORE OF YOURSELF INTO THE

RELATIONSHIP THAN HE IS. FIND SOMEONE
WHO WOULD WRITE THESE WORDS ABOUT
YOU.

Who listens to your sad songs
The shoulder that you cry on
Out on that ledge you walk on
When you're sinking
Who ~~knows your~~ keeps your secrets locked up
When ~~I'm~~ there's no one you can trust
I know it's much more than just wishful thinking
Just say the words and (<u>YOU</u> KNOW) I'll be there

Before I left Mama's with dinner for Graham and
me, I placed the journal back on the greeter's desk with
the same piece of paper just below it. Only this time, I
copied her words in my own writing on the back, warning anyone who saw the journal not to move it.

Chapter Five

Charlie

May 31, 2016

I PRACTICALLY RAN into work the next morning; my footsteps only slowed once I was inside and spotted my notebook where I'd left it the day before. I glanced around at the few workers already inside—none of whom were looking in my direction—and walked up to the greeter's desk.

I took the torn paper between my fingers, and eyed his scrawl in wonder. I didn't realize I was smiling until I had flipped the paper over numerous times, looking at each side and how our words mimicked each other's.

But the smile faded when I read the note he had left for me.

I wanted to write back, saying that I'd thought *he* was listening to me, but knew those words sounded immature and ridiculous given the situation. Just as my excitement to hear back from a stranger had been.

What I had been expecting, I couldn't say, but it had been more than that.

Maybe Grey was right. Maybe I did read too many romance novels.

I started to crumple the torn out paper, but stopped and placed it inside my notebook instead. After closing it up, I placed the notebook inside my waist-apron pocket behind the check holders, and got to work.

FIVE HOURS INTO my shift, on one of the many journeys up to the front of Mama's Café to greet newcomers, something caught my eye.

A napkin on the greeter's desk with a familiar scrawl on it, and the words:

WHERE'D YOU GO? I'LL COME BACK FOR YOU.

I inhaled softly, and a stupid, *stupid* fluttering took up residence in my stomach. One I knew needed to go away because there was no reason for it to be there in the first place, but one that was there nonetheless.

I glanced at the three people in front of me, quickly taking in the confused looks they were giving me before slapping my hand down on the napkin and pulling it close to my body.

I whirled around to see if anyone was watching, waiting for someone who would have a reaction to that note . . . but there was no one. Just residents of Thatch eating, others serving, nearly all people I had known most of my life. None of them paid any attention to me, or the chaos of emotions flooding me.

Again, *stupid* fluttering and emotions that made no sense. Because this person was nothing more than an opinionated stranger, and I was making him and this situation out to be much more than they were because of my obsession with romantic fiction.

"Um, table for three?" I asked through the lump in my throat, and shoved the napkin into one of my pockets so I could grab menus. "Right this way."

By the time I left work that night, my notebook was on the desk, the slightly crumpled piece of paper had been smoothed out, and had my plea not to move the book facing up. No words had been added to Ben's song, but there was a note left to the stranger.

> You gave me relationship advice that was a few years too late; I didn't know you expected a response. Since you want one: Thank you, stranger. I'll make sure to remember your words for the next guy who comes into my life.

I didn't work the next day, but there was a response waiting for me when I came in the day after. And though I tried to watch the front desk as much as possible, I never saw anyone take my notebook. I had studied almost everyone who sat in the café, studied everyone working . . .

no one seemed to touch it, and no one seemed to watch me. But by the time my shift had ended that day, there was already a response.

> IS THIS WHERE I SAY THAT I'M SORRY THAT YOU AREN'T WITH THIS GUY ANYMORE? BECAUSE I'M NOT. I DON'T KNOW IF IT'S BECAUSE THAT GUY WAS A DUMBASS FOR TREATING YOU THE WAY HE DID, OR IF AFTER READING MOST OF WHAT YOU HAVE WRITTEN IN THIS JOURNAL, I'VE DECIDED THAT I WANT TO BE THE ONE WHO GETS TO LISTEN TO YOU.

> *Those are big words, stranger. Words can be deceiving. Are you so sure that once you find me, there will be any words to listen to at all? Maybe this is all I have . . .*

> YOUR WORDS HAVE KEPT MY INTEREST LONGER THAN ANY GIRL HAS EVER BEEN ABLE TO. I'LL TAKE MY CHANCES. WHO ARE YOU?

> *Won't that ruin everything?*

Because it could, and would, ruin everything for me. I was just Charlie. Shy Charlie who struggled to talk to anyone outside of Jagger and Grey, and who definitely couldn't talk to guys. Shy Charlie, who, in the real world, had a toddler and no clue what she was doing with her life.

Chapter Six

Deacon

June 3, 2016

I GROANED INTO my hands as I scrubbed them over my face, and leaned back in the driver's seat of my car. "This thing is gonna be a disaster."

"What?" Graham asked as he shut the passenger door. "The dinner?"

"The dinner. The wedding. The whole damn thing."

A low laugh rumbled from him. "Don't tell me you suddenly hate Harlow again?"

I slid my gaze over to him and narrowed my eyes. "No. But her older sister sure as hell hates me, and I have to be paired with her."

We'd just finished the rehearsal for Knox and Harlow's wedding, and it was the second time I'd ever seen her sisters. I was also hoping it could be the last. But seeing as Graham was walking her younger sister down the aisle, and I was walking with the older one, and we were about to head over to the rehearsal dinner, I knew I still had at least another day with them.

Graham's face went blank for a second before he smacked my arm. "You didn't."

"Didn't what?"

"Dude, she's married and has kids!"

My face pinched. "No. Hell no. I'm not about to have some guy coming after me for trying to sleep with his wife, and no way in hell would I touch a chick with kids. But I flinched away from one of her kids when they came running over to her, and she got pissed."

Graham smirked. "Yeah . . . what'd you say to make her get pissed, though?"

He knew me too well.

I turned on my car and pulled out of the parking spot before I gave a slow shrug. "I don't know, something about kids and Satan and maybe connecting the two."

Another laugh, this one louder. "I'm putting money on it right now. Hundred bucks you'll be the first of us to have kids."

A sickening feeling filled my stomach, causing it to churn. "Fuck that. The day I get married is the day I see the doctor about making sure that shit isn't possible."

"A thousand," Graham amended. "Thousand dollars."

"Done. I will enjoy taking your money when Harlow pops one out."

It wasn't as though I had an aversion to humans under the age of ten, I just . . . okay, I had an aversion to them. A strong one.

They had imaginary friends, which weirded the shit out of me. They never shut up. Constant babble about any- and everything, as long as it didn't make sense. They smelled. They were always covered in food. They sneezed on you. And they pooped on themselves and other people . . . including unsuspecting teenage mechanics holding them while their mom searched for her wallet.

No baby should be able to produce so much shit that it comes out of their clothes. It isn't natural. Almost a decade later, and I still had nightmares about it.

Anyone who wanted kids was out of their damn mind.

We pulled up to Jagger and Grey's warehouse—since it had a big-enough space for all of us—just after Harlow's older sister and her family did. The glare she sent toward my car was enough to make me want to ditch the dinner.

"Do you think we could ask Harlow if we could switch sisters?"

Graham sighed as he opened the door to step out of my car. "If it makes you more comfortable . . . then no."

"Asshole," I mumbled under my breath as I stepped out, and pulled my phone out of my pocket to check the lock screen.

Something like disappointment settled in my stomach when there was nothing new, and I sighed through my nose as I put my phone away. My mind was already away from Harlow's terrifying sister, and back at Mama's

Café. My thoughts on nothing but a journal full of words people just didn't say out loud . . .

My next step faltered when I looked up and caught Graham watching me.

"What are you doing?"

I let my eyes dart around us, then said in an unsure tone, "Walking . . ."

"You checked your phone every three minutes during the rehearsal, and twice while we were driving. I know what phone that is, Deac. Can't you keep it in your pants for a couple nights, for Knox?"

A disbelieving huff burst from my chest. "A couple nights? I haven't gotten laid in—" I cut off quickly, and tried to think back to when the last time had been. "It's been almost a week."

Graham's surprise didn't last. "Doesn't matter. It's Knox's rehearsal dinner and wedding. Put the phone away until after the wedding. Besides, you'll probably find a girl there tomorrow."

I followed him toward the warehouse, but I was already itching to check my phone again.

This thing with the journal couldn't go on forever; it had already gone on long enough without someone else taking it. And I needed to know who it belonged to.

I owned two phones: one for family and friends, another I affectionately called "Candy" for the girls who fell in and out of my bed. It made things easier for me. I didn't want to have to worry about who might be calling when my personal phone rang. On the other hand,

Candy was full of contacts that usually began with "Don't Answer!" and was a way for girls to feel like they could get in touch with me whenever they wanted, but really only could if I wanted them to. I'd been called an asshole for it on more than one occasion . . . I thought I was a genius.

Since I'd put the number to Candy in the journal that morning, I'd been stressing over whether or not I would ever hear from the owner of the journal. Considering how many women in Thatch had Candy's number, I figured there were three options: She already had my number and would know who had been writing to her as soon as she entered it into her phone—and it would all be over then. She would already have my number, still contact me, and it would be over once the message popped up from a Don't Answer contact. Or we somehow wouldn't know each other, and this would continue . . . that is, *if* she decided to contact me at all.

But if I didn't hear from her by the next afternoon, I was going back to Mama's to look for the damn journal before getting ready for the wedding.

Charlie's car came into view then, as we turned into the alley of the warehouse, and my stress over hearing from the girl subsided as something else filled me.

For a year and a half, all I had wanted was to tell Charlie exactly what I thought of her—what I thought of how everyone treated her. I'd thought it would feel like a weight was lifted once I finally did.

I'd been wrong.

Ever since she'd shut the door four days ago, and I'd

left her car only halfway fixed, a nagging feeling had consumed me. I'd told myself at first that it was only because I was waiting for Jagger's call—because I knew it would come. But as the days passed, I knew that wasn't it.

It was the look on Charlie's face after I'd finished laying into her.

Acknowledgment. Agreement. Defeat.

Her expression played through my mind on repeat, and each time I saw it, I felt like even more of a bastard.

Guilt swirled through me when we walked into the warehouse, and I looked over to see Charlie finishing setting up the table. She had her head down as people poured inside, trying to be invisible as she always did. When she glanced up and caught me watching her, she froze.

Her blue eyes pierced mine as the same emotions that had been haunting me flashed across her face.

Maybe if I hadn't been so damn worried about some girl committing suicide, I wouldn't have lashed out at her. Or maybe that was inevitable. Maybe I wouldn't have felt like shit for doing it if I hadn't been reading some other girl's deep thoughts all week. They were making me have feelings. I didn't like it.

"Look who's here," Graham said under his breath. "Have you talked to her?"

"Who?" I asked without looking away from the girl across the room.

"Charlie," he hissed. "Have you talked to her since last weekend at Mama's?"

Yeah, it was no question that I fucked up if I'd refused to tell Graham about my run-in with Charlie on Monday.

"Uh, n—"

"Deaton!"

I looked down as Keith came running through the room toward us, and held out my hand for him. "Hey, kid!"

"Guess who I am!" he shouted.

"Thousand bucks," Graham whispered. I didn't have to be looking at him to know he was smirking.

"He's funny," I murmured back defensively, then bent down to get on Keith's level. "Hmm, I don't know. Are you Iron Man again?"

"No!" Keith said, and bounced on the balls of his feet. "Guess again."

"Spider Man? Magneto?" When he continued to shake his head, I said, "I'm running out of ideas here."

"I'm Mommy's hot dog tonight!" he said as he puffed up his chest, the cheesiest grin covered his face.

"Oh gosh. It's hot *date*, buddy."

My head snapped up at Charlie's voice, so close now to where we were, but she was staring at Keith, and very clearly avoiding looking at me.

"That's what I said!" Keith said in exasperation.

"Charlie," I murmured as I stood.

She tried to smile, but it fell flat. That was when I noticed she was shaking. "Come on, it's time to go."

"Go? You're not staying for dinner?"

Charlie looked up at Graham at his question, and

shook her head firmly once. "No, I was just helping your parents set up in here. Keith and I are going out—"

"Yeah! 'Cause I'm her hot date."

"Right," she said with a flash of a smile, and ran a hand through Keith's wild hair.

"You don't have to leave because you're not in the wedding," Graham said. "I think Knox and Harlow wanted you here. We all want you here."

Charlie pulled Keith closer to her, and took a step toward the doors. Her head tilted slightly and her eyes narrowed like she was studying Graham. When she spoke again, her voice was soft, unsure. "No, it's fine. We already have plans."

"All right. See you tomorrow?"

She nodded faintly in response to Graham's question, but with each step she took away, her head was bowing down more and more—already trying to be invisible.

I took a step forward, and reached out toward her. "Char—"

She lifted her head and narrowed her eyes again.

Acknowledgment. Agreement. Defeat. And a warning—clear as day in those blue eyes—not to say anything more.

I dropped my hand as I choked back my next words. Whether they would have been an apology, or something else to hurt her more, I wasn't sure. With a stiff nod, I turned back around, and tried to ignore the disappointment radiating from Graham.

"Good effort." Frustration leaked from his words.

"Whatever, man."

Charlie

June 3, 2016

I crept out of the room I shared with Keith late that night, book in hand, and made my way to the living room for a little "me" time. Something that had already been a luxury since Keith was born, and something that had been nonexistent in the week and a half that I'd been working at Mama's Café.

But after everything since I'd moved home—or, more accurately, all the crap with Deacon—I needed this time.

I didn't care that I would be dead on my feet for my shift the next morning. Who needed sleep when there were other worlds to get lost in? Made-up lives that you wished could be your own? Fictional men to swoon over—ones that were in no way linked to Marvel Comics or a notebook almost a mile away in a locked-up café?

I moved things out of the way in the fridge until I found my secret stash, and grabbed a cold bar of chocolate before walking back toward the couches.

I'd just gotten a lamp turned on and myself settled under a blanket when Grey plopped down next to me.

I froze from tearing open the wrapper for a few seconds, then slowly resumed what I had been doing as I watched her watching me.

"Hi," I said warily, and handed her a small chunk.

"So who are you reading about tonight?" she asked as

she popped the chocolate into her mouth. "Cinderella? Sleeping Beauty? Belle?"

"None of the above. I told you I don't read fairy tales. Did I wake you?"

She shook her head slowly as she chewed. "Aly just fell asleep a couple minutes before I heard you going through the fridge. He's cute," she said suddenly, and gestured to the guy gracing the cover of the book on my lap.

My eyes narrowed in suspicion. Grey never wanted to talk about the books I read unless it was to make fun of them, and she was sitting and speaking stiffly. I knew her well enough to know she was wasting time before talking about something personal.

"If you've suddenly changed your mind and want to start reading romance, I'll get you a good one to start with." When her face twisted, I continued. "That's what I thought. Why do I have a feeling you're down here for a reason?"

"What's going on between you and Deacon?"

Irrational, betraying heart.

I didn't want to feel anything for Deacon Carver other than the loathing he felt for me, and I hated that just hearing his name could cause this kind of chaos inside me.

My eyebrows rose in surprise at her blunt, unapologetic question.

"What do you mean?" I hoped my tone rang with naïveté rather than the unease I felt over having this conversation with her. I didn't want to talk about Deacon with *Deacon*, let alone Grey.

One of Grey's eyebrows rose slowly, and I knew in the

look she gave me that I hadn't succeeded in seeming clue-less. "Charlie."

"What?" I asked defensively when she didn't continue. "There *isn't* anything going on between us, I don't know why you're even asking."

"No? So I was imagining the hostility emanating from you when he was here fixing your car?"

"What host—"

"And then I guess I just thought I saw you give him a look that could slay the world's strongest man earlier tonight?"

"Guess so."

"So then that also means that Graham is just making up stories about Deacon being a complete asshole to you last weekend?"

My head had been dipping in a nod, but froze half-way. I swallowed my curse and any other response I may have had, and stared blankly at a spot on the floor as Grey waited for an answer I wouldn't give her.

"Right; that's what I thought. What is going on be-tween you and Deacon?"

"Nothing."

"Charlie—"

"Nothing, Grey. There is nothing going on between us, just drop it." My voice was now a plea and a whisper. An indication that I was uncomfortable, and, for Grey, a massive red flag waving through the air above me that I was lying.

"Graham told me what Deacon said to you last week-end."

I bit down on a small rectangle of chocolate.

"How long has he been treating you like that?"

I shrugged, and the movement made me cringe internally. My red flag was practically glowing now, waving more wildly than ever.

"You know—"

"I don't need you to try to be my mom, Grey," I said quickly, my voice still gentle enough that the words didn't come across harshly. "Jagger parents me enough, I just want you to be my friend and sister-in-law."

"I don't want to be your mom, but I want you to talk to me. I don't like that there has been a . . ." She trailed off, and seemed to search the space between us for her next words for a moment. "I don't like that there's been a disconnect between us ever since what happened between you and Ben. There are times you still talk to me, but it's not like it was before. You know that I forgave you a long time ago, and what happened *happened* a long time ago, so I feel like we should already be back to where we were. But a lot of times, I feel like I still have to pull information from you. Like now."

The ache in her voice and on her face hurt my soul. I didn't know she still felt like there was something hindering our friendship. I had thought that once everything came out about Ben and me, things had slowly but surely gotten better.

My brow pinched. "There isn't a disconnect between us, Grey," I assured her. "This—what's going on with Deacon—it's just different. You're so close with him, and I . . . well, I didn't want to talk to anyone about it. I didn't even know why—" I closed my mouth quickly before the words, *I didn't even know why he'd been treating me that way*, could slip from my tongue.

But Grey was too quick.

"You *didn't* . . . which means now you *do*."

A heavy sigh slowly left me, but I didn't respond. For a long minute, we just stared at each other as Grey waited for something from me, and I twisted my hands in an attempt not to shove the rest of the chocolate bar in my mouth.

"Grey, for now can it be okay that I don't want to talk about it? Not just with you, but at all?"

She looked like she was going to argue, so I held up a hand.

"Deacon said things to me that have been building for a long time for him, and I think he needed to get them out. It doesn't excuse it, but I also—well, I can't fault him for his thoughts. And what he said was meant for me, not everyone else."

"I can respect that," Grey said slowly after a moment. "But Deacon will always be in my life, as will you. What am I supposed to do when it comes to all of us getting together, knowing the two of you will be at each other's throats?"

"We won't." I laughed at Grey's disbelieving look, and repeated, "We won't! I promise."

After a weighted sigh, she nodded and snatched a piece of the chocolate as she stood. "All right. Well, if you decide you want to talk about it, I will *try* not to kick his ass for whatever he said to you."

My eyes rolled and a smile touched my face. Just as she turned to leave, I called out after her. "Grey, wait!" But once she turned back, I only sat there staring at her with wide eyes and shaking hands. My heart was racing faster than ever as I tried to force the words from my throat while also wishing to take back the previous ones.

"Yes . . . ?" she said, drawing the word out, making it sound like a question.

"Um, I wondered—well, do you know if—does your . . ." My eyes fell to my lap, and my shoulders bunched up to my ears in a quick jerk of a shrug. "Does Graham go to Mama's a lot?"

Her expression showed her shock and amusement, and I knew she was trying to decipher the reason behind my question. "Uh, yeah, I think so."

"Like, every day?"

"I'm not sure. Have you seen him every day?"

"No, just once." *But I haven't seen the stranger at all*, I mentally added.

Her amusement faded to hesitation. "Do you *want* to see him every day?"

"No. No, no that's not it. I'm just—"

What am I?

I'm incredibly intrigued by a stranger who writes to me in my notebook, and every day I look forward to seeing what—if anything—is waiting for me from him. Wednesday and today felt impossibly long, being away from work, for the sole reason that I don't know if he wrote to me. And your brother has been oddly nice to me the past weeks, nicer than he's ever been before, and it's confusing me and

making me wonder if he's my stranger. Especially consider-
ing some of the things my stranger has written. . .

"I'm asking for one of the other waitresses," I finally
said. My lie felt thick in my throat.

"Uh-huh," she murmured, and took a step back
toward the loft. With a grin, she turned, but called over
her shoulder, "You're blushing, Charlie."

Chapter Seven

Charlie

June 4, 2016

THE GLOW FROM the strings of lights became hazy and faraway, and the faces of the couples dancing on the floor in front of me blurred until they were unrecognizable. Until my thoughts were no longer on Knox and Harlow's wedding reception, or Keith fast asleep in my arms as my fingers trailed over his little back.

Until my mind was consumed with nothing but a stranger's notes, mentally poring over them again and again as I worried over the next response.

It will come, I told myself. *It has to.*

ONE OF THESE DAYS I'M GOING TO COME
BACK FOR YOU, AND YOUR WORDS WON'T
BE HERE.

That had been the note waiting for me when I'd arrived at work that morning. Below, a phone number, and
one final word . . .

PLEASE.

I hadn't responded, and I hadn't left my notebook
when my shift had ended. I'd spent hours agonizing over
whether or not I should message him—because *calling*
him was out of the question—and even longer hating the
giddy smile that refused to leave my face, and the stupid
fluttering in my stomach.

Because that's all this was: stupid.

Because, as he'd pointed out, I didn't know him and
he didn't know me. For all I knew, he was old and married. Or young . . . too young. This was stupid.

But despite every warning I told myself, I sent a message to the number when I arrived at Knox and Harlow's
wedding hours before. One word. Nothing profound; and
nothing that would embarrass me if he'd given me a fake
number.

Stranger. . .

I blinked quickly, bringing the reception back to
focus, when the chair next to me was pulled out and
someone filled it.

I looked over my shoulder, and my hand paused on

Keith's back for a second when I took in Graham, so close to me.

"Having fun?"

After a short hesitation, I nodded. "Are you?"

He stretched back in the chair, and took out the scene before us. "Yeah, still seems weird that it's *Knox's* wedding though."

"Did you think it was going to be the three of you forever?" I asked softly, the teasing evident in my tone.

A short laugh was forced from his chest. His shoulders slid up in the barest of shrugs. "Kind of."

"Deacon, Graham, and Knox . . . the Three Musketeers," I mumbled, my eyes fell to my son as a smile touched my lips.

Graham's next laugh was fuller. "Ah, man. I'd forgotten about that. I can't believe you remembered."

"Hard to forget. Knox tried to rescue me from my bag full of chocolate and ended up ripping my costume in front of everyone. I'm pretty sure that Halloween night scarred me and is the reason I never went to another party. Until now."

Graham leaned closer like he was going to tell me a secret, but stopped a few inches away and nodded toward Keith. "I noticed your dancing partner passed out. Will you dance with me if I promise not to rip your dress in front of everyone?"

The confusion and suspicions I'd been plagued with the past days rose up again at Graham's question, and I felt my body still and my breathing pause as I studied him. Just as quickly as everything had stopped, it all started up again, this time faster than it had been before.

There had been no fluttering in my stomach or racing heart during our short conversation. My breath hadn't caught at his smile or laugh, even though Graham had always been one of the most attractive guys in town. But now, now my pulse was erratic and speeding up with each passing second. I couldn't seem to form words as I tried to make connections between the person sitting next to me, and the one I had been writing to.

"Uh," I forced out.

"Come on, one dance. We finally got you out in public with everyone, we're all having fun, you can't just sit back and watch the party happen."

I nodded slowly, and then more confidently. "Okay."

I stood and gently laid Keith across two chairs, then let Graham lead me out onto the dance floor.

The song was an old one, and fast paced. I didn't have time to let insecurities take over before Graham spun me away, then pulled me closer. A laugh bubbled from my chest before I could attempt to stop it, and then we were moving.

We quickly got lost in the mass of people trying to figure out a way to dance to a song that clearly had no right way of dancing to it. My cheeks burned with heat from trying to let loose for once, as well as the look Grey gave me when she saw me dancing with her older brother.

In that look from Grey, I remembered why I'd let Graham bring me out here at all. But there was no way to try to understand Graham or why he had been so nice lately, and there was no connecting him to a stranger in that moment.

Like before, the fluttering was gone. The racing in my heart was only from our fast movements and the loud music. Even when Graham's hand slid around mine to pull me toward him, or to quickly spin me away again . . . there was nothing.

All of it, every feeling had only been prompted by the thought that I might be face-to-face with a guy who hid behind pages in my book.

The song ended and transitioned into something slower, more intimate, and I felt myself retreating from the reception and the dance floor before my body could begin doing the same. Almost impulsively, my arm curled around my waist as my head bowed. Just as I began to take a step back, a warm voice came from behind me, and a shiver moved down my spine at the sound.

"Charlie Girl . . ."

Irrational, betraying heart.

My chest rose and fell in an exaggerated movement, and a longing to hear those two words rose up inside me at the same time I wanted to demand he never call me that again. Instead of turning around, I looked up at the suspicion crossing Graham's face.

One of his eyebrows lifted slowly, but otherwise he didn't say anything as he stared at his best friend.

"Can I cut in?" Deacon asked.

Graham's lip curled to match his brow. "Can you be nice?"

Something silent passed between the two, and seconds later, Graham's face relaxed and he took a step back.

I glanced over my shoulder to find Deacon watching me patiently, his hand slightly extended toward me.

"What do you say?" he asked gruffly.

"I don't slow dance."

"Neither do I," he responded immediately, but still he took a step toward me and slid his hand around my waist.

Deacon turned me slowly and pulled me closer until our bodies were pressed against each other. He grasped my hand in his, and brought our joined hands between our chests as he began rocking us.

Whether or not we were moving to the music, I didn't know.

Because at that moment, I couldn't look away from his eyes.

For the first time in so, so long, there was something missing from them. Coldness. Anger. Everything I'd come to expect from Deacon, and everything I'd been shying away from was now replaced with guilt and confusion and wonder.

"Why are you doing this?" I asked. My words were so soft they almost got lost in the music filling the outdoor tent.

"I'm sorry."

If it weren't for Deacon leading us, his apology would have halted our movements the way it halted the pounding of my heart.

"I'm sorry for what I said to you. You didn't deserve it—"

My head tilted to the side and shook once in a subtle

plea for him to stop talking. I tried to pull away from him, but he held me tighter, his eyes pled with me to stay as his words tumbled from his lips quickly and quietly.

"—the way you looked at me that day, I can't stop thinking about it. I hate that you looked like you—"

"Please stop." My head shook faster as panic started rising in my throat. My gaze quickly moved through the couples on the floor, searching for Jagger and Grey, making sure they weren't close enough to hear Deacon.

"I shouldn't have said anything. I was stressed out over this—"

"Deacon, *stop*," I demanded, my voice still as soft as a whisper.

I finally succeeded at shoving away from his hold, and turned to walk away from him, but he was still there.

Within seconds his arm was around my waist and he was guiding me from the dance floor, past the tables, and out of the tent. As soon as we were a dozen feet away, surrounded in equal parts night and light from the reception, Deacon pulled me into his arms as if we were dancing again.

"What are you doing?"

"Making you talk to me."

In the back of my mind, I knew it was because he thought I would walk away again, but something about the darkness, his voice, and being with him like this made me shiver again.

Before he could begin talking again, I shook my head quickly to clear my mind of the way he made me feel, and grit my teeth as I focused on my anger. "I don't want your excuses."

"They aren't excuses, I'm explaining why—"

"I don't need explanations for what you said, either!" I hissed, cutting him off. "All I ever wanted was to know why you suddenly had so much hatred toward me. You told me. That's it; it's over. There's nothing left to explain. You don't have to apologize for feeling the way you do. And you didn't have to dance with me to try to make up for some words you said." I pressed my hands against his chest and pushed, but he held tight to my waist, not willing to let me go.

"It was the only way to get you to talk to me."

I hated that a part of me had foolishly believed that he would want to dance with me.

Irrational, betraying heart.

"Both were unnecessary. I'm a big girl, Deacon, and as you reminded me, I have a spine; I know how to handle you and move on with my life."

Deacon's shoulders sagged, but his eyes burned into mine. "Fuck, Charlie. I'm sorry. I'm sorry for what I said. Can't you hear that? Can't you *see* that?"

"When have you ever been sorry for anything you've said or done in your entire life? That's part of who you are—that's part of *Deacon Carver*—unapologetically arrogant and unaware."

A few seconds of silence passed between us before a mumbled "Christ" slipped from his lips. Instead of loosening his hold on me, his fingers contracted slightly, bringing us impossibly closer together. "Where did shy, sweet Charlie go?"

"You'd be surprised what I can say when I think it

long enough." It also helped tremendously that we were mostly hidden in the darkness.

He huffed. "Clearly." But there was something in his voice that caught me off guard. Instead of the sneer I had come to expect from him, it sounded like a mixture of amusement and pride.

And I didn't know what to make of it or him or the fact that he was still holding me and my heart was beating loud enough that I was sure he could hear it.

"I'm ready for you to let me g—"

"Your face on Monday," he said softly, his voice gruff. "I can't stop thinking about the way you looked at me."

"I already asked you to stop." I pressed harder against his muscled chest, but my strength suddenly gave out at his next words.

"Just tell me if you're okay with what happened to Ben."

"What?" I asked breathlessly.

"Tell me if you're okay. With what he did to you, with his death . . . all of it."

"Why . . ." I stared at my hands and blinked slowly as I replayed his words, then lifted my head until I was looking into Deacon's eyes. Mine narrowed in suspicion. "Why would you ask me that?"

"I've known you most of your life, Charlie, and—"

"We live in Thatch. Everyone has known everyone for most of their life."

"You know it's different with us. But I always saw you as shy, sweet Charlie, who hid behind her brother and Grey so she wouldn't have to talk to anyone. When I found out about you and Ben, and the way everything was handled after, I thought you were selfish and immature. It looked like you didn't care, and let Jagger always take care of your problems. That look on your face this week—like you agreed with me—has fucking haunted me because I know I had it all wrong."

"So because I agreed with you, suddenly you want to apologize and check on me?" I said with a disbelieving laugh.

Judging from his expression, he knew it didn't make sense, either. "Charlie, I just want to know if you're okay."

My head shook subtly, but instead of responding, I asked, "Why are you doing this? This isn't you and this isn't us. We aren't friends, Deacon. So why don't you go back to being your unapologetic, arrogant self, and I'll go back to not speaking to you, now that I've gotten out everything I've been thinking all week."

Deacon's brow pinched in frustration and hurt, but just as he opened his mouth to respond, a deep voice came from a few feet away.

"Everything okay out here?"

I whipped my head to the side, and stumbled back a step when Deacon suddenly released me.

A freezing feeling shot through my veins as I stared into my brother's narrowed eyes, and my stomach rolled as if he'd just caught me doing something I wasn't supposed to.

Deacon cleared his throat and shifted his weight. "Jagger."

Jagger didn't look at him. He folded his arms across

his chest and tilted his head as he asked me, "Again, is everything okay?"

"We were just talking," I said quickly, and bit back a groan when Grey stepped up behind Jagger.

"Uh, so . . . hey, everyone," she said slowly, and looked quickly among the three of us. "Charlie, my parents are going to take Aly home. Do you want them to take Keith too, so you can—"

"No, no, I'll get him. It's late, I was about to leave."

"Looked like it," my brother mumbled.

"Jagger . . ." I released a sigh and glanced over at Deacon, but his eyes were on the grass. Without saying a word to any of them, I started walking in the direction of the tent.

I hadn't taken more than three steps before Deacon called out, "Char—"

"Good night, Deacon," Jagger said roughly, and turned to follow me when I passed him.

Despite Jagger's constant questions about what Deacon and I had been doing, and Grey's questions about what she had walked in on, I remained silent as I collected my son and walked to my car.

"Deacon isn't the kind of guy you should—"

I shut the back door of my car once I had Keith in his booster seat, and whirled on Jagger. "We were talking, Jagger. Literally *talking*. Nothing more. But even if for some insane reason there had been *more*, you cannot do what you just did."

Jagger shot his arm out behind him. "Do you know how close you two were? Do you know what it looked like I interrupted? And with *Deacon*, of all guys!"

"I don't care!" I cried out. "He was holding me because he was trying to keep me there so I wouldn't keep walking away from him while he apologized for what he'd said last week."

That stopped Jagger from whatever he'd been about to say. His head jerked back as he took in my words, and Grey's eyes widened as she looked from Jagger to me. It was clear in her look that she hadn't told Jagger that there had been tension between Deacon and me. Not that I'd thought she had. Jagger would have brought it up to me as soon as Grey mentioned it.

"Apologize?" Jagger asked softly, darkly. "For what?"

"It doesn't matter; and you're still doing it. Jagger, you are my *brother*. Just be my brother! I appreciate what you did for me growing up more than you will ever know, but I am an adult now. You don't need to keep parenting me. You don't need to force your way into a situation and act like my father when you don't even know what the situation is. Do you know that people think I hide behind you? Do you know that people think I pawned Keith off on you because *you* forced me to go away to college alone? All I wanted was to be with my son, but because you think you know what's best for me, I missed out on so many months with him!" I nearly yelled. "Jagger, I love you, but just *stop*!"

I rounded my car, ignoring Jagger's protests, and slid into the driver's seat.

"Are we mad at Uncle J, Mommy?" Keith asked softly from the backseat once I was pulling out of the parking spot.

I sagged against the steering wheel and put the car in drive, but just sat there with my foot on the brake for a few seconds. He'd still been asleep when I'd put him in the car. I hated that he'd heard us yelling. "No, buddy. No, we're not," I finally said.

"Then why we yelling at Uncle J?"

"Sometimes . . ." I trailed off, and tried to think of what to tell him. "Sometimes grown-ups don't listen to each other very well. And sometimes when that happens, we raise our voices to get another grown-up to finally hear us, but that doesn't mean it's a good thing. It wasn't nice of me to do that to Uncle J. I'm sorry you heard that."

Keith was silent for so long that I'd thought he'd fallen back asleep, but he suddenly said, "So Uncle J hears you now?"

I nodded. "Maybe."

"Okay then, Mommy. Then it's okay."

I smiled though he couldn't see me, and whispered, "Thanks, buddy."

ONCE WE GOT home, I got Keith in his pajamas and in bed, then changed into something comfortable. I'd just finished taking off my makeup when I heard Grey and Jagger get home.

I checked my phone again, and tried to hide the disappointment that there was still nothing from the stranger, then walked out into the main room to talk to Jagger.

I knew he would be waiting for me, and I found him

sitting on the couch, forearms resting on his knees and head dropped.

Long seconds passed in silence after I sat down next to him before he looked up at me. His expression was withdrawn and full of worry, but a small smirk tugged at his mouth when I sent him a shaky smile.

"I'm sorry," I whispered.

His head was already shaking before I finished getting the second word out. "Don't be. Apparently I still think you need me for everything. I think I've chosen to forget that you were raising Keith and dealing with Mom on your own while I was away at college. In my head, you still need me. I know that you can make all of your own decisions, Charlie, but I feel like I still need to make them for you. You know?"

"I want your opinion," I said quickly. "I want your opinion, but I just want my brother. I don't like when you say things and that's the final decision for *my* life. Part of the agreement was that I needed to find my own place, but the times I've even mentioned that I've looked at places, you *still* say that it would just be easier to stay here in a way that hints that you don't want us leaving. Yes, it would be easier, but I need a place with Keith, and you and Grey and Aly need this place to yourselves."

Jagger nodded slowly. "I know." He sighed slowly, and said, "I know. Grey and I were talking on the way home about what you said. I don't think I realize all that I've been doing all these years, and I swear to God I'll step back." He made a face, and the corners of his mouth pulled up in another grin. "*Try* to. But there's one thing

I need to know. Do you resent me for making you go to college?" When I took too long to answer, he laughed sadly. "Got it."

"No, I don't. Really, Jag, I don't. I was trying to think of how exactly I felt." I looked away as I tried to gather my thoughts, and when I spoke again, my words started off slow and unsure. "I was upset, yes, but I knew why you did it. I knew that going away was something I had wanted growing up, and I think you were just trying to make sure I still had that. My wants changed after Keith was born though, and I don't think you could fully understand that until Aly was here. But honestly, I'm not mad that you forced me to go, I'm mostly mad that I allowed you to. Like I said, some people think I pawned Keith off on you, and that's how I feel too. It felt like as soon as he got to be mine, I abandoned him. I feel like I'm no better than Mom."

"You're nothing like her," he argued gently.

I chewed on my bottom lip as dozens of responses and insecurities came to mind, but didn't voice any of them.

Jagger exhaled heavily as he stood, and leaned down to kiss the top of my head. When he straightened, he asked hesitantly, "Can I ask about one more thing?"

I looked up and lifted an eyebrow in silent response.

"Deacon."

My face fell. "What about him?"

"What's going on between you two?"

"I don't—" I started to tell him it wasn't something I wanted to discuss before I realized that Jagger's tone was different from Grey's earlier that week. "Um. Wait, how do you mean . . ."

"I'm not gonna be able to sleep if I think there's something going on between you and Deacon fucking Carver. I get that you want me to back off, Charlie, and Deacon's a great guy . . . but not in that way. Never in that way, and especially not for you. I know Grey would say the same."

I forced a laugh and tried to ignore the way my stomach swirled with heat. Jagger's worries were unnecessary because Deacon would never look at me like that, and I hated that I felt anything for him at all. "It's not—there's nothing—no, you have it wrong. Deacon and I fought earlier this week. He was trying to apologize tonight. That's all."

"Apologize." Jagger's tone was full of disbelief. "Do you have any clue how close the two of you were tonight?"

Yes. I knew exactly how close. I could still feel Deacon's body pressed against mine, the way his fingers curled against me . . .

Irrational, betraying heart.

"I didn't want to talk to him. I'd already walked away from him. He was trying to keep me there so I would listen to him."

Jagger's eyes narrowed. "Are you gonna tell me what he was trying to apologize for?"

"No."

He nodded, as if he'd expected the answer. "All right. And you swear there isn't something else going on between the two of you?"

"Jagger, I have only ever been with Ben. I've never had a boyfriend, and I have a son. Do you really think the next guy I'd choose would end up being one of the two remaining town man-whores?"

Jagger shrugged. "You surprised me before."

I deserved that. "There's nothing there, but whenever—if ever—I find someone to be with, trust me to make the right decision for me and Keith. Okay?"

After a short hesitation, he nodded, and then turned to walk toward the loft where his and Grey's room was.

I pulled myself off the couch and headed toward the bedroom, ready to crawl into bed and sleep for the few hours I had before I needed to wake up for my shift. I checked on Keith, and smiled at the way he was sleeping, completely sprawled out with all of the covers pushed all the way down.

As I was pulling the comforter back over him, my phone vibrated on my nightstand, and my heart skipped a beat.

I stared at it until the screen went black again, then slowly straightened and walked around the room to retrieve it. With shaky hands, I picked up my phone and held my breath as I prepared to check the lock screen.

The air ripped from my lungs and my heart took off when I read the message that waited for me.

Stranger: *And here I'd thought you'd taken your words away from me . . .*

Chapter Eight

Deacon

June 5, 2016

"Jesus Christ, dude, stop yawning," Graham said with
a groan the next morning, and kicked at my leg.

I ran my hands through my hair and bit back another
yawn. "Shut up, you don't look any better than me," I
grumbled, and picked up one of Keith's crayons to fix
some things on his kid's menu before he woke from his
nap on the short drive over.

"I need coffee," I said distractedly as I colored. "It was
a long night."

"Ew," Grey said, then pretended to gag. "Ew, I don't
want to know."

"Did you really take home someone from the wedding?" Knox asked, and shook his head. "Come on, man. It was my wedding."

"He didn't," Graham answered for me. "But he probably had a line waiting when we got home. I made him turn off Candy for a couple days until the wedding was over."

Knox barked out a laugh, and everyone else sitting at the table looked among the three of us with clueless expressions.

"Didn't," I said through another yawn. "Just . . . I just couldn't sleep."

"Yeah, I bet you couldn't," Knox said through his laughter.

I'd spent the entire night and morning texting the owner of the journal while working on Charlie's car outside the warehouse. After the bullshit that had gone down at the wedding with Charlie, I probably would have done exactly what Graham and Knox thought—I would have gone down my list of waiting girls in Candy. But that message, that fucking message with that one word had changed everything.

Stranger . . .

I hadn't been able to respond fast enough.

I also hadn't responded to anyone else, or given a shit that hours had passed or that night had turned to day as we'd texted.

I still didn't have a name, but I didn't care. I knew she was somewhere between the ages of twenty and thirty, so at least I knew she was legal. And I knew she was single . . . that was all I needed to know to not put a stop to this now. The rest of the specifics didn't matter.

Her words and everything else I learned about her through them mattered more than specifics ever could.

The fact that I had been able to open up to her in a way I never had with anyone else meant fucking everything.

Because to her, to this girl, I wasn't Deacon Carver. I wasn't the guy everyone in Thatch knew me to be.

"Hey, everyone. What can I get you?"

My head snapped up at that voice, and my gaze locked with eyes so blue, it was hard to look away.

To this strange girl, I wasn't what Charlie had so perfectly described me as: Unapologetic and arrogant.

A chorus of "Heys!" went up around the table, and as soon as they died down, Jagger cleared his throat.

"Well, apparently Deacon needs coffee to get through the morning after the marathon of women from last night."

My eyes shot to Jagger, but he was looking at his sister pointedly.

"Ew," Grey and Harlow said at the same time, and after a slight pause, I heard Charlie mumble under her breath, "Disgusting."

Before I could say anything in my defense, Charlie looked at Harlow and said, "Shouldn't you be on your honeymoon?"

I didn't pay attention to Harlow's response, or anyone else as they gave Charlie their drink orders. I couldn't stop watching Charlie and the way she was once again so obviously trying not to look at me.

Without realizing it, my gaze slowly dropped from her face down her body, and settled on her waist. My hands curled and the tips of my fingers tingled, and I had the strongest urge to pull her against me again.

I flexed my hand and mentally shook my head, and told myself it was because I wasn't used to having someone who didn't throw herself at me. But when I looked back up and noticed the way her eyes kept darting over to Graham, and how her cheeks filled with heat, my hand curled into a fist. Irritation flashed through me, and something white-hot settled in my stomach and pulsed through my veins, just as it had the night before when I'd seen Graham dancing with her. I didn't understand it, and I didn't like it.

And I needed to stop thinking about the way her body had felt against mine.

Before I knew I was moving, I was out of the booth and following her as she walked away to get our drinks.

"Charlie Girl," I murmured when she slowed at the POS to enter in the drink order.

She faltered for a second, but she didn't turn to look at me, and her voice was calm when she asked, "Why are you following me?"

"Is that really how people see me?"

She looked over her shoulder, her brow pinched and eyes full of confusion.

"Unapologetic and arrogant," I clarified.

"And unaware," she added softly.

"Of what?"

"Exactly." Her eyes bored into mine for long seconds before she spoke. "Deacon, why are you asking me this?"

"Because I need to know if that's what people see when they see me."

"Isn't that how you want people to see you?" She looked down again to punch our drinks into the screen, and when she finished, she just stood there. She didn't have to look to know that I hadn't left. With a sigh, she turned, already speaking as she did. "You've created this image, Deacon. The three of you did. Knox got out of it, but that was different because he'd had Harlow before any of you ever became—well, the way you are."

"And what's that?" I asked, my tone slightly taunting, mostly curious to see if she would say it to my face.

Charlie's cheeks blazed red, her head shook slightly. "You sleep with every legal female close enough to touch—"

"Not every."

"—and you brag about it. You act like no one can touch you. And if you hurt any of those women, you don't care. It isn't in you to care."

I lifted an eyebrow and reminded her, "I cared about hurting you."

"That's different, Deacon. You would also care about hurting Grey or Harlow or Knox's sister."

I had never fantasized about touching any of them though. And I still didn't know what to do about wanting to touch the girl in front of me.

"So to answer your question, yes, that's how people see you. But I think that's only because you created *this* for them to see. And I also think that you have deep and confusing thoughts when you're going off little sleep. That, or one of the girls from last night made you think about who you are far too much. Which . . . actually might be a good thing for you. Maybe she'll be a change for you, like Harlow was for Knox. But go sit down and I'll bring your coffee regardless of whichever one it was."

I bit back my automatic response, because, technically, she wasn't wrong, and blew out a heavy sigh as I took a step back. Before she could turn away, I asked, "Why does it have to depend on a girl? Why can't there just be different sides to me?"

"Such deep and confusing thoughts," she murmured again. "Why are you coming to me with this?"

"Because I've seen different sides of you in just the last week. I've seen the shy, sweet Charlie I grew up with, and I've seen the one who stood up to me and for herself."

Embarrassment flashed across her face. "You can't compare us, Deacon. All you've ever wanted was to be seen, and I'd rather not be seen at all." She walked away, leaving me there, staring at the place where she'd been standing.

Just as I turned, she called out my name, and I looked over my shoulder to see her walking back toward me with a mug of coffee in her hands.

"Here, so you can get started." She smirked, but it died as soon as I took the mug from her hands. "And, Deacon? Keith might be sleeping right now, but he repeats everything, and he's obsessed with you lately. Keep that in mind when you talk about your *nights*, okay?"

I'd never realized how much people expected me to have a night with a random girl, or multiple girls, until this week. I'd also never realized how much this image that Charlie said I'd created for myself would piss me off when I found that I could no longer get away from it.

I huffed in frustration, and stared into the dark depths of the coffee for a moment before looking up at her again. "Would you believe me if I told you that I was alone last night?"

Charlie's face was etched with disbelief, and it was the only answer I needed.

"Right." I cleared my throat and took a step back, and raised the mug in her direction. "Thanks, Charlie."

I had barely gotten settled back into the booth before Jagger said in a low, warning tone, "Man, stay away from my sister."

I glanced up, and everyone else at the booth was frozen and looking at either Jagger or myself . . . but Jagger wasn't paying attention to me. His focus was on his daughter.

Just when I started to think I'd imagined his warning, and imagined everyone's stares, he said, "I love you, Deac, but I'm so fucking serious." His eyes finally flicked in my direction, the look in them drove home his words.

"Jagger . . ." Grey said, her voice almost too soft to hear.

"What the hell are you talking about?" I asked. "We were just talking."

One of his eyebrows ticked up, a huff burst from his chest. "Yeah, I keep hearing that. As long as it stays that way, then that's fine. I mean it; you're like a brother. But Charlie has Keith, she doesn't need to get involved with someone like—"

"Jagger, stop," Grey said, this time louder.

"Yeah, no, I got it." I tried to laugh, but it may have come across as a sneer. One of my phones chimed then, and I didn't even pay attention to which one it was when I pulled it out of my pocket and held it up. "Because of this, right? They call, and I go willingly."

I downed the hot coffee as fast as I could and slid out of the booth, more than ready to get away now that no one was speaking and everyone was staring at me with a mixture of shock, confusion, and sympathy.

"See the two of you when you get back from your honeymoon," I said to Knox and Harlow, then nodded in Grey's direction. "When Keith wakes up, tell him I already covered up the ladybugs on the menu so they can't take his superpowers away." When her sympathetic expression turned confused, I said, "He'll understand."

I turned and nearly ran into Charlie as she carried the drink tray toward the booth.

"Sorry," she said quickly, her eyes already darting over me. "Are you leaving?"

My mouth opened to say, "I have to go live up to my reputation," but shut again. Instead, I simply mumbled, "Charlie Girl," and walked past her and out of Mama's Café.

As soon as I was back home and in bed, I opened up the conversation with Words, the journal girl, on my phone. And as I tapped out a message, I realized I needed this more than I'd thought. If the people I was closest to wouldn't allow me to be anything other than this image I'd created, then at least I had this.

Words, have you ever thought about how people move to places like Thatch to start their lives over, but the people who grow up in those towns can't start over unless they leave?

Charlie

June 9, 2016

Stranger: *At all.*

My jaw dropped in disbelief as I hurried to respond a few days later.

I'd spent every night since the wedding talking to Stranger, and in that time, I'd come to know him better than anyone, and he me. And sometimes it was hard to believe that he hadn't been in my life for years, because I'd never been able to talk to anyone like I could this.

What do you mean? How can you not believe in love?

Stranger: *No, I mean, I do. Just . . . not like . . . I don't know. I love my family and my closest friends because they're like family. But the other? I think it's something people have made up over the years. It's wants and needs and infatuations that people glorify into a relationship and marriage that you either stick out for your life or decide you don't want to deal with anymore.*

Stranger: *I don't think we're meant to fall in love with* *someone and spend forever with them. I think the whole "the one" thing is just bullshit.*

"That's depressing," I whispered, then tapped my words out to him.

That is incredibly depressing.

Stranger: *How did I know you wouldn't agree with me? Even after the guy from years ago that treated you the way he did, you still believe in it?*

Of course I do.

I don't think it's always easy, and the journey to find the person you're meant to be with can be messy, but I think there is at least one person for everyone. And I don't say "at least" in the instance that we get bored, but if there's a death, or something like that . . .

And, yeah, it can start with wants and needs and desire, but you never know when it might end up turning into something so much more than that—when your soul recognizes theirs. I feel like a part of our souls are dying away every day until we finally find the person who holds the other half.

Stranger: *Soul mates, huh? If that even exists, I think people are quick to put that label on someone. Just like I think people are too quick to say those three little words.*

True, some people are.

Stranger: *Not you?*

I had only ever told one person that I had loved them, and I hadn't even said the words "I love you." I'd simply told Ben that I'd been in love with him for as long as I could remember. Those three words had never left my lips, though I had fantasized for years about the day they would.

No, but I envy them. I think it's a beautiful thing to be a lover.

Stranger: *You and your words . . .*

Stranger: *So you're a romantic then?*

Obviously, as if you expected me to be anything less.

And I will say I'm kind of disappointed in your lack of belief in love.

Stranger: *Sorry, Words. No white knight waiting to sweep you off your feet here.*

Ha ha. Shame.

I fought off a yawn as I tapped out my response, and glanced up when something caught my eye out of one of the large windows of the warehouse. I blinked quickly, squinted, then smiled at the pinkish gray sky.

Good morning, Stranger.

Stranger: *Christ. Already? Morning, Words.*

I don't know why you always sound so surprised when you won't ever let me go to sleep.

Stranger: *I'm sorry.*

Stranger: *I like your words, what can I say?*

My chest moved with my silent laugh, and my lips pulled into a smile.

Yeah, but I think people at work are starting to worry about why I can't function.

There was such a long pause before the little dots popped up, indicating he was typing, that I'd thought he'd finally fallen asleep.

Stranger: *I'm really struggling not to ask where you work. Or who you are . . .*

I wouldn't tell you even if you did.

Stranger: *Ever?*

My thumbs stilled above my screen as I thought. What we'd had with my notebook last week, and now with texting all night every night, was safe because we knew nothing about each other. And yet, in the past week and a half, I'd told him everything about myself.

He didn't know my name, my family, the specifics of my past with Ben, or about Keith . . . but he knew more about me than anyone else ever had. And I knew that was because there was this sense that he wasn't actually real. Like he was fictional. It was as if I was falling for the hero of a book, except he was real.

Something told me that if we were ever put in front of each other, what we'd had would end, and I wasn't ready for it to. I'd never had this, and I didn't know if I ever would again . . . so I wanted it for as long as it could last.

I'm not sure.

Stranger: *Right . . . probably best, yeah?*

Yeah . . .

Stranger: *Before I let you go, can you tell me something?*

Of course :)

Stranger: *What ever happened to that not-so-suicide note that started all of this?*

Ha . . . the song?

Stranger: *It was a song?*

The beginning of one, yes.

Stranger: *. . . were those all songs?*

My cheeks burned with heat as I quickly tapped on the screen.

Songs and poems, yes . . .

Stranger: *So did you finish it?*

I blinked slowly as I realized I couldn't even think of anything to say about my nights with Ben other than what I'd already said. I'd been thinking about those nights for years before I finally allowed myself to write about them, and then my Stranger came and made me wonder why I was still waiting for a guy who wasn't even alive to love me.

Actually, no. I'd forgotten about it with our notes and everything.

Stranger: *Are you saying my words can make you forget? ;)*

Stranger: *Are you going to?*

Yes. That's exactly what I was saying. I chewed on my bottom lip as I thought, then finally responded.

Ha ha. I'm not sure. I thought I had an entire song about what I was for him, and what he never was for me— but now I'm not so sure.

I flew up to a sitting position on the couch, and glanced back up at the window. The sky now a mixture of pinks, purples, and oranges.

Stranger: *He didn't deserve a song anyway*

Hold on. I'll be back with something, but then I really need to get ready for work.

I ran through the warehouse and tiptoed into my room, and snatched my notebook up before running back out to the couch. I flipped to the first clean page since our notes had taken up so much of the others, quickly wrote out what had been Ben's song, and then added a little bit below. Once it was done, I took a picture and sent it to Stranger.

Who listens to your sad songs
The shoulder that you cry on
Out on that ledge you walk on
When you're sinking
Who keeps your secrets locked up
When there's no one you can trust
I know it's much more than just wishful thinking
Just say the words and you know I'll be there

You can't believe it's daylight
We stayed up again all night
~~Just ta~~ Talking just cause you like the way I make the words sound

I waited for what seemed like hours but was really only a minute before those little dots popped up. My heart raced and I bit at my lip as I worried about what he would say.

Stranger: *That's not about him, is it?*

No . . .

Stranger: *Will there be more?*

I guess that depends.

Stranger: *On?*

Our conversations, and if they continue.

Stranger: *Words . . . you're not getting rid of me.*

My cheeks burned as my lips stretched into a smile.

Then eventually.

Stranger: *Good. Go get ready for work. I'll talk to you later.*

Have a good day, Stranger.

I stood from the couch and started walking back toward the bedroom when my phone vibrated in my hand again.

Stranger: *Hey, Words? Having what you wrote about him at the beginning makes it seem like that's what is happening now. He's your past . . . I think he should come after us.*

Us. I stared at that word for the longest time as those stupid, stupid butterflies took up residence in my stomach again, then I tapped out a response.

Okay then.

Chapter Nine

Deacon

June 11, 2016

I GLANCED AT Charlie's car as Graham and I walked up to the warehouse, and shifted the bags in my hands when he knocked on the door. After knocking again and not getting an answer, Graham tried the door, and sent me an annoyed look when it opened.

This was Thatch, but Jagger and Grey really needed to start locking their door.

Loud music was blasting through the warehouse, and from experience, we knew that meant Jagger was drawing in the back.

"Jagger," we mumbled at the same time.

"I'll go let him know we're here," he said, and set off in that direction, but I didn't bother to respond as a flash of blond caught my attention.

I hurried to set the bags of food on the table before quietly walking toward the couches, where Charlie was curled into a ball on her side; her finger still holding her place in a book even though she was asleep.

My mouth curled into an amused grin as I squatted next to her. "People actually fall asleep like this?" I said under my breath, and carefully took the book from her.

Once I had it set down, I looked back down at her, and was struck again with the intense urge to touch her. To feel her body against mine again.

Before I could do something as stupid as either of those things, her eyes shot open and she jerked away from me. Her hand went to her chest, and she exhaled roughly.

"Oh my God, Deacon," she whispered, her voice hoarse.

"Charlie Girl."

Blood rushed to her cheeks, and though she opened her mouth, it took her a few seconds to get the words out. "Why are you staring at me while I sleep? It's creepy when Keith does it, and I actually expect him to be there when I wake up."

"I . . ." I blew out a slow breath, and sat back on my heels when I faltered for a reason that I could give her. "I was going to wake you up. You beat me to it."

"Room."

My brow furrowed. "What?"

She placed her hand against my chest, and pushed. "Give me room so I can sit up." Once she was upright, she ran a hand through her long hair and looked around the large room as she blinked slowly, like she was trying to orient herself.

"How did you sleep through Jagger's music?"

She lifted a shoulder. "I don't know. Years of getting used to it, I guess."

Jesus Christ. Why the hell did this tired, rumpled version of Charlie make me want her more?

This was Charlie. *Charlie Girl*. Jagger's shy little sister. Shy, sweet Charlie who had always been in the background my entire life. No man could deny that she was gorgeous, but she wanted to be invisible, and she usually succeeded in it.

I'd never once thought of her in any way like I had the past couple weeks. I'd never wanted to touch her. I'd never wanted to push her back down and cover her body with mine. I'd never wanted to know what she felt like beneath me.

This had to be what it felt like to lose your damn mind. Because this was fucking *Charlie*.

It had never been that she was untouchable; it was just that there was no thinking of her at all. I didn't know what to do now that I couldn't stop. Ever since that night, that damn night outside these very walls had changed something. And I wanted to change it right back.

"Why are you here?" she asked softly.

I glanced up to find her studying the ground with her arms wrapped securely around her waist.

There she went, trying to be invisible again . . . but I'd never seen anyone so clearly.

"Graham and I brought breakfast from Mama's," I said as I nodded toward the kitchen area, even though she still wasn't looking at me. "Speaking of, I figured I would've seen you there."

"I switched with someone, so I'm going in later today." She looked over her shoulder toward the kitchen, and said, "But I should get ready because I have to walk to work."

"Walk?" I asked as she stood.

Charlie gave me an odd look just as Keith came running in.

"Deaton, Deaton, Deaton! Guess who I am!"

I huffed when he slammed into me, then held him away from me to look at his face. Across his forehead was a large *A*.

"Uh . . . Ant-Man?"

Keith sighed. "No, I'm Captain America."

I laughed. "Of course you are. Where's your shield?" But Keith was already running away, and my attention went to the girl backing away from me. "Why are you walking to work?"

Again, that odd look. "My car doesn't work. You didn't finish fixing it."

"Yes, I did," I said, disagreeing with her. "I stayed up—" I cut off quickly before I could tell her that I'd stayed up talking to some girl, and instead said, "I didn't sleep at all after the wedding, so I came here and finished working on it. There's no real fix for your car unless you want to spend thousands of dollars, and honestly, your car isn't worth it. No offense, but it would just break down again in a year if you're lucky, probably six months. So there are temporary fixes that *might* help it run for a couple days at a time. I did what I could."

She stood there for a few seconds without saying anything or looking at me, and finally, her blue eyes flickered up. "Really?"

"Yeah. If I can get it into the shop, I might be able to get it to run for longer periods at a time, but I think you should look into getting a new car."

Charlie sighed, and mumbled, "Now you sound like—"

"At least someone agrees with me," Jagger said as he came into the main room from the back halls.

I hadn't even realized his music had turned off.

"Deacon," he said in a low tone. His gaze went from me to his sister, then back again.

"Jag." I dipped my head in his direction, and tried not to follow Charlie's movements as she left the room.

"Deaton, Deaton! Guess who I am!"

I pulled my attention away from the entrance to the halls, and watched Keith as he raced toward me with a piece of a cinnamon roll in his hand.

"Uh," I sucked in a quick breath as I glanced as his forehead. The *A* had been wiped away, leaving only black smudges. "Definitely *not* Captain America. Let's see . . . Loki!"

"No! I'm Darf Vaber!"

My head jerked back. "What? Darth Vader isn't a superhero. He isn't even with Marvel, kid!"

Keith sighed like he was getting annoyed that I wasn't

keeping up with him. "Supaheroes can't defeat the lady-bugs 'cause they take away the supapowers, memember?"

"So you need to be Darth Vader in order to get rid of ladybugs?"

Another long, drawn-out sigh. "Yes, Deaton," he said as he went to go sit at the table. "One day you'll undas-tand."

"You're right, kid. Maybe one day." I caught Graham smiling impishly at me, and my smile abruptly faded. "What?" I demanded.

He gestured from Keith to me. "Thousand bucks, man."

I flipped him off, but held back any verbal retort as I slipped quietly from the room while Jagger's eyes were off of me.

I set off toward the hallway to try to find Charlie, but as soon as I turned the corner, I nearly knocked her over.

"What—" Charlie began as she danced out of my way, and hurried to finish pulling her hair on top of her head. "Deacon, what are you doing back here?"

"Looking for you."

She bit down on her full bottom lip, and her cheeks turned pink. "Uh . . . I have to get to the café."

"Right, about that. I was wondering if I could take you."

Her steps abruptly halted, and she turned slowly to look up at me. "Why would you want to?"

If only she knew it was the least of the things I wanted to do with her at that moment. Pushing her up against the wall and tasting that lip she kept biting on came close to the top. "I can take you, and then I'll take your car into the shop—try to figure out something else to do with it."

Surprise settled over her features. "You're really going to do that?"

"Charlie Girl," I said with a laugh. "Yeah. But I was serious; it's *really* temporary. It's just something that will have to continue being fixed. You need to look for a new car."

Her surprise faded into defeat. "I know, I just . . . I know." With a sad sigh, she began walking again, her voice trailing behind her. "I will."

I followed her back out to the main room, and tried to ignore Jagger's warning glare when he found out I was taking Charlie to work. Graham's assessing gaze that kept bouncing back and forth between Charlie and me was harder to miss. Each time he made the pass back to her, the mixture of confusion and worry in his eyes grew.

I was already struggling with trying to understand why I couldn't stop thinking about the girl standing just a handful of feet from me. I didn't want to spend time trying to understand the way Graham was looking at her, or why it was bothering me.

But I thought about that damn look the entire drive to Mama's.

Fucking Graham. Whatever was going on between them, I knew it hadn't been like that before, and it was pissing me off more each time I saw them together.

"Hey, Charlie, what time do you get off today?" I asked before she could get out of her car once I pulled up in front of the café.

"Oh, it's a weird shift, I get off at three thirty. But don't worry about it if you're not finished with my car, I can walk back."

"No, I'll be here no matter what; my car or yours. Since you get off early enough, do you want to go to some dealerships in Richland after?"

"With you?" she asked, clarifying.

"Yeah."

For long moments she studied me as her head slowly shook. "Why do you keep doing this? Why do you—I don't understand why you've been talking to me the way you have been, or trying help me. And now—"

"Would it really be so hard for you to believe that I just want to spend time with you?"

Her cheeks turned red as my question hung in the air. "Yes," she finally replied.

"Why?"

"Because you're Deacon Carver, and the minute I believe that you *do* want to is the minute I find out this is one huge joke to you."

An agitated huff left me. "And you can say that because—"

"I know you."

"Do you?" I challenged. "I've already proved that you were all wrong about me the night of the wedding, didn't I?"

Whatever response she'd had waiting for me died, and her lips pressed firmly together. After a few seconds, she nodded distractedly, and whispered, "Why, Deacon?"

"Why? I told you, I just want to spend time—"

"No. Why *now*?"

The silence in the car felt like a living thing as I searched for an answer, but I'd been searching for an answer for over a week now, and I still hadn't found one.

"I don't know, Charlie Girl," I said honestly.

For some reason, my answer seemed to surprise her. After a second's hesitation, she nodded, and said, "Okay."

"Okay?"

"If you want to take me, let's go. Jagger and Grey are leaving for Seattle for a little over a week, so Grey's supposed to drop Keith off at the babysitter. I'll just ask her to keep him longer."

I tilted my head slightly at the mention of Jagger. "Your brother's going to kill me."

"For taking me to look at cars?" she asked, her tone both curious and testing.

My eyes slid down her body, and before I could stop myself, I said, "Let's just say he has every reason to tell me to stay away from you, Charlie Girl."

By the time I was looking at her face again, her eyes were wide and her cheeks were the brightest red, and it looked like she was fighting a smile. "Um, okay. I'll, uh, I'll see you then. After work. When I get off," she stammered as she opened the passenger door of her car.

"If I'm not here to pick you up, then I'm still at the garage working on your car. I'll get your number from Grey and text you so you have mine in case I'm not here."

Charlie still looked like I was speaking some foreign language to her, like she didn't believe this was happening as she turned and walked into Mama's. I didn't blame her. I was still trying to make sense of it myself.

It wasn't until Grey sent me Charlie's number twenty minutes later, and I automatically sent Charlie a message from my regular phone, that it clicked.

I hadn't once thought about adding Charlie's number to Candy. I hadn't even used Candy other than to talk to Words since the wedding. Actually, I hadn't used it for its designated purpose for almost a week before that.

From the day I'd walked into Mama's Café and found that journal, I'd been so consumed with Words that I hadn't had sex in nearly two weeks. On top of that I'd been trying to apologize to Charlie for how I'd treated her, and somehow . . . somehow those two things had started affecting how I now saw her.

Charlie—*Charlie* of all people. A girl I'd never looked twice at, I now couldn't stop thinking about, and I now had no doubt that it was because I'd gone from having sex nearly every day to not at all. Because I was addicted to a girl who was real, but would never be real to me. And now I knew I needed to put an end to this before I did something that ruined fucking everything.

Chapter Ten

Charlie

June 11, 2016

I CHECKED MY phone for what had to be the twentieth time since I'd last tried calling him, and after looking out into the parking lot once more, called Deacon again. But like the first two times, it just rang until his voice mail eventually picked up. And again I hung up without leaving a message.

It was one thing to be ten or fifteen minutes late, it was even okay to be twenty minutes late if there was traffic on the freeway. You know, if we had freeways or traffic in Thatch. But even then, you expected a call or a text from the person you were waiting on explaining why they were late. That's what normal people did anyway. Normal people probably also only waited for about fifteen minutes before leaving.

I was the idiot waiting for Deacon for nearly an hour and a half, sure that he would be coming in "just a couple minutes." I could've walked the length of the town multiple times in that amount of time.

My fingers drummed agitatedly on the table I was sitting at in Mama's, and I wondered again what I was doing sitting there.

I had nothing to go home to at the moment. Keith was at the babysitter's house. Jagger and Grey were already on their trip to Seattle. I could have spent the time possibly messaging Stranger, but every time I'd gone to message him I'd told myself that Deacon would show up as soon as I did, and I knew I wouldn't want to give up talking to Stranger so soon.

With one last look around the café, I slid out from the corner booth and finally left. After a quick scan around the parking lot to be sure I didn't see my car or Deacon's, I started walking in the direction of Danny's Garage.

My chest tightened uncomfortably when I passed by and found it deserted. A sign hanging on the door stated they were closed and, being a Saturday, had been for hours. Instead of calling Deacon again or turning around, I continued on in the direction of Deacon and Graham's house.

I kept thinking of different scenarios as I walked. Most of them began with me being the one to find out that something had happened to him; the others with

Deacon apologizing over and over again for forgetting to pick me up, and showing me in more ways than with just his words how sorry he was.

Irrational, betraying heart.

Those scenarios made my eyes roll, and left me re-thinking tonight altogether. Like I'd told Deacon, I was so sure that the minute I agreed to spend time with him, I would find out this was nothing more than one huge joke to him. What I hadn't said was that I'd been *afraid* that's what I would find out.

The more Deacon had forced himself into my life lately, the harder it had been to ignore that I liked when he did it. I liked knowing that when I walked away, he couldn't help but follow me. I liked knowing that when I tried to leave, he would do everything to keep me to stay. And I liked the way he couldn't seem to figure out what to say when he was around me.

And, damn him, I liked the way he was with my son. For someone who claimed to hate kids, he always knew what to say and do with Keith.

No one else would have thought to cover the ladybugs on the kid's menu at Mama's.

I still didn't understand the sudden change in him, and that made me want to guard my heart and myself. Because I knew all it would take was Deacon proving to me that he was nothing more than *Deacon Carver* to make me regret ever letting my guard down—even for a second.

The sound of a sultry female laugh caused me to do a double take just as I was rounding the corner onto

Deacon and Graham's driveway, and I stumbled to a stop. I wanted to turn around and run, but couldn't stop looking at what was happening in front of me.

Deacon was shirtless and buttoning his pants, and the girl I'd heard laughing had pulled him close to kiss him before walking toward her car.

My stomach sank and chest ached. As much as I wanted to make myself believe that I'd come in at the wrong time and was taking what I was seeing the wrong way, I knew I wasn't. I'd waited for him, I'd let myself believe that maybe . . .

That was the problem.

I'd let my mind run wild with the possibilities of what *could* be with a guy like Deacon. One huge joke to him, or not, Deacon Carver obviously hadn't changed. I wouldn't waste my time waiting around to see if he ever would, and I refused to let myself fall into a place where I allowed myself to be another girl that Deacon would never remember.

I wrapped an arm around my waist and took two hesitant steps back as the girl's voice floated over to me.

"I had fun. Call me," she said over her shoulder as she slid into her car, but got too busy checking her face in the mirror to realize that Deacon never responded.

Not wanting to be found staring at them like some deranged, lovesick girl, I turned around and headed home as fast as my legs would take me without breaking into a run. I hated that my vision kept blurring, because I knew Deacon wasn't worth my tears, but it was hard to stop them.

I hated that the first time I thought I could move on after years of hanging on to Ben's memory, I once again felt like I wasn't enough. Despite everything he'd told me, Ben had needed Grey. She was his safe place, his comfort. And Deacon needed a different face every night, and a girl willing to be used for a few minutes of pleasure.

But I have Stranger. . .

The thought made me laugh sadly.

Unfortunately, tonight only reaffirmed why Stranger should stay a stranger.

Because there was something safe in keeping him *fake*. The screens of our phones helped guard my heart because I knew that no matter how much I loved our conversations, I would never be able to get invested enough to the point where he could break it.

I was only five minutes away from home when my phone began ringing. I didn't have to look at it to know who it was, but I was disappointed that it took him that long to check his phone and realize what he'd done even after the girl had left. Seconds after the ringing stopped, it started up again, and again, and again.

My fingers twitched to grab my phone and answer it, to let him attempt to give me some bullshit explanation, but the tears came faster with each time he called. And that made me angrier at him—that he somehow had enough of a hold on me to make me cry harder at the thought of letting him explain away why he'd forgotten me for another girl.

This was Deacon Carver! I didn't want to care if there had been another girl at all. I should have expected this. I should have never let myself feel anything for him in the first place.

I'd barely made it two feet inside the door before Grey was rushing toward me from where she'd been looking in the fridge.

Crap.

"What's wrong?" Grey asked loudly.

"I thought you were going out of town," I said as I quickly wiped at my wet cheeks.

"What happened?" Jagger's worried voice sounded throughout the open space from upstairs, and within seconds he was looking over the rail.

"I thought you were going out with Deacon," Grey said, ignoring both Jagger and me.

Jagger bit out a curse as he ran down the stairs. "Deacon? You were going out with fucking *Deacon*? What'd he do?"

"*Nothing*," I said firmly, then repeated, "I thought you were going out of town."

Grey's eyebrows drew together as she studied me. "We started to, but Aly got sick on the way there, so we're going to leave in a few days. Now what's wrong?"

I laughed and waved them both off, and tried to walk toward my room in the back. "Again, nothing. I'll be leaving again soon, can I take your car?"

Grey held on to my hand to keep me from walking away. "What happened? Did he say something to you?"

My body deflated, and I huffed at my own stupidity. "He would've had to actually show up in order to say something," I whispered. "But he was busy."

"Busy with what?" Grey asked at the same time Jagger growled, "When were you two going to tell me that you were going out with Deacon?"

"Jag, now is not the time to be like this, okay? Don't— just don't." Grey had let go of me to try to calm Jagger down, and I used that to my advantage to walk toward the hall again. "And since when is it a *what* with Deacon, Grey? It's always a *who*."

"He wouldn't when he had plans—"

"He would," I said, cutting Grey off. "I called him a few times, but he never picked up. I walked over to the house, and he was seeing a girl out while buttoning up his pants." I tried to sound like it didn't matter, but my voice cracked more than once during my explanation.

Jagger's face fell, but he didn't say anything else, and I knew from his silence that he was now truly pissed off.

Grey looked like she couldn't decide if she was more upset at Deacon or sad for me, but she mouthed, "I'm sorry."

"Again, not a big deal. I mean, it's Deacon, right? But is it okay if I use your car tonight? He left mine in the shop."

"Of course," she said, and tugged on Jagger's arm when he continued to stand there staring at a spot on the floor.

I hurried back to my bathroom, and groaned when I saw my face. It was more than obvious I'd been crying, and if my brother knew I was crying over Deacon, then he knew tonight meant a lot more to me than I'd let on. Which explained his silence just before.

After washing my face, I did my hair and makeup and was finishing getting dressed when I heard Jagger start yelling.

"You really think fucking someone is more important than whatever plans you had? Or making sure she had a ride home?"

My head dropped and mortification slid through my body at the thought of my big brother calling Deacon, before I heard another voice.

"Just tell me if she's here. She's not answering her phone!"

"Did you answer yours?" Jagger countered.

"Charlie!" Deacon's booming voice echoed through the warehouse.

I wanted to hide, but instead of actually attempting to, I froze in place as Deacon and Jagger yelled at each other all the way down the halls. My body jerked when Deacon began pounding on my bedroom door and calling my name. After taking a deep breath in and giving myself a second to school my expression, I walked over to open it.

"Charlie, I'm sorry," he began, but Jagger cut in.

"You don't have to talk to him."

I shrugged and smiled. "Why wouldn't I? And you don't have to apologize."

"The hell he doesn't," Jagger growled.

"Yes, I do. I'm sorry, I—I—I lost track of time and crashed, and when I woke up it was two hours after I was supposed to get you."

"You fell asleep?" I asked, but kept the smile plastered on my face.

"Bull—"

"Jagger," I bit out, but didn't stop looking at Deacon.

"I'm sorry," Deacon said in response. "I'll make it up to you, I swear to God. Let me—"

"That really isn't necessary, and actually, I need you to leave. I have a date tonight, and I'm running a little late now that you're here."

His eyebrows shot up, as did Jagger's, and for the first time since I opened the door, Deacon's eyes slowly trailed over my body. "Oh . . . you have a date?"

"Uh-huh. So if you wouldn't mind, I need to finish getting ready."

He nodded absentmindedly and took a step back, but didn't take his eyes off me. "Then, uh, I guess things worked out tonight."

"Yeah," I agreed. "Funny how that can happen for both of us."

Deacon's gaze had been traveling down again, but snapped back up at my words. From the way he quickly looked away, but kept opening his mouth like he wanted to say something, it was clear he'd assumed I had somehow guessed the real reason why he hadn't been there for me today. But I wasn't going to make it easier for him by saying anything else. He'd hurt me without even trying or caring.

Unapologetically arrogant and unaware.

Well, I guess now he was apologetic at least.

"Deacon," I prompted when he continued to stand there, and tried to ignore the chaos his light eyes caused inside me when they finally rested on my face again.

My heart was racing so fast it felt like it would beat

out of my chest, and it was taking every ounce of strength to stand still when my body was craving the feel of his against mine again.

"Right, well . . . I'll, uh, I'll see you." After another pause, he turned and walked down the hall. And with a worried look, Jagger reluctantly followed.

I released a ragged breath and slumped against the doorframe, and tried to ignore the way my hands shook from the chaos that Deacon left in his wake. After I heard him leave, I waited in the hall for a few minutes before grabbing Grey's keys and leaving as well. And soon I was at the babysitter's house picking up my son.

"Hey, thank you for understanding," I told her as I handed her some cash, and took Keith's hand and started backing up toward the driveway. "After what happened today, I really just need to spend the night with my favorite guy."

"Not a problem! Call me whenever you need me again."

"I will." Once Keith was in his booster seat, I kissed his cheek and asked, "Who are you?"

"Mommy!" he said with a laugh and a cheesy grin. "I'm Spider-Man!"

"What do you say to Spider-Man taking me out on a date tonight? I think other guys just make our lives too complicated."

Keith held out his fist, and I bumped it. "All right! Hot dog!"

My laughter bubbled up, genuine and free. "Hot *date*, bud."

"That's what I said!"

Chapter Eleven

Deacon

June 11, 2016

YOUR TURN . . . COME *back to me, Words.*

I sent the text, then walked into the kitchen to look for something to eat, but I didn't know if I was hungry. I couldn't even focus on what was in front of me. So much so that it took way too long to realize that I was staring at the closed refrigerator door instead of inside it.

All I could see was Charlie. Still.

The way she'd looked when I'd gone after her earlier. The way her blue eyes had been guarded.

What she'd said. *"Yeah. Funny how that can happen for both of us."*

She knew . . . I don't know how, but somehow she fucking knew about my afternoon.

I knew I'd fucked up. All I'd wanted was to forget about her, and to knock some sense back into my head. I'd still planned on picking her up and taking her to look at cars once her shift was over.

But one girl had led to another.

By the time I'd gotten the second to leave, I was ready to slam my head into the wall over and over again, if only to get the thought of Charlie out of it. Because she was still there, just as she had been for nearly two weeks, only now it was paired with this overwhelming sense that I'd done something wrong. To Charlie, to Words . . .

But I'd done nothing more than what I'd done nearly every day for years, and Charlie meant nothing, and Words was . . . Words wasn't real. And yet, as soon as I grabbed my phone and saw the missed calls and the time, my stomach had dropped and I'd felt crippled from the guilt that tore through me.

I'd known that I needed to leave, to get to Charlie. That I had to explain everything and nothing because I refused to let her know what I'd done in an attempt to erase her. But I hadn't been able to force myself to move.

I'd stood frozen with my hair gripped tightly in my fist as I'd called her over and over again.

I'd thought if I allowed myself to want Charlie, I would do something that ruined everything.

Each call that went unanswered drove home the realization that I'd already done that.

I barely registered the sound of the front door opening from where I was lying on the carpet in the middle of the living room. I didn't remember walking in there or lying down, but there I fucking was, scrubbing my hands over my face again and again, trying to wash away images I couldn't keep.

My hands stilled and body tightened when I felt someone settle down next to me. I slowly lowered my arms and turned my head only enough to take in the person next to me when they pressed themselves as close to me as possible.

A shock of red hair met me seconds before her voice did, and I felt myself instantly relax.

"If I hadn't witnessed what just happened in my home, seeing you right here would clue me in to the fact that something is wrong." Grey turned her head to look at me, her gold eyes dark in the room, the only light filtering in from the entryway.

"What do you mean?" My voice was hoarse, as if I'd actually been yelling and screaming at myself the past hour the way I'd wanted to.

"What was it you and Graham said?" She trailed off, and resituated herself so her head was now on my shoulder. "Right . . . you always said Knox was murdering the carpet when all that stuff was going down with Harlow, back before he told you about it. And now for the first time ever, I find you lying here in the dark. I think this carpet means bad things for some of my favorite guys."

A low, dark laugh vibrated in my chest. "Just a carpet, Grey."

She didn't respond for a long time, and when she did,

hesitation crept through each word. "Jagger . . . Jagger's so mad, Deacon." There was an uneasy pause before she admitted, "And I was too, but then I saw you when you came looking for her, and more importantly, I saw you when you left. I know there's something going on that neither of you are telling me, and you don't have to tell me if you aren't ready, but I had a feeling that you needed me."

" 'Course I need you. You're the love of my life." It was meant to come out teasing, but my tone only sounded defeated.

"That was so depressing I can't even roll my eyes," she murmured. One of her arms suddenly flopped over my chest and tightened around me.

I lifted my hand to her forearm and squeezed back.

Her face was buried in my shoulder, muffling her voice. "I can always count on you for a bear hug when I need it most."

My next laugh was louder, more genuine. "Is this your version of one of my hugs?"

"Shut up. You're too big to bear hug, and it really doesn't make it any easier when you're lying on the floor."

I squeezed her arm once more, and said, "Exactly what I needed, Grey."

She released me and rolled back so her head was barely resting on my shoulder, and blew out a slow sigh. "It wasn't one of your bone-crushing, breath-stealing hugs, but I tried."

We laid there in silence for a few minutes as my turmoil mixed with her unspoken questions, filling the darkness above us.

I opened my mouth nearly a dozen times to say something I didn't want to allow to leave my tongue. As if speaking the words would give them power, would make all of the chaos in my mind real.

"I said you didn't have to tell me if you weren't ready, but I know you're ready. So this is me telling you that you have to tell me."

Amusement tugged at my mouth for a second before it fell again. "She went on a date tonight." The words finally tumbled out before I could stop them.

I felt Grey nod. "So I heard. And, no, before you ask, I don't know who she went with. I found out after you did. But I also heard that you had a, uh—you had . . . you had time with someone of the opposite sex today, as well." A barely audible gag sounded next to me. "Ugh, God. You, Graham, and Knox have me in a constant state of wanting to throw up."

I didn't respond, because at that moment, I was ready to find a wall again. My head needed something hard to come in contact with.

"Deac, tell me why it matters to you that Charlie went on a date tonight."

"It doesn't." My reply was instant; the lie was thick on my tongue, and more than obvious to Grey.

"I'm almost positive I know the answer, but I think *you* need to hear yourself say it. So why does it matter?"

Christ, why did Grey have to know the three of us so well? Knox kept Harlow from Graham and me, but hadn't been able to keep her from Grey. And I knew Graham and I were the same—we couldn't keep shit from Grey because she already knew it anyway. She knew us better than we knew ourselves.

"I have no damn clue," I said honestly. "I don't understand it."

"Not a whole lot to understand," Grey murmured.

"It's fucking Charlie, Grey. *Charlie*."

"And?"

"She doesn't talk to anyone."

"She talks to me," Grey countered.

"Well, she can't stand me."

"You are kind of obnoxious."

I let her joke roll off without so much as a hint of a smile. "She would hide behind her books if she could."

"You hide behind a never-ending line of women."

That stung.

A comment that would normally have me feeling pretty damn proud of myself now made me wince.

"She's young—she's so fucking young."

Grey snorted. "It's not like she's underage, Deacon."

"It doesn't matter. In my mind, she's Jagger's little sister. I remember her in elementary school and middle school and—"

"We all remember each other during those times."

"And, again, she's *young*. I gave Knox so much shit over Harlow's age, and Charlie is . . . Charlie is . . . what, twenty?"

"Twenty-two," Grey informed me. "Four years younger than you. It isn't crazy."

It *was* crazy, even if the age difference wasn't. Because no matter what Grey said, it was still Charlie Easton.

"I think I've hated her for the last year and a half," I admitted suddenly.

I felt Grey shift to look at me, but I didn't meet her stare.

"How do you go from hating someone—from having that much anger directed at them—to *this* in a matter of days?"

Day. Hours, I mentally corrected.

Grey sucked in a breath, but it got caught when she tried to speak again. After a moment, she said, "First, why on earth would you ever hate Charlie?"

I finally turned to look at her. One of my eyebrows arched as I waited for her to understand.

It didn't take long.

There wasn't much that pissed me off; Grey knew that.

"Deacon, no. No . . . you didn't—you told her, didn't you? That's what the two of you fought about, isn't it?"

"I love you, Grey."

And I meant it.

Grey was family. My baby sister even though I was an only child. She was one of the only females who weren't blood that I would ever love.

"People can't fuck with the lives of those I love, and expect me to be okay with them or what they did."

"Oh, Deacon." Disappointment coated her voice. "You can't . . ." She trailed off; her head shook against my shoulder. "If you knew exactly what happened, you wouldn't have ever been able to hate her."

"Grey—"

"It was messed up, and she was old enough to know

what she was doing. She knows that, I know that. But what Ben did to her, the way he messed with her mind with the things he said to her, and after all those years of her feeling the way she did." One of Grey's shoulders lifted. "She made a mistake, but it's impossible to hate her for it knowing what happened to her—especially after."

The anguish in Grey's voice for a girl who had slept with her fiancé cut straight through me. As if I hadn't already known that I'd pegged Charlie all wrong. As if I hadn't already been rethinking everything I thought I'd known about her. Now I was hearing straight from Grey that I still had no fucking clue at all, that there was still so much I didn't know about the girl who haunted me, waking or sleeping.

"Look, I already know I was wrong. In thinking that way about her, in saying it to her, all of it."

Understanding lit in her eyes. "You were apologizing at the wedding."

A huff of frustration left me. "Trying."

She nodded absentmindedly. "Well if you hated me and let me know, I don't think I'd give you a chance to apologize. I still don't know why Harlow forgave you and Graham for the way you both treated her." Before I could try to defend myself, she continued. "Okay then. Second, what is the 'this' that you mentioned? What has your hatred turned into?"

I looked back up to the darkened ceiling. "Something I don't understand," I said after a second, but the confession sounded more like an accusation. "Something I'm not okay with."

"Why?"

"I already said it, Grey. It's Charlie."

I felt her studying me for a long time before she looked up at the ceiling as well. "Is that really it, or is it the fact that for the first time, you're actually falling for someone, and that scares you?"

"Falling for—no. I'm just—"

"Falling for her."

"Confused," I argued, my voice bordering on a growl.

"You've spouted off a list of what sounds like your reasons why you shouldn't be with her. You came storming in and *shoved* Jagger out of your way to get to her tonight, and looked defeated on your way out." She paused, then reiterated. "*Defeated*, Deacon. I've never seen you look like that in my life. You're Deacon Carver, nothing can bring you down, let alone *defeat* you."

I was rethinking my love for Grey. She was too perceptive. Too right.

"But a conversation with Charlie did," she added softly. "I'm not going to pretend to understand what's going on, and I'm not going to tell you that I'm okay with it. Because even though I'm here right now with you, I know that you have the capability of breaking her heart. She doesn't need her heart broken again after how hard she fought to put it back together after Ben."

I ran my free hand through my hair, gripping at it as I did. "I don't want—" I cut off with a growl. "I don't want her heart, Grey. I don't want her in that way. I just . . . I just want her out of my goddamn head."

Silence engulfed the room again for a long while

before Grey sat up and spun around so she was facing me. "I'll let you keep denying everything to yourself after I leave, but know this: you can't have it both ways. Charlie isn't someone who falls in and out of a bed. Charlie is a girl who falls into arms and stays there. So this girl you ditched her for—"

"Girls," I corrected, my throat thick. Revulsion churned my stomach.

Shock covered Grey's face and quickly morphed into disappointment.

The front door opened, stopping Grey from speaking, and Graham came walking in with a satisfied look on his face. He did a double take when he spotted us, and walked back a step to flip on the light in the living room.

"What the hell, man? She's married and has a kid!"

Grey rolled her eyes without looking back at her brother.

I didn't have it in me to mess with him tonight.

"Does Jagger know you're here?" Graham demanded as he walked up on us.

"Yes, Graham, he does, and I'm sure he's totally worried about what's happening since he let me come alone."

Graham mumbled something about Jagger needing to keep an eye on Grey, then said louder, "Hey, is Charlie okay?"

The second her name left him, my attention shifted from Grey to Graham, my jaw clenched as I thought of the way Graham seemed to always go after Charlie lately.

Grey's brow tightened in confusion as she looked up at her brother. "What do you mean?"

"I mean, it seemed like there's something bothering her."

"Wh—"

Suspicion flooded me and leaked out when I spoke. "When did you see her?" I asked quickly, cutting Grey off.

Graham gestured over his shoulder, as if Charlie would be standing in our entryway. "Just now at Bonfire."

Before either of us could respond, Graham pulled his ringing phone out of his pocket, and slowly started backing out of the room as that same satisfied smile covered his face.

I didn't hear him answer the call, my mind was racing, trying to figure out if there was a key word I had missed just now, or earlier when I'd seen Charlie.

Grey's wide eyes came back to me again, and this time, the silence between us felt strained and awkward.

Like the times I'd seen Charlie with Graham in the previous weeks, my blood felt white-hot as it pulsed through my veins. I gritted my teeth against the surge of anger that flared up. The feeling so foreign and sickening.

Jealousy.

I was jealous.

Of my best fucking friend.

"Would she . . ." I began, but didn't continue.

Grey looked at me helplessly. "I'm not sure. Before she came home from college, I would've sworn that she would have never been involved with either of you. But I saw her tonight, and she *has* asked me about Graham."

Shock hit me as fast as the jealousy had.

"How's it feel, Deac? How does it feel knowing a girl can hurt you like this?" Disappointment and sympathy and sorrow swirled in her eyes. "I don't know what happened between you two when you got to the warehouse tonight, but I saw what your actions did to Charlie today. Remember that you can hurt her, remember that you have. Think hard about what you want, and if you decide to go for what you've never had, know that you are not allowed to hurt her again like you did today."

I ground my teeth to keep from saying anything, and nodded.

My phone chimed twice from wherever I'd dropped it next to me, and Grey used the distraction to stand up and move away from me.

"I mean it, Deacon, think really hard about what you want from her, and the consequences that come with that decision. I'll only help you out with Jagger this once. If you do it again, I'll let him come visit you afterward."

I nodded again, and scrambled up to walk her out. When she was stepping out of the house, I asked, "Do you think this is all I can be?"

Grey slowly lifted an eyebrow in question.

"*This*, how people know me now. Is that all I will ever be to everyone else?"

The confusion left her face and was replaced by a smirk. "A man-whore?"

Again, a title that would have normally had me feeling damn proud of myself left me irritated.

"No, Deac. But that's all you'll be until you're ready to force them to see something different." She took slow steps backward, and shrugged. "Knox did it, I have no doubt that you can too, just like I have no doubt that Graham will be trying to do it soon too."

A dent formed between my brows. Suspicion, confusion, jealousy, anger—everything I wasn't used to, and everything I hated when it came to my friends. "Graham? Why?"

Another shrug. "There have been more than a few times in the last couple years when Graham and I have talked about *hypothetical* scenarios, and somehow he always ends up with a girl he grew up with. I've just been waiting to find out which girl these not-so-hypothetical scenarios are about." She pointed to the house, and said warily, "Unless that conversation was my first clue."

My hand curled around the door frame.

"Night, Deacon."

Once Grey was in her car and pulling out of the driveway, I had to force myself not to go talk to Graham about whether or not he'd been out with Charlie, or had just run into her with her date. I was too pissed off to talk to him rationally, and I was too confused to understand why I needed to know at all.

I started walking toward my room when my phone caught my eye where I'd left it on the floor of the living room. I felt my frustration seep away when I saw the name on the notification screen.

Words: *I'm here.*

Words: *Are you okay?*

I had no fucking clue if I was okay, but I knew I needed her and needed this. I didn't know what to think about the fact that just seeing her name on my phone could instantly make me forget about everything that had happened today, but I was thankful for it.

Yeah, just need you. I don't know how, but I've somehow missed talking to you since this morning.

Words: *Those are dangerous words, Stranger.*

But it's true. My day . . . Christ, everything in it feels wrong and goes wrong without you.

Words: *Don't. Don't say that. What you're saying does dangerous things to my heart.*

Heart. There was that word again.

The thought that I had the capability of doing anything to Charlie's heart made me feel uneasy—wrong. Because not only was I not the kind of guy who had anything to offer to her, but I had a feeling that I wouldn't know how to stop hurting her if I had her.

With Words, it didn't feel so dangerous. She knew what she was getting with me, and I knew she wouldn't willingly put her heart anywhere close enough for me to touch.

Words . . .

How do you have me rethinking everything I thought I wanted, and wanted to stay away from?

Words: *. . . There you go being dangerous again.*

Words: *Say it.*

Words: *Say it before you ask me for something I can't give you.*

What do you want me to say?

Words: *That you're okay with keeping us strangers because you know it would ruin everything if we weren't, and you're afraid of losing what we have.*

So what exactly are you saying you can't give me?

Words: *Stranger . . .*

Despite the way I craved having Words directly in front of me, I did a great job of fucking up things in person without even trying, and had no doubt I would do the same with her.

And she was right: after tonight especially, I knew I wasn't ready to lose this.

I blew out a slow sigh as I fell onto my bed, and tapped out my response.

I'm starting to think it's necessary for us. But I think I would lose more than you if this ended. You would probably be happy to get some sleep.

I'd gladly lose sleep for the rest of my life if it meant listening to you.

Words: *My heart . . .*

Words: *Damn you, Stranger.*

Words: *I thought you weren't going to sweep me off my feet. A guy who doesn't believe in love shouldn't be allowed to be as romantic as you are.*

My mouth curved up in a bemused grin as I reread what I'd sent her so far this evening. Not once had I tried to be romantic, I was just being honest for the first time in too long.

But her reactions to my honesty? Yeah, I fucking liked those.

My apologies?

Words: *Don't apologize.*

Wasn't sincere anyway. ;)

Words: *You were wrong, by the way. About who would lose more.*

Really.

Words: *My entire life has revolved around words and love. In less than two weeks, a man who doesn't believe in the latter has destroyed the way I view relationships and myself, and raised the bar incredibly high for any man who comes into my life in the future. And after such a short time, I'm dreading the day you walk out of my life.*

I stared at her message for a long time, just reading it over and over again. Absorbing every word and the meanings behind them.

Words . . .

You and your words . . .

Unable to stop myself, I tapped out the words that were so desperate to be said, even though I knew no matter how real our conversations felt, *she* never would be.

Walk away from you? I don't know if I'll ever be able to.

If anything, you should be waiting for the day I decide to finally find you.

Words: . . .

Words: *I dare you.*

Chapter Twelve

Charlie

June 15, 2016

"GRAHAM, HONEY, I'M so glad you were here to help today. I was thinking about Caroline—"

Graham's face pinched with irritation as his mom stepped up beside us that next Wednesday. "Mom, no. No Caroline, no Melissa. No more lists of girls." He jerked his hand away when his mom tried to put a piece of paper in it. "I don't want her number. One of these times I'm just going to show up with a girl so you'll stop doing this."

Mrs. LaRue sighed. "Well she can't be just any girl you found on the street."

"She won't be, Mom, Christ. I'll probably have known

her my entire life. This *is* Thatch. As much as I love talking to you about all the girls you want me to settle down with, I need to finish talking to Charlie about the house."

His mom kissed me on the cheek and squeezed my shoulder. "We're going home. Enjoy your new place, sweetie!" Before I could thank her, she turned her thoughtful gaze on Graham. "Known her your whole life, huh? That narrows down my lists."

"I didn't mean—Mom, I still have to find her—you know what? Never mind. Yes, go narrow down your lists." Graham let out a slow breath when the door shut, then dug in his pocket to produce a ring of keys for me. "Here, before I forget to give these to you."

My pulse was racing and my mind reeling from his words. I repeated them to myself as I stared at the keys in my hand, and tried to keep my tone light when I asked, "You still have to *find* her? Is this mystery girl hiding from you?"

Graham winked, and the corner of his mouth pulled into a lopsided smirk. "Something like that."

I tried to keep my heart in my chest, but it felt impossible, when it was entirely *possible* that I was standing just inches from my stranger.

It had been four days since I'd dared Stranger to find me. Each night I asked if he was any closer, while praying he wasn't.

Stranger allowed me to be someone I could never be in real life. I couldn't attempt to voice the things I wrote to him without my words getting caught in my throat. I couldn't try to speak to men that way without needing to find someone or something to hide behind.

With Stranger I had my voice because I had my phone to hide behind. His beautiful soul endlessly pulled me out from behind the walls I'd built around myself; all the while I remained invisible to him. Every day he helped show me how to trust someone with my heart again, even though he and I both knew that, in reality, he would never hold it.

But now with Graham's cryptic and oddly similar words, I wanted to shout that I was standing right there.

But I needed to keep Stranger at a distance. I needed to keep him fictional, or everything we had would shatter. Our deep conversations that meant everything, and even the innocent flirting and teasing . . . all of it would be gone.

Graham's voice pulled me from my internal conflict, and I blinked quickly to clear my head as he handed me a piece of paper.

"I'm sorry, what?" I asked breathily when I realized I'd missed everything he'd just told me, and hated that my tone gave away everything I was feeling.

"There's a security system already set up throughout the house, but the owner had it shut off when he moved. Everything to get it turned back on is on that paper."

"Oh. Right," I said quickly, still wanting nothing more than to get away from him, and to say things I knew I shouldn't.

"All right. Anything else you need to know?"

Only about a thousand things, starting with what the word "stranger" means to you.

But I knew that wasn't what he was asking.

I'd run into Graham during my date with Keith the weekend before, and he'd told me about one of his friends who needed to rent out his house.

The owner had moved across the country for a year-long transfer with his job. I was told there was a possibility of it becoming permanent, but I wasn't going to focus on that now.

Because that wasn't important at the moment. Either we would find somewhere more permanent in a year, or we would stay there. What was important was that I had a two-bedroom house in Thatch with a backyard for my son and me.

We'd just finished getting moved in, with the help of Jagger and the LaRues, and tonight would be our first official night there.

"Uh, no." I shook my head and looked around. "No, just thank you so much for helping me with this. I can't tell you how excited I am."

"Ah, Charlie. Don't thank me. You know I'd do anything for you." He leaned forward and pressed a hard kiss to the top of my head.

And it ended.

The breathlessness. The racing heart. All of it . . . ended.

Because there was nothing behind that kiss from him, and there was nothing I felt from it other than the protectiveness I always felt from Graham.

"Sorry I'm late."

My body stilled and my next inhale was sharp and audible when the deep, rough voice sounded behind me.

I turned though I told myself not to face him, and was overcome with everything I *didn't* want to feel from the man in front of me.

Deacon.

I'd seen him twice since I'd asked him to leave the warehouse, and had heard from him at least once each day since.

The next morning he'd shown up for breakfast at Mama's with Graham, as they always did on Sundays. And since I worked the front on the weekends, I worked their table. I didn't say a word to him, and he didn't speak to me, but those eyes of his never once stopped following me from the moment he entered the café until they left.

I'd tried like hell not to look at him, but I could still feel his stare . . .

Searching, begging, asking and telling a hundred things I refused to hear.

By the time they left, I was shaking from forcing myself not to look at him.

When I got off work on Monday, my car was in the parking lot of Mama's with a note tucked into the windshield. I'd taken one look at the black smudges from the grease on the paper, and thrown the paper away without opening it.

Tuesday he'd walked into Mama's with purpose, right up to where I was waiting on a table in the back. White shirt, straining against his muscular form and stained with grease, every inch of him demanded attention and screamed for me to touch.

I'd turned my back on him and forced myself to focus on taking my table's order.

My breath had caught in my throat when one of his hands went to my hip and his lips brushed against my ear. Goose bumps covered my arms and my stomach swirled with heat as his deep voice rumbled.

"Keep pretending I don't exist. Keep ignoring me. Keep acting invisible if it makes you feel better, Charlie Girl. In case you haven't noticed, I fucking see you." His fingers flexed against my hip as if to prove his point. "I'm not giving up until you talk to me."

When I didn't respond to him, he'd turned and left.

Each of those days, there had been a text from him asking me to call him.

I hadn't.

I also hadn't asked him to help me move in.

But there he was, standing in front of me, looking the same as he had the day before. Demanding attention and screaming for me to touch.

I curled my hands into fists and wrapped an arm around my waist.

At least he'd changed before he'd come, though the streaks of grease that he'd missed on his arms made it clear that he'd come from work. Not that what he had changed into hid his size or strength any more than that tight white shirt had.

"Charlie Girl," Deacon murmured, his voice barely above a growl.

His mouth was set in a grimace and his light brown eyes were conflicted; when they flicked up at something behind me, they flashed with rage.

"Dude, it's almost eight. I told you we were moving her in two hours ago," Graham said from behind me.

Not something, I realized. *Someone.*

"Got held up at the shop with an emergency. I can see I missed a lot."

Heat crawled up my cheeks at Deacon's meaning, and I realized he'd come in when Graham had kissed me.

If somehow Graham had missed the implication of Deacon's words, it would have been impossible to miss the glare that was clearly directed at him.

Bold, unyielding.

"Yeah, the whole thing," Graham said slowly, awkwardly.

I forced myself to look away from Deacon, and turned back to find Graham tapping away on his phone, completely oblivious to Deacon's anger.

"I'm about to head out, you headed home?" Graham asked Deacon without looking up.

"Deaton, Deaton, Deaton!" Keith screamed as he tore through the living room. "Guess who I am!"

"Hey now." I gave Keith a curious look and pointed from him to the hall he'd just come running down. "I could've sworn I just put you in bed."

Keith's shoulders sagged. "But Mommy! Why I hafta sleep when my people are here?"

I bit back the laugh that so desperately wanted to escape, and said, "Nope, sorry. Back in bed plea—" My heart stuttered, and I froze when I heard my phone chime from where I'd left it charging in my room at the same time that Graham put his phone in his pocket. "Uh . . . say good night to Deacon and Graham, and I'll be in your room in just a minute to tuck you back in," I finished quickly, then slipped away from the boys to head toward my room in search of my phone.

It was one thing for Graham to say things that linked him to Stranger, it would be another if the message waiting for me was from Stranger after having watched Graham text someone. I could feel it, that end when all of this became real, and I wasn't ready for it. I wasn't ready to lose this person who had helped me learn so much in such a short amount of time. I wasn't ready to lose this person that I had such a strange connection with. And I wasn't ready to find out that Stranger was Graham LaRue, when I so desperately wanted him to be someone I knew he never would be.

Irrational, betraying heart.

I blew out a relieved breath when it ended up being only a message from Jagger letting me know he was happy for me, and was sorry for having to leave earlier.

Not that I blamed him. Since Jagger and Grey had to delay their trip to Seattle last weekend, they were leaving early the next morning to see friends and catch the last few days of an art show that Jagger had some pieces in.

Truthfully, I was ready for them to finally go to Seattle. I was worried that even with a place separate from them, I would still have to endure Jagger's endless questions about Deacon, like how I was feeling, and what was I thinking planning something with him in the first place.

In other words, the parental-type talks had been in full force ever since Saturday night, and I needed a break.

I left my phone on the nightstand so it could continue charging, and walked back down the hall toward the living room. My footsteps slowed when I found it empty, but then I heard Deacon and Keith's voices coming from Keith's new room at the opposite end of the house.

Graham was already gone.

"What? No way, kid! Batman can't beat Superman!"

"Yeah huh! 'Cause I'm so supa strong."

"But Superman's stronger. Like, ladybugs can't even touch him, he's so awesome."

I peeked into the room in time to see Keith smack his forehead with his open palm. "Ladybugs can't touch *Darf Vaber*. How many times I hafta tell you?"

"What if Superman just used his laser eyes to kill all the ladybugs in the world?"

Keith sucked in a huge breath, then faltered. "Whoa."

Deacon nodded slowly. "Yeah, kid. Whoa."

I froze against Keith's doorjamb when both boys looked over at me, and stammered, "Uh, it's t—you rea— it's bedtime."

Keith sighed exaggeratedly, but shuffled over to me for a quick kiss, then to his bed when Deacon said good night.

I swallowed thickly and tried to ignore the way Deacon's eyes devoured me as he ate up the distance separating us.

Those same eyes held so many unspoken questions when he stepped close to me, but before he could voice any of them, or I could ask him to leave, the doorbell rang.

"Whoa cool! Mommy! Did you hear it?"

"I did," I said uneasily as I wondered who could be at the door. "Get under the covers, buddy, I've gotta go—"

"I've got it," Deacon murmured, cutting me off.

"It's my house."

"And it's for me," he argued gently, and stretched his hand out behind him to hold me back.

It worked. I was so terrified of what I would feel the second he touched me that I nearly jumped away from his touch.

I still followed a few feet behind him after shutting Keith's door, and listened intently when he answered my door.

After a minute, he shut the door and sent me a challenging look as he stood there holding a pizza box. "Knew I wasn't going to make it in time to help, and figured if you let me in at all, you were going to kick me out as fast as you could . . ."

"And you think pizza will stop me from doing that?" I asked when he didn't continue.

"No, but I'm hoping it'll help." I would have expected him to look smug then, but he was just standing there waiting. His expression showed that he was waiting for me to make him leave.

I grabbed the box from him and turned to walk to the kitchen. I didn't look back at him, but I knew he followed me. "I find it incredibly convenient that you didn't show up until Jagger was gone tonight, especially considering I didn't know you were coming at all."

"Graham asked me to come help, and, like I said earlier, I got caught up at the garage."

I glanced at him from over my shoulder and forced a smile as I dropped the box on the kitchen island. It felt like a sneer. "Did you?"

"Fuck, Charlie . . ." He grabbed my forearm and turned me around, his shoulders now sagging with the weight of some invisible stress as his large hands moved up to grip mine. "I'm sorry. I'm so damn sorry."

The depth of his apology stunned me, but it didn't change what I saw. What I'd felt and let myself believe . . . how he'd lied to me and forgotten about me. My head shook, but he continued.

"I fucked up, I know. I have never been more aware of anything in my life than how much I've messed up with you. I got stuck at the garage tonight, I swear to God."

"I'm sure you can understand why I don't believe you," I bit out, and hated that my eyes burned with unshed tears.

Deacon Carver hadn't deserved my tears then, and he most certainly didn't deserve them now. Not when he could see them, not when he could get a glimpse into how much he'd hurt me.

"Give me a chance to make it up to you."

"No!" I huffed sadly and shook my head furiously. "You told me exactly what you thought of me. You forced me to stand there so you could apologize and somehow got me to agree to let you make it up to me. And then you made me look like an idiot because I so stupidly let myself believe for one second that you might actually care about someone other than yourself! Because I believed that you would actually show."

"Charlie, I do, and I meant to," he ground out. "I nev—"

"No, you don't get to try to tell me how you *intended* to be there for me *after* you finished screwing someone else."

His large hands tightened around my shoulders, not uncomfortably, but like he was pleading with me through his touch alone.

But I wasn't finished.

Deacon should know better by now. If I thought about something long enough, if I imagined how a conversation would go in my mind enough times, once I finally started talking about it I wouldn't stop until I said every last word.

"And now look where we are . . . with you forcing me to stand still so you can apologize and ask me to give you another chance." I forced a laugh from my chest, but it sounded wet from my tears. "How many times can you make me look like an idiot before it stops being some sick, hilarious joke to you?"

He flinched as though I'd slapped him across the face. "You think I find this funny? You think this is a joke to me?"

"What else could it be?"

My breath came out on a rush when my back suddenly hit a wall. Deacon's body was flush against mine, pinning me in place, his face was a breath from mine.

And, God, I hated him for making me want to beg him to close that distance.

Every rough breath brushed my chest against his.

Every touch incited something inside me I had been so sure I would never feel again.

His hands moved slowly across my shoulders, the tips of his fingers barely grazed against the slope of my throat until his large hands were cradling my neck and his thumbs were brushing along my jaw.

His eyes followed the movements of his hand, as if he was memorizing the path they took, the curve of my neck.

My heart beat wildly in my chest, begging to be freed. Begging to be seen by this man.

"Tell me, Charlie Girl," he said roughly as his nose brushed against mine. "This . . . does this feel like a joke? Because the hell you've been putting me through for the past two weeks sure as fuck hasn't felt like one."

I blinked up into those eyes, those eyes that were once so cold and unforgiving but now held a heat unlike anything I'd ever seen before.

"That I've put *you* through?" I whispered in disbelief.

One of his hands moved up so his thumb could brush across my cheek, but I was so captivated by his stare and the feel of his hands on me and his body pressed against me that I couldn't find it in me to be embarrassed that he'd wiped a tear away.

"I can't stop thinking about you," he admitted gruffly. "I can't stop seeing you even when I try to force the thought of you away. I can't stop wanting you, needing you. All I've thought about since Knox's wedding is feeling you like this again." His body pressed harder against mine, emphasizing his words. "To go through all of that day in and day out with a girl I know I should never have, with a girl I've forced to hate me, has been the purest form of hell."

His words were ecstasy and agony all at once.

A girl I know I should never have. Deacon's words swirled around and around in my mind until they were all I knew.

So similar to ones Ben had said so many years ago before he'd destroyed my heart, and yet so different coming from the man holding me.

My heart and my mind and my body were screaming so many different things I couldn't think straight. I wanted to hate him and kiss him and slap him and beg him to say it all again so I would know I hadn't imagined it.

My head shook faintly. "You . . . no. The girl. I saw her . . ."

Deacon flinched and his eyes shut. When he looked at me again, he looked like he was in pain. "I said I tried to force away the thought of you."

"You disgust me," I breathed.

It was all coming back to me.

Ben telling me he loved me even though he knew he shouldn't. Taking my virginity and promising me a future with him, then asking Grey to marry him two days later because he was afraid to lose the years he'd had with her. Calling me a mistake because he wasn't *in* love with me.

Watching as he pushed the thought of me, of us, away because he was scared.

And now Deacon forgetting about me because he was

having sex with some nameless girl—all because he was trying to force the thought of me away.

I didn't understand what it was about me that made guys want to drown out the thought of me with another woman, but it hurt.

God, it hurt.

"That's nothing I don't already know, Charlie Girl."

My head shook harder. "You're disgusting. Let me go and get out of my house," I said through gritted teeth as another tear fell, and then another. No matter how hard I tried to keep them away, I couldn't stop them.

I *hurt*.

I wanted to be wanted, wholly and unconditionally. Just once.

"Christ, Charlie, I'm sorry. I'm sorry, I'm sorry," he whispered soothingly, and wiped at my cheeks. "I'm sorry, please stop crying."

"*Leave*." I pressed against his chest, but he didn't move away. "Let go of me!"

Deacon's hands immediately left my face and landed on the wall on either side of my head, but his body didn't leave mine. Instead, he dipped in closer until his lips were at my ear, just like the day before, and said, "I'm an asshole. I've lived the last—God, I don't know how long, just waiting for the next girl, and the next. Names and faces didn't matter, just as long as they were gone as fast as they got there. You want me to go, then I'm gone. But I know I won't get this chance again, so just listen.

"I've never been haunted by a girl the way you haunt me, Charlie Easton. It wasn't because I hadn't had you, or because I knew I shouldn't. That knowledge and everything I felt scared the shit out of me, and I knew I had to do something to put an end to it. So, yes, I fucked up. I will apologize forever if I have to, but know that I've never hated myself, or how I am, more than I did that day. And you? All I saw was you, more than ever."

One of his hands slowly fell from the wall back to my cheek, and he pulled back to look into my eyes. Indecision, fear, and need swirled in their light depths.

"Hurting you has killed me. Unaware . . . yeah? I get it now. Maybe with everyone else, but I've never been more aware of anything or anyone."

My body sagged against the wall when he pushed away, and after another second, he turned and stepped away.

I needed to let him go.

Step.

A guy like Deacon Carver would only do what Ben had done, and more.

Step.

But my body was screaming in protest the loss of his touch, and I'd only lost it seconds ago.

Step step.

I swallowed past the tightness in my throat and dropped my head to stare unseeing at the floor.

Step.

I pushed down all of my fears—of rejection, of getting my heart broken, of simply speaking my mind on a whim, and said, "This is usually the part of the book where the hero kisses the girl."

Silence.

"I don't know how to be that hero, Charlie Girl."

I slowly lifted my head and found Deacon facing me. Chest moving with each exaggerated breath, hands slightly flexing like he didn't know what to do with them.

"If you want me to be that guy, I would only hurt you more." But even as he spoke the words, he took a couple steps back toward me. "I can't compete with whatever it is you read."

If only he knew that he wasn't so different.

I lifted a shoulder. "This is also a house of superheroes."

Deacon smirked. The slant of his lips challenged and warned and promised.

My stomach warmed at the sight, my body was already buzzing with anticipation.

"Now *that* I can compete with."

He ate up the distance in two steps, and pulled me from the wall as his mouth fell onto mine.

One of his hands pressed against the small of my back, molding our bodies closer and closer, the other curled around my neck again. Cradling and guiding, strength and tenderness.

I clung to his shirt as our mouths moved in perfect sync, trying to hold on to this kiss that was everything.

Everything I'd dreamed of.

Everything I'd craved.

Everything I'd never had.

Because Deacon was holding me like he was afraid of letting me go, and I wasn't trying to hold him closer, afraid he *would*.

His thumb pushed against my jaw to tilt my head back

farther, and his tongue hesitantly brushed against the seam of my lips. Asking. Begging. Creating chaos within my body.

My mouth opened with an inhale, and a soft moan slid up my throat when his tongue met mine in a perfect dance. The push and pull, the desperation and need, all in a space that felt as though time would stand still at any moment.

The kiss slowed, Deacon's lips moved across my jaw and down my neck until his mouth was at my ear. "If I don't stop myself now, I'm taking you to the couch and laying you down, and I know I won't want to stop then." His teeth grazed the skin just below my ear when he finished, and a growl rumbled in his chest when a shiver moved down my spine. "Christ, Charlie."

I continued to stare at his chest as I wondered what would happen now that the kiss was over. My world felt like it was tilted, just waiting to find out which way it was supposed to turn next. That kiss had been more than I ever expected it could be, but this was still Deacon.

He could still leave.

I couldn't figure out if I needed to guard myself and my emotions, or allow myself to stay in this surreal moment for a little longer.

"What now?" I asked softly.

Deacon pulled away from me, his light brown stare bouncing all over my face and staying on my lips longer and longer each time, as his eyes darkened with heat. Without warning, he pressed a quick, rough kiss to my mouth, then spoke against my lips. "Now . . . I take you on a date to your kitchen table, and hope like hell that you give superheroes third chances."

Chapter Thirteen

Deacon

June 15, 2016

KNOX AND GRAHAM'S loud voices met me as soon as I set foot inside the house that night, and, for a second, it felt like it always had. Back before Knox had found Harlow again, and married her. Back before I would have done anything to make Charlie Easton mine—back before I wanted to make any girl *mine*, period. Back before I had to constantly talk myself down from punching one of my best friends.

I curled my arm around Harlow's neck, and pulled her in so I could kiss the top of her head when I found her walking out of the kitchen. "Hey, Warrior."

Harlow narrowed her eyes suspiciously when she pulled away, and looked me over quickly. "That was one of the quietest, most unenthusiastic greetings I've ever received from you. You okay, Deacon?"

I had no fucking clue.

Yes, yes I was. Because I'd just spent the past few hours with Charlie. Because I'd kissed the hell out of that mouth and held her as close as I could stand before I gave in to a need I knew she wasn't ready for yet.

But I still didn't know what I was doing. I had never been this guy before, and, again, I couldn't be the kind of guy she wanted. I wasn't some hero in one of those books she hid behind.

As I told Words, I wasn't a white knight. I didn't sweep girls off their feet.

After a few hours, I already felt like I was stumbling around, fucking terrified for when I hurt Charlie again.

Graham laughed loudly, the sound echoing through the house and pulling me from my thoughts only to remind me of what I'd walked in on earlier that night.

I forced a quick smile in Harlow's direction. "Yep. Just gotta take care of some stuff."

I followed her into the living room where Knox and Graham were sitting on the couches, and clapped Knox's back as I passed him to sit in the only chair.

"Where've you been?" Graham asked with a sly grin.

One of my eyebrows ticked up in response, and I stared at him like he should already know the answer. "Charlie's."

Graham's grin fell. "This whole time?" He looked at

his wrist, then grabbed for his phone to get the time. "Deac, I left you there over two hours ago."

"Oh, did she find a place to live?" Harlow asked excitedly.

But Graham didn't respond, and when I spoke, it was directed at him. "You're my best friend, I refuse to compete against you for her."

"Compete—what?" Graham stammered.

"But I'm gonna give you right now to tell me if there's something going on before I ask you to back the fuck off."

"Whoa," Knox said with a hesitant laugh. "What did we miss while we were gone?"

Graham looked floored. "What the hell are you talking about? Are we talking about Charlie? *Little* Charlie Easton?"

I winced. "Don't call her that."

Knox's laugh boomed throughout the living room. "Oh man . . . this is rich."

"What do you mean, *compete*?" Graham asked, confusion still covering his face. "What the hell would we be competing for when it comes to her?"

"You're the one who is always checking on her, making sure she's okay. You were the one who got her to dance at the wedding. You helped her find a place to live," I added, going down the list of things I thought of on repeat. I would have asked about the date this weekend if Charlie hadn't told me earlier that Keith had been her "date." "Tonight I fucking walked in and you were kissing her."

"Oh!" Knox hissed as Graham jerked back and clarified, "Her head. I kissed her head. Let me remind you that you kiss my sister's head all the damn time."

"And Harlow's," Knox murmured.

"Where is all of this coming from anyway?" Graham demanded. "You've been treating her like shit."

"Yeah, no need to remind me; I do that enough myself." I sighed roughly and scrubbed my hands over my face. "Look, I just need you to tell me if there's something going on between you."

He laughed hard once. "Deac . . . it's *Charlie*. I mean, don't get me wrong, some time in the last few years she's grown up and she's fucking gorgeous, but she's still little Charlie Easton. She's my brother-in-law's little sister."

I shook my head slightly. "Stop with the *little* thing."

Knox huffed, his chest moved with his silent laughter. "I don't know, I kind of want to focus on it. I mean, Harlow and I had to endure years of bullshit from both of you because she's two and a half years younger than me, and Charlie is . . ." He trailed off, waiting for me to finish. When I didn't, he guessed, "Five years younger than you? Six?"

"Four."

Knox smiled knowingly. "How's that crow taste, Deacon? Eat some more."

"Man, I already apologized for that shit long ago."

"Yeah, but I think you're just now realizing how wrong you actually were to use her age against me."

If that wasn't the truth. I sat back in the chair, and mumbled, "Bitter. Tastes really fucking bitter. I'm sorry, for all of it."

I knew from Knox's expression that I hadn't needed to apologize again, he was just enjoying tormenting me a little more than I already was.

"For the record," Harlow said, speaking up to break the silence that had fallen between us, "I think Charlie is a very sweet girl, and I think her quiet would be the perfect balance for a guy like you."

I sent her a thankful smile, but it fell when Graham said, "You know, Charlie isn't the kind of girl you screw once or twice, then never talk to again."

"I don't know why people keep saying that, like I'm not already completely aware of that."

Graham sent me a knowing look. "Because I know how you are, just as you know how I am."

My head shook as I tried to figure out what to tell Graham, as I tried to figure out what was going on between Charlie and me at all. "This is different," I finally said.

My phone chimed in my pocket, and without thinking, I pulled it out to look at who had messaged me.

My body locked up when I saw her name with a picture below, too small to make out on the lock screen.

Words.

I immediately opened up the messages on my phone, and stood from the chair to head for my room, but stopped when Graham's voice ricocheted off the walls.

"Deacon, what the fuck?" He was pointing at the phone in my hands, his face set with a rage I'd felt all too often when I'd seen him lately. "This is exactly what I just meant! I *know* you, man! Is that Charlie?"

"No, she has my real number," I said automatically, defensively.

From Graham's expression, it was both the wrong and right answer. "I told you that Charlie isn't the kind of girl you screw and then leave, but she also isn't the girl that you keep screwing around on, either. You come home and try to start shit, demanding me to tell you about something that wasn't even happening, and all the while you still have Candy? You get up and leave the second it goes off? I mean, thank Christ you didn't put Charlie's number in *that* phone, but are you kidding me?"

I didn't know how to defend myself or Words to them, when I knew they wouldn't understand. I wouldn't even know how to explain it. Like everything else in my life lately, I was still trying to figure it out. One day, one message, one mind-blowing kiss at a time.

"You wouldn't understand."

"Deac," Knox said warily. "I'm all for you being with Charlie if it meant what we all thought it did just a couple minutes ago. But this?"

"No, this isn't okay," Graham finished. "You can't do this to her."

"Even if I could explain it, you wouldn't understand. Just trust me, the last thing I'll be doing is sleeping around on Charlie."

"Deacon—"

"I gotta go." I ignored Graham trying to call me back as I headed to my room. The entire time my body was vibrating with anticipation as I hurried to pull up the picture Words sent.

It was another shot of her journal, like I'd gotten a week ago. My eyes skimmed quickly over the top that was scratched out, then to what was written below.

~~You can't believe it's daylight~~
~~We stayed up again all night~~
~~Just ta Talking just cause you like the way I make the words sound~~

You can't believe it's daylight
We stayed up again all night
Talking just cause you like the way I make the words sound
I triple-double dare you
Fess up and make the first move
You need me like I need you
That's why you come around here
Cause you know I've always been the one

Who listens to your sad songs
The shoulder that you cry on
Out on that ledge you walk on
When you're sinking
Who keeps your secrets locked up
When there's no one you can trust
I know it's much more than just wishful thinking
Just say the words and you know I'll be there

I read the new lines over and over again before saving the picture and swiping it away so I was back in the messages. She'd sent nothing else, just the song. It wasn't like her.

I glanced at her writing again in the smaller version of the picture on the text, then tapped on my screen as the weight of my conversation with the guys fell off my shoulders.

The one?

Words . . .

I thought her response would never come. My amused smirk slowly fell as the minutes passed, and I'd nearly gotten to the point where I started messaging her again when the dots suddenly popped up on the screen.

Words: *It's just a song.*

Words: *No need to let a couple words in it freak you out.*

A crease formed on my brow, and I hurried to respond.

They didn't.

Words: *I'll change it.*

Words: *I wrote the new part this weekend because of our conversation, I just hadn't sent it to you yet.*

Hey, stop. What's going on . . . are you okay?

I was messing with you when I sent those first texts. I wouldn't have done it if I would've known that this would happen.

Five minutes passed without a response.

And then another five.

Words, talk to me. I'm here listening to you. Remember?

With each minute that passed, I got closer and closer to doing something I swore I would never do—calling her. I wasn't ready to lose her. I knew I couldn't keep her, but I couldn't let her go yet, either.

Words: *I think tonight might not be a good night to talk, Stranger.*

Words: *I'm sorry.*

What the fuck. Words, what's wrong? Fucking talk to me.

If it was how I responded, then I'm sorry. I was teasing you about it. You and I both already know how the other feels about it, that hasn't been a secret.

Words: *It's not what you said.*

Words: *I'm sorry, but I have nothing that I can say to you.*

That hurt more than it should have. It was the smallest glimpse of what it would feel like when she disappeared from my life, and it fucking hurt. I stared at her response for long seconds before typing back.

Tell me what I did so next time I can avoid it. Tell me what to do so I can try to make it up to you. Tell me something, anything, so I can stop thinking that you're about to walk away from this.

Watching those three dots, waiting for her response, was agony.

Words: *Nothing, Stranger. Nothing. And walk from you? Like you said, I don't know if I'd be able to.*

Then talk to me.

What could have happened between when you sent the song and when you next texted me?

Words: *A lot . . .*

Words: *I don't know how to talk to you tonight. I don't know what to say to you. Everything that is running through my mind right now is too personal, and we don't do personal.*

You know me better than anyone. I know you, Words.

Words: *Not like this. This would change things.*

Try.

Long minutes passed, but this time I gave her the time she needed and tried to stay patient as I waited.

Words: *To put it as simply and vaguely as I can . . .*

Words: *I was asked something, and it made me want*

to tear myself away from every happiness that I've recently found, and any I could possibly find in the future.

Words: *It was innocent, really. The person had no clue what kind of devastation they would inflict on me by asking, but it feels like even my soul is crying now. Everything hurts. It hasn't hurt like this in so long.*

I felt helpless. I needed to reach through the phone and grab her, pull her into my arms and not let her go. But she wasn't real.

You're not going to tell me what the question was, are you?

Words: *I can't.*

Words: *And that's why tonight isn't a good idea. I don't have anything I can say to you.*

I think that's why tonight is a perfect idea. I can't leave you when you hurt.

Words: *I won't be any fun.*

I doubt that.

Words: *I'm crying.*

You have no idea how much I wish I could be there to dry your tears.

Words: *My heart . . .*

Words: *Stranger, don't. Don't. Didn't you just hear me? I already want to tear myself away from the happiness that I've found. Don't make me wish that you would hurry up and find me just so I could rip myself away from you, too.*

Fuck if you think I'd let you rip yourself away from me, Words. If I find you, I'm not letting you go.

Words: *There you go sweeping me off my feet again, Stranger . . .*

Words: *How is it possible that I'm unreasonably jealous of the girl you'll one day leave me for, when you can't leave what you never found?*

I dropped my phone on my chest and let my eyes shut. I wanted to swear that I wouldn't leave. I wanted to tell her that I would find her.

But I couldn't.

Words was my outlet. She was the only person who had allowed me to be *me* without judging me for my past. In the last weeks she had unknowingly forced me to see what I really wanted out of life, when I'd spent years thinking I was happy in my repetitive life. Letting her go, closing that connection, scared the hell out of me. But I knew one day I would.

Because when I thought of Words, I only ever pictured one thing. A thousand faces blurred into one. Always one.

One I could reach out and touch.

One who was real.

One I would give up everything for.

Charlie.

Chapter Fourteen

Charlie
June 18, 2016

DEACON SIGHED AS he unfurled his large frame from under the hood of my car. "It'll run for a day or two . . . maybe." He turned his light eyes on me, and looked at me guardedly. "Charlie Girl, I'm serious. You—"

"Need to get a new car," I finished for him, then let loose my own sigh. "I know. You and Jagger keep reminding me."

He wiped his hands on a rag, and pulled me close with one arm. His lifted my chin with his knuckles to press his mouth first to my jaw and then my lips.

I felt his mouth spread into a slow grin when I shuddered from the warmth that moved down my spine at the contact.

After four days, I still wasn't used to it. To this.

If it would always feel like this, if it would always leave me breathless and weak, then I wasn't sure that I ever wanted to get used to it.

"Speaking of Jagger, what do you think he's going to say?"

My eyebrows rose in question, and Deacon's smile grew.

"About us, Charlie Girl. About the fact that I can't stop kissing you and don't know how to let you go."

I pulled my bottom lip into my mouth when he pressed me tighter to his large, muscular frame. And as I had the last few days, embraced the way my heart beat wildly in my chest. One of these times it was going to break free, and I wasn't going to attempt to stop it.

All of this was happening fast, I knew. But I had a feeling that all those years I'd felt betrayed by my irrational heart around Deacon had been leading up to this. When I would be ready to trust someone with my heart again. When Deacon would be the one to take it.

"Does it matter?"

Deacon looked at me with open disbelief.

"If what Jagger said really mattered to you, then you wouldn't be here. You wouldn't have been here yesterday, or the night before . . ." I trailed off, and lifted one of my shoulders. "You would've never come after me."

I knew from Deacon's expression that he couldn't deny what I'd said. "Still, it's going to matter to you, and that will matter to me."

"He doesn't always know what's best for me." I trailed

my fingers over his lips, then pushed up on my toes to press my mouth to his. "Besides, they won't be back from Seattle until late tomorrow night. I still have until Monday morning to prepare for whatever he'll say."

The corner of his mouth slowly lifted in a mischievous smirk. "Guy isn't going to know what hit him if you've been preparing your comeback all this time."

I laughed and pushed at his chest, but he just pulled me back in for another searing kiss that made my head spin before he released me.

Deacon stepped back to push down the hood of my car when I started toward my house, and continued to stare at it for a few seconds before following me. "Tell me what's stopping you from getting a new car. I know from talking to Grey and Jagger over the years that you have money from your grandparents, so why?"

The daze that Deacon's nearness and his kisses had put me in abruptly disappeared. My blissful smile fell, my stomach dropped, and my palms suddenly felt clammy.

I'm not like her. I refuse to be her. I'm not like her. I refuse to be her, I chanted over and over again as a tremor of unease slid through me.

"Um." I swallowed thickly and studied the ground for a second before taking a step back. "I need to go. I have to wake up Keith and get him over to the babysitter's, then get to work," I mumbled, then took another two steps back.

Deacon's brow furrowed, and in one step, he closed the distance I'd managed to put between us. "Charlie—"

I turned and hurried toward the front door, calling

over my shoulder as I walked. "Thanks for coming over so early."

"Charlie, damn it, stop," he demanded, and wrapped his arm around my waist, pulling me close to his chest. "Why do I have to hold you still to get you to talk to me?"

"Why don't you understand that when I walk away, I'm not ready to talk?"

"That's not how this works. Not with us. Not with you." His large hand pressed firmly against my stomach, his fingers spread so wide that his thumb brushed the underside of my breast with each breath that I took. "I may not have been paying attention to you all these years, but that doesn't mean I don't know you. That doesn't mean I don't know what you're doing when you walk away from me. It's just another form of hiding for you."

His hold loosened. His hands went to my arms, and slowly slid down. The tips of his fingers teased my own before he released me completely and took a step back. He was giving me every opportunity to try to leave, only now I couldn't move.

"You've spent so long trying to be invisible, but I told you, I can't stop seeing you. Stop trying to hide from me. Stop walking. Talk to—"

"I don't want to be her." The confession tumbled from my mouth like a dirty secret. Fast, soft, and full of shame.

"Who?" Deacon asked after a few seconds.

I turned to look at him, shaking my head as I did. "My mom blew through all of her money. If it weren't for our grandparents, we would have starved. If it weren't for Jagger, we wouldn't have made it. If she had a dollar, then she spent five. I don't want to be her, and I'm so terrified of turning into her. I have to think of Keith, always."

"Charlie, buying a car isn't going to turn you into your mom."

One of my eyebrows arched, and a sad laugh sounded in my chest. "Are you sure? I mean, it's like you said, I've already pawned my son off on my brother. I already took a huge step toward being like her."

Deacon's shoulders sagged as I threw his words back at him. As he finally understood why I didn't want to have *this* conversation with him. His face tightened with regret and pain. "Fuck . . . Charlie. No, that—you can't . . ." He trailed off and scrubbed his hands over his face. "God damn it."

I tilted my head back toward the house. "Sometimes, when I'm walking away, you should let me *walk*. I can forgive you and try to forget things that you've said or done, but that *trying* becomes so hard when your words fueled lifelong fears."

"I don't expect you to forget what I said that day, but you have to know that I was wrong. All of it, everything was wrong." He gestured to me, his eyes pleading with me. "*Clearly*. I was mad when I didn't have the right to be. When I only had a fraction of the story. I get that now. But, Charlie, turning into your mom? That won't happen. In the last three weeks alone, anyone could see that that won't happen."

I gritted my teeth when my jaw began to tremble, and blinked through the burning in my eyes, determined not to cry. But my voice shook with every emotion I felt, giving me away. "I have less than a week, Deacon. One week until we go back to court. I need to get my son, do you understand?" I gestured to the house with a hand. "He's here. He's with me, but I need him to be mine. I can't risk messing that up."

Confusion swept across Deacon's face, and something close to panic filled his eyes when my voice broke on the last word. He reached out for me, and I let him pull me close as he struggled for something to say. "Charlie . . . what are you talking about?"

With how close he was to Grey, with how often they saw each other, I was sure he would have already known. "Keith. I don't have custody of him, I never have."

"What do you mean? Who does?"

My head slanted to the side as I tried to understand the frustration and determination that wove through Deacon's words. "You really don't know? Grey never told you?"

"Why would she have? If it had to do with Keith she probably knew I didn't want to know. It's not really a secret I don't like kids." When I flinched, he hurried to say, "You know he's different."

I blinked quickly and mentally shook away the quick stab of pain from his declaration. Like he'd said, it wasn't a secret. "Um, my mom," I began, and looked back up into his eyes. "Before I had Keith, she kept telling me that I wouldn't be able to handle it, that I wasn't ready, that I would ruin the baby's life, that the baby would one day resent me. It was just . . . endless, and repeated every day until I believed her. Until I finally signed custody over to her. When Keith was two and Mom left, we went to court to try to change custody over to me. We had more than enough proof that my mom hadn't ever been a fit mother anyway, but the judge said that he wasn't sure that *I* was either."

"What the hell?" Deacon growled in a dangerous tone.

"I was living in the back room of my brother's warehouse and I didn't have a job. I'd never gotten one because I needed to be there to take care of Keith since my mom always randomly left. The judge thought I needed to finish school and get my life in order before I was ready to get custody of Keith, and granted Jagger and Grey temporary custody until then."

"Charlie Girl," he whispered; his head shook subtly. "Fuck, Charlie, I'm sorry. But you're not your mom."

I smiled weakly. "Jagger felt like the judge helped his argument to get me to leave. So I left and finished school. I have a job, thanks to your grandma. And thanks to Graham, Keith and I now have our own place. I did exactly what the judge said, and I'm terrified that if I do one thing out of line, he'll stop me from getting custody again. Keith is three and a half, Deacon. I want my son to be mine."

Deacon's hands cradled my face gently as his face dipped closer to mine. "So wrong about you," he whispered against my lips, then pressed a feather-soft kiss there. "So damn wrong."

I gasped against the force of his next kiss, and clung to his muscled forearms as he walked us toward the house. My back had barely touched the door before it was falling open and Deacon was moving us inside and kicking the door shut behind him.

Heat pooled low in my stomach when his mouth made a line down my throat, and cool tingles spread across my skin when he gently bit down there. The conflicting combination made me feel more alive than I had in years.

His lips replaced his teeth, but instead of continuing, he paused for a few seconds. His low laugh and voice rumbled against my throat. "Who are you today, kid?"

I blinked my eyes open, and tried to orient myself.

Before Deacon's question could register in my mind, a soft, anxious voice came from beside us. Ice filled my veins when I heard Keith ask, "Are you gonna go to the grassy place?"

Keith, no!

All the air in my lungs came out in one fast, rough whoosh, and I shoved Deacon away from me as quickly as I could.

For once I was able to move him.

Deacon stumbled back, caught off guard by my sudden movement, but I couldn't look at him.

Agony pierced at my chest and made it hard to pull in a breath at that innocent, *innocent* question.

I'd been so careful not to kiss Deacon in front of Keith the last few days, because one good-bye kiss from Deacon that first night had nearly devastated my son, and had absolutely destroyed me.

"Keith," I said breathlessly. "When did you wake up?"

He looked up toward the ceiling for a second, then shrugged. "I donno. Deaton, are you—"

"Keith, stop!" I pled, and fell to my knees with the grief that slammed into me. I gripped Keith's shoulders and pulled him close so Deacon wouldn't hear the shaking in my voice. "Buddy, stop. Remember what I said? Remember? We don't ask that. That isn't going to happen."

Again, it felt like my soul was grieving. I wanted to tear myself apart, rip myself away from Deacon and any man that might come into our lives in the future.

Keith's nearly identical question on Wednesday night had destroyed me. I'd barely made it from his room to mine before I'd crumbled under my grief and the torrent of sobs.

I didn't want to go through it again. Not now. Not when I couldn't escape him or Deacon.

"What's the grassy place?" Deacon asked warily, and my eyes shut in pain.

"Deacon, don't," I whispered my plea.

There was a pregnant pause before he asked hesitantly, "Does he want me to take him there?"

"Deacon!" I meant to shout his name, but I would have been surprised if he heard it at all. My head fell so I was staring at the ground when I said, "If I could, I would walk. Let me walk away."

For once, Deacon didn't push, and I was thankful for it. I felt so beaten down from the past five minutes that I didn't know if I could get myself standing again, and I knew I wouldn't have been able to keep it together if Deacon forced me to talk again.

I drew in two deep breaths, trying to steady myself, then looked up at Keith. "We have to go. Do you need to use the bathroom?"

He shook his head quickly, and whispered, "Mommy. I don't want Deaton to go to the grassy place. Is that okay? Mommy, don't make him go."

A choked cry forced from my chest before I could stop it. I didn't know if I was nodding or shaking my head, only that it was moving. "Yes, that's okay. I won't, baby. I swear I won't."

I stood on weak, shaking legs, and avoided Deacon's questioning stare as I left to go help Keith change clothes.

A few minutes later, when I approached the front door he was holding open, I glanced up and forced a smile that he didn't return. "I'll talk to you later."

He nodded slowly. His face was guarded, but his eyes were searching, begging, questioning everything he'd just seen and heard.

I couldn't give him an answer to any of the questions he had. Instead, I grabbed Keith's hand and walked to my car.

. . . which was now no longer working again.

Deacon didn't say anything about my needing a new car, or say anything at all. He just waited silently as I got Keith's booster seat into his car, and kept quiet during the drive. By the time we got to Mama's, I was ready to run from the awkward silence of Deacon's car, but he gripped my hand in his as soon as he pulled into a parking spot.

He waited until I was looking up at him to say, "I will never force you to talk to me in front of Keith. If you want to walk from me in front of him, then I'll let you walk— even if you physically can't. But watching you go through that . . . damn it, Charlie. My fucking heart was breaking for you and I had no clue what was going on. I just had to stand there and watch because you pushed me away."

My head shook slowly as he spoke. "This morning . . . I *cannot* handle this morning. It's been one thing after another, and it isn't even eight, Deacon."

He arched a brow, and gently challenged, "So you're gonna push it away until it comes back up? Keith normally doesn't stop talking, and I couldn't get him to talk or even look at me after the question about the grassy place."

I swallowed past the tightness in my throat, and whispered, "It's because he saw you kissing me."

Deacon didn't say anything for a few seconds. And I knew he was thinking back over the last four days. His confusion was apparent when he spoke again. "He saw me kiss you the night you moved into that house. He was coming out of his room when I was leaving. He didn't care then."

"He did. When I was putting him back in bed after you left, he asked if you were going to have to go to the grassy place. Then he asked me not to kiss you anymore." I could see that the unknown half-answers and vague responses were starting to overwhelm Deacon. Before he could ask, I hurried to explain. "Die, Deacon. He thinks you're going to die because I kissed you."

Light brown eyes bored into mine, trying to uncover the meaning behind my words. "Why do I have a feeling that for once, what Keith was talking about had nothing to do with mutants or ladybugs?"

A startled laugh bubbled up from my chest, but

quickly faded away to nothing. "No, Keith calls the cemetery the grassy place. He doesn't understand why or how Ben died; he just knows that his *daddy* is in the grassy place. The night he saw us kiss, he asked me if you were going to have to go to the grassy place since I'd kissed you. I nearly lost my mind when that question left his little lips, but I tried to stay calm and just told him I didn't understand.

"To Keith, only daddies kiss mommies, and since he saw you kiss me, he was making that connection. When I tried to explain to him that kissing didn't necessarily mean people were married, he said that he couldn't have a daddy because his daddies would always have to go to the grassy place." I tried to steady the shaking in my voice when I continued, but knew from Deacon's expression that I didn't succeed. "Then he asked me not to kiss you anymore, because I'd already made 'his Ben' go there, and he didn't want me to make you go to the grassy place too."

"Charlie," Deacon murmured, shock and pain for my son and me clear in that one word. "Shit, Charlie Girl, I'm sorry."

"He doesn't understand what he's saying, but God, it hurts."

Dozens of questions and emotions swirled through Deacon's eyes and passed over his face as my words hung heavily in the space between us. When he finally settled on one, he was looking at me like he'd never considered the possibility of whatever it was he was thinking.

"What?" I nearly begged.

"He really meant a lot to you too, didn't he?"

"Ben?"

But Deacon didn't respond, just continued watching me, waiting.

"He meant . . ." I trailed off; my head shook quickly. "I loved him the way Jagger loved Grey: deeply and wholly, silently and from a distance."

Again, clearly something Deacon hadn't ever considered, and now, something else was mixing with the surprise and confusion. The corner of his mouth lifted and fell, and he exhaled quickly through his nose. "I never expected to be jealous of someone who wasn't alive."

"Jealous of Be—Deacon, why? He's been gone for four years."

"Doesn't matter, Charlie. The way you reacted to what Keith asked, knowing now what it all meant . . ." He trailed off. "You were able to break my damn heart just by watching yours break, and it was over another guy."

I shrugged weakly. "What do you want me to say? I won't lie to you about—"

"No, Charlie, don't you get it?" His brown eyes warmed and lit with amusement. "I've never been jealous of a guy in my life. And now I've had to restrain myself daily from punching one of my best friends, and I hate that a guy who died four years ago touched you."

I jerked my head back and flattened my body against the door. "Punch one of your best friends—which one, and why?"

"Don't let Graham kiss you again," he said flatly. His eyes narrowed on my cheeks when blood quickly rushed to them, and a growl rumbled deep in his chest. "And don't do that when I mention him."

I tried to stop my blushing, but I had no control over it. Considering Graham made me think of Stranger, and when there were thoughts of Stranger, there was never-ending blush paired with a racing heart; I knew it was going to be impossible to get it to stop. Just like it was nearly impossible to stop thinking of Graham as Stranger when nearly every time I saw him, he said something that echoed Stranger's words.

But there were no romantic feelings between Graham and me. No fluttering stomach or racing heart. No heat racing through my veins or deep, secret ache.

Everything I felt in Deacon's presence, and the reason I only imagined the man sitting in front of me when I texted Stranger.

It didn't matter that I knew it wasn't Deacon; that wouldn't stop me from wishing that he could be the kind of guy to say those things to me.

Again, Grey was probably onto something: romance novels were ruining the way I viewed men and relationships.

"Deacon, Graham's done that forever. So has Knox. So did you until you started hating me."

He leaned over the center console and gripped my chin in his fingers, and brought our faces so close that I was silently begging for him to close the rest of the distance between us. To press his mouth to mine and make me forget everything about this morning except the way he made me feel.

"For my sanity, and for the sake of our friendship, don't let Graham kiss you again." He passed his lips across mine in a kiss so soft, I wasn't sure it happened at all. "Say 'okay.'"

"Okay."

He smiled against my lips, and whispered, "You're late." His deep laugh filled the car as I scrambled to get out of it, and his voice followed me out. "I'll be here when you get off."

I paused from shutting the door; an ominous feeling slid through my veins like ice. I turned my head slowly to look back at him, and asked, "Promise?"

"Where else would I be, Charlie Girl?" Deacon shot me a look that seemed to stop everything. Time, sound, my heart.

My breath caught in my throat, and a chill spread over my skin like a lover's caress. I wanted to experience the feeling again and again.

Awareness came flooding back in with a rush, and I hurried to memorize the set of his eyes and his smile. Because I knew . . . I knew a look like that, I wanted to remember forever.

Chapter Fifteen

Charlie

June 24, 2016

I watched Keith from across the table at Bonfire, the grill in Thatch, my smile impossibly wide as he recounted his version of what had gone down today—complete with use of the Force, since he was, of course, Darth Vader.

He couldn't go into the hearing unprotected against the ladybug judge, after all.

And I didn't care.

I didn't care if he wanted to be Darth Vader or Iron Man or Captain America or Wolverine. He could be whoever he wanted, fight whatever ladybugs he encountered.

Keith was officially mine.

The judge had barely asked more than a handful of questions, and had only glanced at the proof that I'd actually done all that he'd asked. He'd mostly relied on Grey and Jagger's word, and had talked to Keith without any of us in the room.

Again, I didn't care.

I had broken down outside the courthouse, tears of joy unlike anything I'd ever experienced streaming down my face, and hadn't let go of Keith until Jagger had forced me to stand up and walk to my car.

Even then I'd carried Keith, not willing to let him go yet.

Keith had smiled the cheesiest smile and patted my cheek. "Silly Mommy. You've always been my mommy!" he'd said after he'd climbed into his booster seat.

"See?" Grey had asked softly from behind me. "Some papers and a judge's signature never meant anything to him."

I didn't know if anyone would be able to understand the significance of today for me, but that was okay, because it wasn't for them. It was for Keith and me.

As Jagger and Grey pointed out, I had mostly raised Keith. Something I would always be grateful for. But they still didn't know what I'd gone through. They didn't know the extent of what Mom had said to make me give up custody. They didn't know that my mom had often threatened me with taking Keith and running away.

Jagger had thought he was keeping our mother's true nature from me.

Grey thought she was keeping how evil our mother was from her children.

I'd thought I was keeping Mom's sick, twisted mind from Jagger.

She hadn't ever fooled any of us. She'd just fooled us into believing that each of us was the only one who knew what she really was.

After two years of living in fear for that I would wake up and my son would be gone, and knowing I wouldn't be able to do anything because he wasn't mine on paper, and then having a judge tell me that I wasn't fit to have custody transferred to me, the fear that he could disappear at any time never left.

It didn't matter that I knew Jagger and Grey would never do something like that to me . . . mothers have irrational thoughts when people try to keep them from their children.

But that was all over now.

Keith made a noise as if his lightsaber was powering down, and took an exaggerated breath. "Safe from the ladybugs."

"Whew, buddy. I don't know if we would have made it out of there without you."

He nodded seriously. "Good thing I'm Darf Vaber."

"Yeah, good thing. If you would've woken up as Magneto, we might still be trapped."

Keith gasped wildly, and my chest shook with my restrained laughter. "Mandeeto! Mommy! Ladybugs control metal! Mandeeto is a ladybug!"

I drew in a shocked breath and let my face fall as I glanced warily at the table. "Oh no," I breathed, and slowly reached toward the spoon that lay forgotten next to his bowl of soupy ice cream. Lifting the spoon, I looked into Keith's worried eyes, and whispered, "We need to leave before the ladybugs come after us."

He nodded vigorously, and I hurried to grab cash out of my wallet. As soon as I had it placed within the bill-fold, I took Keith's hand and helped him slide out of the booth, then pretended to run out of the restaurant with him.

I didn't care about the strange looks or laughs from the people inside—this was the best day of my life.

I slowed Keith down when we got into the parking lot, then helped him get into my new car so we could head for Jagger's.

Yeah, I'd done that too.

After Deacon and his dad had done everything they could to get my car to run for more than a few minutes at a time, I'd let Deacon take me to look at cars earlier that week.

It was a mid-size SUV that had great gas mileage and didn't make me want to die when I looked at the price. And most of all, Keith loved it and my mechanic had approved.

The only thing that had helped ease my fears through buying it was the knowledge that I didn't have Jagger or Grey's cars to rely on anymore. And now that my car was working less and less often, I needed something that was reliable for Keith, and figured the judge would probably have made it a requirement anyway.

He hadn't asked.

I pulled Keith's sleeping form out of the car once we

got to the warehouse and carried him inside. But I froze when I was unexpectedly bombarded with screams as soon as I set foot in the door.

"Congratulations!"

Keith jerked awake from the unexpected noise, and scrambled out of my arms and toward the group of people standing in the main room of the warehouse.

Heat crept up my neck and into my cheeks as I looked from my brother and his wife to Grey's parents, and to Knox and Harlow.

The only person not watching me was Jagger, but that didn't surprise me. With the exception of a few clipped sentences during and after the court hearing, he hadn't spoken to me once that week. He and Grey had somehow already known about Deacon before they'd gotten back from Seattle, and every time I'd seen them that week, that calm silence that meant Jagger was well and truly pissed off had radiated from him.

"Uh," I said on a breath, and let my head drop slightly.

Grey walked up to me, and pulled me into a hug. "I didn't think you'd be here yet."

"I didn't know I wasn't supposed to be here," I whispered, then moved so Grey was blocking me from view. The way everyone was still staring at me made me feel lightheaded.

"You are, crazy. I just thought you'd be another twenty minutes or so. Graham and Deacon are still on their way." Her eyes narrowed on me when she realized what I was doing. "You'd think after working at Mama's, you'd be a little bit better with attention."

"That's different. They look at me for a few seconds, then go back to talking to each other."

She sighed slowly. "Well, just breathe. After they all tell you they're happy for you, they'll talk to each other. Okay?" She stepped away from me, then turned to push me forward.

I accepted hugs from Harlow and Knox, and tried not to show how uncomfortable I was with everyone else in the room still watching me as we talked.

Mrs. LaRue stepped up to hug me from behind, and said, "This is such a special day, honey. We're so happy for you. It's been a long time coming."

I looked over my shoulder and sent her a shaky smile, and opened my mouth to thank her, but was cut off by Jagger.

"Probably would've been even longer if the judge had asked about your current *relationship*."

My gaze snapped over to him in time to see him take a long swig of his beer. My brow furrowed. "What?"

"Jagger," Grey hissed.

"What is that supposed to mean?" I demanded.

Jagger gestured toward the door with his bottle, as if Deacon would be there. "You honestly think the judge wouldn't have hesitated if he knew about you and Deacon? For fuck's sake, Charlie, even Graham has been telling us that you two shouldn't be together. His *best friend* is warning us to get you away from him."

Shock hit me like a punch to the chest at that piece of news, but I couldn't react to it. I couldn't believe Jagger was doing this, and most of all, I couldn't believe he was doing this in front of other people.

I eyed the bottle of beer in his hand, and wanted to snatch it away, but I couldn't move. Jagger never drank, and I knew he wouldn't be doing this to me now if he hadn't been then. I'd known that he was upset. But when Jagger got that angry with me, he waited until he was calm before he brought up what was bothering him. And we always had those conversations in private.

My breathing became shallow and rapid, and the lightheadedness increased as I became acutely aware of every pair of eyes on me in that moment.

"You're with a guy who sleeps with a different girl every night, and is just going to use you up the way he does them. You're with a guy who *hates* kids, and today we were at a hearing so you could try to get *custody of your son*. Yeah, I'm sure any judge would have thought that was a great choice of a guy for you to have around your son. Great role model."

"Jagger, man, I think you should chill for a while," Knox said firmly, and held his hand out for Jagger's drink, but Jagger didn't hand it over, and he wasn't finished talking.

"I've been telling you for so long to get a new car, and you've shot down my suggestion every time. You're with Deacon for a few days and let him talk you into it. Is this starting to sound familiar, Charlie?"

"Stop," Grey pled, and managed to pull the bottle from his grasp.

A high-pitched ringing started up in my ears, and my legs began shaking. I didn't know if I was still breathing too rapidly, or if I wasn't breathing at all anymore. I just knew that I didn't have long before it felt like I would faint.

"You always talk about not wanting to turn into Mom, but you're choosing the exact same guys she did. The same guys she constantly brought around, the same guys she married before they left her not long after."

I'm not like her. I refuse to be her.

He ticked off each likeness on his fingers. "Hates kids, gets you to spend your money, fucks anything with tits."

"Jagger!" Knox barked out.

"If you don't want to be her, stop making her mistakes! You already got the first kid, Charlie, should we be expecting the second soon?"

My palm connected with his face before I acknowledged that my arm was moving. Afterward, you could have heard a pin drop in the warehouse.

No one moved. No one breathed.

Deacon

June 24, 2016

Graham and I glanced at each other warily as we stepped up to the door of the warehouse. The voices were muffled, words indistinguishable, but the last thing I'd expected when we'd gotten there was yelling.

I hurried to open the door, and stepped inside with Graham right behind me.

I only had a split second to take in the scene and absorb that Jagger was screaming . . .

At Charlie.

Knox, Harlow, Grey, and her parents were all gathered around with looks that ranged from shock to anger as they watched Jagger get in Charlie's face. She stood with her back to me, but even from where I stood fifteen feet away, I could see that she was shaking.

Jagger's hand was in Charlie's face as he continued to yell, " . . . kid, Charlie, should we be expecting the second soon?"

Charlie slapped Jagger's face so quickly that if it weren't for the sound of flesh connecting with flesh and the stunned look on Jagger's face, I wouldn't have been sure it happened.

Silence filled the open space of the warehouse.

Everyone standing in the middle of it was either staring at Charlie or Jagger, none of them had even noticed Graham and me coming in.

"What the hell did we miss?" Graham asked quietly.

Instead of responding, I took a step toward the group of people, at the same time Charlie took a shaky step back and then stumbled back another two.

I rushed forward and reached out as if I could have helped her from where I was, but she paused to steady herself.

Just as I got to her, she turned and started off in the direction of the hallway. I reached out to grab her arm, but the second my fingers touched her skin she yanked her arm from my grasp and hurried away.

I watched her until she was gone, then started to turn toward the group, when I caught a pair of blue, watery eyes looking at me from where he hid on the couch.

I didn't know what I'd just missed. But I knew Charlie had never slapped me, and I'd deserved that and more. If she'd hit her brother, then it had to be bad. And he'd done it front of everyone. He'd done it in front of her son.

Forcing myself not to speak, I let my eyes say more than my words could as my glare met Jagger's, and walked over to where Keith was hiding.

My face fell into something neutral and less menacing when I rounded the couch, and I dropped into a squat so I was eye level with Keith. "Hey, kid. Who are you today?"

He sniffled a few times, and with each one his shoulders jerked up from the force. "I don—I donno. I fink—can I be Keith?"

"You can always be Keith."

"Deaton, are we mad at Uncle J?"

I hesitated, not knowing what to say. I knew I sure as shit was, and I still didn't know what had happened. "I don't know, kid. Are we?"

Keith's eyes looked everywhere but at me for a few seconds. When they finally settled on me again, he looked sheepish as he nodded. "I fink so."

"All right. Well, I need to talk to your uncle J. So can you do me a favor and go find your mom, and stay with her?" I waited until he nodded, and then helped him from the couch. "I'll be back there in a little bit."

As soon as he was running toward the hall, I looked back up at Jagger, my jaw clenched, and gestured toward the kid running away. "Nice. Who wants to tell me what happened?"

Knox shook his head slowly, both in response and disappointment.

"Knox?"

His eyes darted to me before looking away. "I don't want to struggle to pull you off Jagger so you won't kill him. And I have no doubt that's what we'll be doing."

I arched an eyebrow, curiosity and rage and surprise swirling through me.

"You aren't good enough for her," Jagger finally said. "You never will be."

A huff of frustration burst from my chest. "This again?"

"You can't keep lying to her to keep her until you get whatever the hell it is you want from her!"

"Lie to her?"

His arm shot out in front of him, toward the couches that were now empty. "Pretending with Keith. Who the hell are you pretending for? Who the hell are you kidding, Deacon? We all know how you feel about kids!"

"That isn't a damn secret! She knows too!"

"So who's this performance for then, huh? Like you said, it isn't a secret. Why act like you care about him?"

I ran a hand through my hair and shot out an annoyed laugh. "He's cool; he's a cool kid. I thought that before anything ever started between Charlie and me. It isn't an act. Why am I always trying to prove myself to you? You know what? Fuck it, I'm done." I lifted my hands in the air and stepped back toward the hall. "If she can believe me after all the shit I've put her through, then that's all that matters."

Jagger's top lip curled in a sneer. "Yeah, looks like she's the only one who does."

Grey's eyes shut. "Jagger. Why—"

"Your own best friend doesn't even believe you . . . with any of it."

My steps faltered, and I glanced to Knox, then Graham.

Knox was staring at the floor. Graham's eyes were wide, his mouth set in a hard line.

"Graham hasn't just told us that Charlie shouldn't be with you. He's been *warning* us to get her away from you. And why's that, Deac?"

But I couldn't respond. I couldn't stop looking at Graham. I knew what Jagger was going to say before he continued. I knew, and I fucking hated Graham for it.

"I mean, this other phone you have . . . I don't know if I'm even surprised because it's just so *you*, Deacon. But the fact that you still talk to other girls on it? And who knows what the fuck you're doing with them?"

Girl, I thought. *Just one. And we only ever talk.*

Fear seized me. I didn't know if they'd told Charlie about it or not. Didn't know what she thought about me at all now.

I didn't know how to give up Words, but to lose Charlie? That . . . that I couldn't do.

I swallowed thickly, and shook my head once. Looking Jagger in the eye, I growled, "You don't know what the hell you're talking about."

I turned to go find Charlie, but paused, and let my right hand curl into a fist. "Knox, tell me something."

"It's not my—"

"All those years ago when you and Harlow were first talking, I said something to her to piss both of you off, and you punched me."

From the corner of my eye, I saw Graham stiffen.

"Yeah . . ." Knox said warily, drawing the word out.

"Was it worth it?"

When he answered, I heard the smile in his words. "Hell yeah."

I nodded, then started to take a step toward the hallway. At the last second, I turned and closed the distance between Graham and me with two quick steps. Grabbing the collar of his shirt, I forced him closer just as my fist smashed into his nose.

I held on to his shirt for a second when he was forced backward, then let go and watched him stumble back a step.

"At least I gave you warning, asshole." I flexed my hand a couple times, then shot Knox a grin. "Yeah, that felt pretty damn good."

He shrugged, and bit back his own smile.

Looking at Jagger one more time, I met his challenging glare, and said, "Whatever it is you said to her, I'm not gonna hit you. She did that; she can fight for herself. As for you and me? Look, I get it. You think any of us wanted Grey with Ben? Or with you?" I scoffed. "You wouldn't have been okay with Charlie and Ben, and you won't be okay with Charlie and anyone. Do I have a history? Yeah.

Knox does too, but Harlow doesn't remind him about it every damn day."

I took a step away and ran a hand roughly through my hair, and then laughed agitatedly. "Do you know what Keith said to me over there? He asked if it was okay if he was just Keith today. Look, I get you've all known this guy who wanted to party and sleep his way through the surrounding cities. But I don't want to be *that guy*. I'm never going to get away from my past if you don't let me. So fucking let me. Let me just be *Deacon*."

No one said anything, and Jagger's glare didn't lessen, but Grey was beaming at me by the time I turned around and went to find Charlie.

When I turned the corner in the first hall, I saw her sitting at the very end with her back against the wall, legs out in front of her and crossed at the ankles, with Keith in her arms.

And I stopped.

I don't know why, and I didn't know what the feeling was that suddenly hit me when I saw them sitting there like that, but I felt pinned to where I was standing. I just knew that I needed to see that every day for the rest of my life.

And that thought confused and terrified me.

Keith's head snapped up, and he squirmed in Charlie's arms until he got away from her.

As soon as he took off toward me, I forced myself to walk again, and met him a little over halfway down the hall.

I dropped to a crouch, and stared into those eyes that looked so much like his mom's. "Hey, kid. I think there's something that we need to talk about. Can we have a grown-up talk?"

He puffed out his chest and nodded quickly.

"You know the grassy place?"

Keith's chest immediately deflated. "My Ben is there," he said softly.

"Yeah, he is." I didn't have to think long about my next words, I'd been trying to figure out a way to have this conversation with him for nearly a week. "I know you think that if your mom kisses me, then I'll go to the grassy place."

He nodded slowly, his eyes darted around like he was worried about what I might say next. But when I was about to continue, he leaned forward to whisper, "Don't go. Supapowers can't bring you back from the grassy place, Deaton. Please."

Fuck. My throat and my chest felt tight, and it took me a few tries to be able to talk again. "No, they can't." I swallowed past the tightness in my throat, and hoped like hell he wouldn't misunderstand me. "Keith, I need you to understand something. When I go to the grassy place, it will be because I'm really, really old, or because of something that is out of my control. But I swear to you, it won't be because I kissed your mom."

His wide eyes searched mine for a few seconds. "But what 'bout my Ben? He's in the grassy place 'cause he kissed my mommy."

"No, that was out of his control. It had nothing to do with your mom. Sometimes dads just have to go to the grassy place before they grow old, like Ben did." I waited a few seconds before saying, "I need to make sure you really understand."

After a short pause, Keith nodded. "You won't leave me for the grassy place."

This kid. This goddamn kid. How could he break my heart and make me want to scoop him up while talking about grass?

"Hopefully not for a long, long time, kid. But do you understand what I said about your mom?"

Keith's next pause was longer, and his face pinched like he was trying to figure out a difficult problem. Finally, he hesitantly said, "Mommy didn't send my Ben to the grassy place."

"Right," I said, relief coating the word. "And just because your Ben is in the grassy place, doesn't mean you can't have another dad someday, okay?" I waited until he nodded, then jerked my head toward Charlie, and said, "Now I need to go kiss your mom, if that's okay?"

He sighed heavily and shrugged. "I guess so."

I messed with his hair when I stood, and walked the rest of the way toward Charlie.

She had a hand pressed firmly to her mouth, with tears streaming down her face and over her hand.

I dropped to my knees in front of her, and gently pulled her hand down and brushed her wild blond hair away from her face. "Charlie Girl . . ."

"You," she began, but didn't continue as her head fell. She tucked her chin to her chest as a soft sob forced from her chest.

I was ready for it, for whatever she would say. I didn't

know what all they had told her, but I was ready to fight for her, just as I had been for the past three weeks.

"What are you doing to me?" she choked out when I lifted her face back up so I could wipe her tears away.

Her makeup was smeared, her cheeks were wet and red, and her bottom lip was swollen from where she'd bit down on it too many times.

And she looked so fucking gorgeous.

"I'm wiping your tears away."

"No," she said with a soggy laugh. "What are you doing to my heart?"

My thumbs paused on her cheeks when her words triggered something inside me, but then her blue eyes slid over to something down the hall, and that trigger disappeared as I followed her line of sight.

Keith.

"How much of that did you hear?" I asked softly when I faced her again.

"All of it."

Her hand gripped my shirt and pulled me close, her mouth pressed against mine roughly and greedily for a few seconds before she silently begged me to take control of the kiss. Her grip loosened, and her palm flattened against my shirt until just the tips of her fingers were curled into my chest. She melted against the wall and sighed into our kiss when she opened her mouth to me, then teased me with the smallest taste of her before she put the slightest pressure against my chest.

"We still have an audience," she whispered against my mouth, then pushed harder.

I glanced to the side to see Keith standing there, waiting patiently. "Right. Time to put distance between us then." I cleared my throat, then glanced back at Charlie. "Uh, well this whole thing was supposed to be for you today. But I walked in just in time to see you hit your brother. So tell me what you want to do."

Her face pinched in pain and her eyes fell to her lap. "I want to go home."

"You want to walk instead of talk it out with him?"

"He said that if the judge would have known about you, he might not have given me custody. He said I was making our mom's mistakes."

Her biggest fucking fear, and he threw it in her face on a day that was supposed to be one of the happiest for her.

"I'm one of those mistakes," I assumed.

Those blue eyes flickered up to me before falling away again.

I nodded once and gritted my teeth. "Considering I told him I wouldn't hit him, I'm ready to leave whenever you are."

"Now."

I stood and pulled her up with me, and pressed my mouth firmly to hers. "Congratulations, Charlie Girl."

Chapter Sixteen

Charlie

June 26, 2016

MY EYES SLOWLY blinked open, and for a moment I stilled as I tried to remember where I was before I relaxed deeper against the body holding mine. Deacon's deep, rhythmic breathing made my eyelids feel heavy, and I wanted nothing more than to close them again. But I also didn't want to miss this.

Because this? There were no words for it.

Deacon had come over after he'd finished working out, and we'd curled up on my couch. As the night had gotten later and later, he'd stretched out his large frame across the entire thing, and repositioned me so I was lying on top of him as if I weighed nothing.

After fighting the blush that had filled my cheeks, I'd grabbed my book off the table and tucked my head under his chin when he curled his large arms around me.

Just as I had then, I felt protected and cherished and like nothing could touch me. Like nothing could find me under the barrier of his arms. I wanted to hide in the safety of his arms forever.

My eyes zeroed in on the book still in my hand, face-down on Deacon's chest, but I didn't make an attempt to move it again.

This was more perfect than any love story I could read.

This meant more than any song I could write.

Deacon's fingers twitched against the small of my back, then made slow, lazy circles against the little piece of skin showing there, from where my shirt had ridden up.

A shuddering breath slipped past my lips as they eased into a smile.

His chest rumbled beneath my ear when he murmured in a low tone, "Charlie Girl."

I twisted my neck to look up at him, and planted my chin on his chest.

Those brown eyes were light and full of warmth, and looking at me as though he was trying to commit this moment to memory. I understood that look far too well.

The tips of his fingers moved up slightly higher and higher with each set of lazy circles, dragging my shirt with them, and I shivered against the onslaught of chills that raced across my body at the feel.

His hands paused, and those eyes darkened. "You're gonna have to stop doing that when you're lying on me."

Heat filled my face, and I pulled my bottom lip into my mouth. Deacon's fingers curled into my back possessively for the shortest second.

"Christ, Charlie. You're gonna have to stop doing that, too."

Except I couldn't.

Not when he was still holding me like he didn't want to let me go. Not when my mouth was just inches from his. Not when our bodies were flush and I could feel what this was doing to him.

Warmth swam low in my stomach as I fought with promises I'd made myself, and a need Deacon created inside me.

A need for him, a need to be touched. A greater need to be wanted and loved, completely and without reservations.

The feather-light touches resumed, instantly my skin was covered with goose bumps, and a shiver crawled down my spine, slow and warm.

The deep rumbling in Deacon's chest and possessive curling of his fingers against my skin were the only warning I had before his hands were suddenly under my arms, hauling me up.

My book slid from my grip an instant before Deacon set me back down so I was sitting on his stomach. And then his hands were on my back, pressing and pleading as he bent me down.

Deacon's mouth met mine with a force that both shocked me and fascinated me. Just as quickly there was the slightest bit of hesitation as he sought entrance along the seam of my lips, and I knew then that Deacon would always hesitate with me. Would always wait for me to give. Because as soon as I opened to him, he took and took, and, God, it made my head spin in the most exhilarating way.

My fingers traced the curve of his jaw, then wove into his thick hair, looking for something, anything, to hold on to as he sat up.

His hands moved from my back to my waist as I slid to his lap, and tightened when I moved against him. "Charlie," his deep voice rumbled in warning, and he took my bottom lip between his teeth before devouring my mouth again.

But that fight within me was raging, stronger than ever. His thumbs were brushing the undersides of my breasts, and I wanted them to move higher. I wanted that shock of pleasure when I rocked against him again. I wanted everything, but I wanted more than I knew he could give me then.

Unable to stop myself, I moved my hips against his, and whimpered into his mouth at the feel of him beneath his mesh workout shorts.

"Fuck, Charlie," he growled, and forced me back.

One second I was on his lap, the next my back was pressed to the couch and Deacon was lowering himself onto me.

He pressed a searing kiss to my mouth before he was moving, leaving a trail of hot kisses down my neck and chest as he slowly lifted my shirt.

My grip in his hair tightened as that fight raged and raged and raged.

"Deacon," I breathed as his mouth touched the bare skin on my stomach, then moved down another inch.

I trembled beneath his touch and his lips as he moved lower still, and placed an open-mouthed kiss just above my shorts. "Oh, God. Deacon. Deacon, wait," I said quickly when he gripped the top of my shorts in his hand.

Immediately he released the fabric and his body stilled.

"I'm sorry. I'm sorry, I'm sorry," I repeated over and over. Embarrassment coursed through me, and I hurried to cover my face with one of my hands.

I was afraid to know what his expression would say when he looked up at me, I was afraid to know what he would think.

My shirt was moved back into place, and a soft kiss was placed high up on my stomach before my hand was pried from my face.

Deacon's eyes were still dark with lust and need despite the questions that hid there, but his face was full of patience. "Don't apologize. You can say 'wait' at the last second, and I'll fucking wait. You understand?"

I nodded quickly as I tried to figure out what to say to him—how to explain.

I could only imagine from his unspoken questions that he was wondering why I had stopped us since there was a three and a half year old asleep in his room that proved I wasn't a virgin.

"I just, I'm sorry, but I—"

"Stop," he begged, cutting me off. "Stop apologizing. You don't have to, and you don't have to explain yourself."

His eyes searched my face, still full of so many questions, making it hard to believe that he didn't *want* to know why. His voice dropped, and his tone turned cautious. "Charlie, who was the last guy to touch you?"

My heart stuttered and skipped a beat before settling into a too-fast rhythm. A lifelong heartache echoed in my chest no matter how I tried to push it away. I opened my mouth to respond, but the name got caught in my throat.

Saying his name was one thing, though it always hurt. Saying his name like this? My body rebelled against the action.

Deacon's head dipped in acknowledgment, the faintest look of surprise on his handsome face as he let my silence answer. "Who was the last guy you kissed?"

I looked at him hopelessly because I couldn't answer, and prayed he would understand exactly what Ben had meant to me, and how completely he'd shattered me. What allowing Deacon into my life and my heart meant now.

He buried his face into my stomach and mumbled a curse. His arms slid beneath me until he was hugging me like he wouldn't ever let go of me. Another curse vibrated against my stomach before he lifted his head, but he wouldn't look at me. "I shouldn't have pushed you. I'm sorry."

A startled laugh bubbled up my throat, and I let my hands move from his hair to his face so I could force him to look at me. "Push me?"

Didn't he realize that Ben hadn't even waited ten minutes after telling me he wanted me before he'd taken me to my bed and taken my virginity?

Not that I'd asked him to stop. I'd thought my lifelong dreams were coming true. But for a shy eighteen-year-old who had never been kissed, it had been too much too fast. Unfortunately, I hadn't realized that I'd needed *slow* until it was far too late.

"You didn't push me, and you wouldn't have been if you continued. I just . . . I promised myself something, and I want to keep it."

Deacon glanced at my warming cheeks, then back to my eyes. "I said you didn't need to explain, but if there's a promise you're trying to keep, then you're gonna have to."

Now it was my turn to look away. "The next time I'm with someone, I don't want to be second to another girl, or just an option," I admitted quietly. "I want to be the only option. I want to know that whoever I'm with loves me, and only me."

His chest heaved against my legs. "That word."

I risked a glance at him, and saw him staring vacantly at my stomach. "What word?"

"Love," he said after a few seconds, then shook his head. "Charlie, I don't . . . I don't even know what that is. I don't know how to love someone; I'm not even sure if I believe in it."

I felt my brow draw together as I listened to him. His words so familiar that it made my heart race as confusion filled me.

If I didn't already have proof on my phone that Stranger and Deacon had different numbers, I would have grabbed my phone and texted Stranger right then and waited to see if Deacon's phone went off.

Deacon's expression fell as he misinterpreted mine, and he hurried to say, "You have to understand, Charlie. My mom left my dad for my uncle when I was young—not that he didn't deserve it—and you know he's still single. My grandpa was such a dick that my grandma left him and started over here in Thatch and never remarried. No one in my family believes in love." He shrugged. "It's just not something I know, it's not something I'd ever be able to give you."

I pushed away thoughts of Stranger, and forced myself to ask something I wasn't sure I wanted to know. "Why are you here, Deacon?"

"What do you mean?" he asked, his tone low and cautious.

"I mean, what did you expect to come of this? What was your plan if it wasn't to make me want something more with you?"

He looked lost. He blew out a slow breath and shook his head once. "There was no plan, I just knew that I needed you."

"And what happens when my son falls in love with you?" My eyes searched his, my voice dropped to a whisper. "What happens when I fall in love with you?" *Because both are dangerously close to becoming realities*, I thought.

Keith already loved Deacon; there was no question about that. And me? I loved the way he made me feel and the way he treated my son. I loved the way he kissed me and held me, and the way he refused to let me hide in front of him.

Instead of looking terrified at the thought, instead of jumping off the couch and leaving my house, Deacon stared at me, unblinking.

"Don't give me your heart, Charlie Girl. I'll break it without even trying."

My eyes fluttered shut, and his mouth fell to my stomach one last time as his hands gripped at my back, silently begging me not to let this end.

And I loved the way he loved me, even if he didn't realize it.

Chapter Seventeen

Deacon

July 4, 2016

"You know, honey, I've been thinking about—"

"Mom, I don't want your lists! I don't care which girls
you think I should marry," Graham groaned, and jumped
up from where his mom had sat down between us on the
couch, and took off for the kitchen.

I smirked when she sighed, and nodded in the direction of the kitchen, but didn't take my eyes off the TV.
"The food smells amazing, Mrs. LaRue."

"It will be ready soon," she said in a dejected tone, but
out of the corner of my eye I saw her sit up and turn her
attention to me. "Deacon, honey."

"Mm-hm?"

"What about you?"

I slowly looked over at her and eyed the paper in her hand like it was poison. "Uh, I thought you knew that I'm . . ." I trailed off, not knowing what to say about Charlie. Because I didn't know what we were.

We weren't anything, but at the same time, it felt like we were something significant.

So significant I'd been trying to figure out a way to tell Words for four days now that I was about to walk away. But every night when she responded to me, the words wouldn't come.

I knew I couldn't have both, the guilt that crept through me at the thought of Charlie finding out told me that, and more. I knew which one I couldn't stand to lose, so why was saying good-bye to Words proving to be so difficult?

I didn't understand it, and I didn't know what to do about it.

Mrs. LaRue patted my arm with the hand that was holding the list of names and numbers.

I also didn't know how to tell my best friend's mom that I didn't want her help in finding a wife. I wasn't sure I ever wanted a wife anyway. "I'm not exactly looking—"

"I'm just waiting for the day when you or Graham realize it's time to settle down so you can have families of your own. Don't you see how happy everyone is here with their families? Don't you want that too?"

A laugh escaped me before I was able to stop it. Sucking air in through my teeth, I cocked my head to the side, and said, "Ah, yeah, 'settling down' and 'family' are about the last thing on my list. They aren't even in my vocabulary. You know I hate kids."

She pursed her lips, studying me curiously. "I thought that . . . well, never mind," she said with disappointment as she stood, then turned toward the kitchen. "However, I will get through to one of you, one of these days!"

"She never stops," Graham grumbled when he snuck back into the living room. "It's constant. She already has Aly, and pretends Keith is her grandkid too. She's not waiting on me for anything, but it's as if she thinks I'm a woman all of a sudden and I'm not going to be able to have kids or some shit if I don't get married yesterday."

I laughed when he did, but it sounded distracted. My attention had left Graham the second he'd said Keith's name. Charlie and Keith were supposed to have gotten there twenty minutes ago. I didn't hear or see either of them, so I pulled out my phone and sent Charlie a message.

Where are you? Do you need me to pick you two up?

"I noticed Candy's been gone," Graham mumbled.

I stilled, and slowly let my eyes drift over toward him. It wasn't, but I was thanking God he hadn't seen it.

There was that guilt again, creeping through my body. I knew it would continue to slowly consume every part of me until it overwhelmed me.

Tonight, I vowed. *I'm walking away from Words tonight.*

Graham glanced at me, the bruising from where I'd broken his nose already gone. "You really like Charlie? You really changing for her?"

I gave him a look, and huffed. "Has it really taken you a month to come to grips with that?"

I glanced down at my phone when it chimed in my hand, and pulled up the messages.

Charlie Girl: *Already here. In the kitchen.*

Graham was talking again, but I stood up and walked toward the kitchen without looking back at him. We were fine, even though things had been a little strained between us around the house for a while, but I saw him all the time. For now, I needed to see my Charlie Girl.

As soon as I rounded the corner into the LaRues' kitchen my eyes found her, and I couldn't stop myself from taking her in as I closed the distance between us.

"You're here," I said when I took the final step up to her and tried to pull her into my arms, but Charlie took a step to the side.

She held her body stiffly, and never once looked up at me. "You knew I would be."

My forehead pinched at her cold tone and body language, and it was then I noticed what she was doing.

Her head was bowed and her arm was wrapped around her waist.

She was trying to be invisible. She was fucking hiding. From me.

"Why didn't you come say hi or let me know you were here?"

A soft exhale blew past her lips, and she finally glanced up at me. Those blue eyes raged with anger . . . I just didn't know who she was angry with or why. "I didn't know I had to check in with you when I went places, especially if you were going to be there too." Her glare darted to something behind me before touching on me again. "Besides, you were busy."

When she started turning around again, I grabbed her arm and pulled her back a few steps with me so we were away from everyone else in the kitchen.

"Let go," she demanded, her voice just above a whisper, but still firm.

"What the hell? You just got here and you're already mad at me? There's no way I could've done something to piss you off when this is the first time I'm seeing or talking to you all day."

She shook her head and tried to force a smile, but it immediately fell. "I'm not mad at you, Deacon."

"Charlie."

"I'm not," she said again.

I didn't believe her, but I knew with all of our friends and her brother in this house, she wasn't going to tell me the truth right now. With a sigh, I looked around and asked, "Where's Keith?"

"In the downstairs guest room," she replied protectively. "He's still sleeping from the drive over."

I wanted to question her tone again, but before I got the chance to, a familiar voice called out, and I turned to look at a chalk-white Keith.

"Mommy? I don't feel—" He abruptly stopped talking, and his eyes widened.

Charlie hissed a curse as she took off toward Keith and scooped him up in her arms. She kept running with me right behind her. They made it to the bathroom, but only to the tub before Keith started throwing up, and I froze.

I didn't know what to do.

Keith was sick, and I needed to help him and I needed to help Charlie, and I didn't know what to do.

"It's okay, baby," Charlie whispered over and over again as she helped Keith lean over the tub.

"What do I do?"

"Get out," she said harshly before whispering to Keith again.

"Charlie, let me help."

She turned her head to glare at me, and repeated, "Get out."

Soon Grey was in the bathroom with us, and with a gentle push of her hands, I stumbled out to the hall to wait.

And wait.

After a few minutes, Grey left with a suggestion that sounded more like a warning not to go in the bathroom, and about ten minutes later, Charlie came out carrying Keith.

"I need to take him home," she said as she walked past me. "He's burning up, I don't want anyone else to get sick."

"Okay, then let me help you. I can drive y—"

"I've got it," she said in a monotone voice.

And it was driving me fucking crazy.

"At least let me carry him for you, Charlie, Christ. Why won't you let me help you?"

Instead of responding to me, she reached out to grab

her purse and keys from Grey, and thanked her. "I'll text you if it gets bad. But we'll be fine, really," she said to Grey, finishing what must have been a conversation from the bathroom.

I opened the front door and followed them outside, but when I tried to help Charlie by opening the back door to her SUV, she turned on me and snapped.

"I said I've got it!"

"God damn it, Charlie! What?" I yelled, and flung out my arms. "What did I do to piss you off this time?"

"Just go back inside," she begged.

"Why won't you talk to me?"

Her lips formed a tight line when her chin started shaking, but she didn't say anything until she had Keith in his booster seat and the door shut again. "I am not mad at you, can you *please* just stop and go back inside?"

I huffed and looked around before focusing back on her. "Stop what? Trying to help you?" She started walking around the car to the driver's side, so I grabbed her wrist to stop her.

She whirled around, and yelled, "Stop pretending! You're not pissing me off, you are breaking my heart!"

I dropped her wrist, and my face fell when I saw the tears streaming down her cheeks. "What?"

She took another step away, but turned back around to face me when she said, "You're doing exactly what you said you would if I gave you my heart. Breaking it. You hate kids? *Still*, Deacon, really?"

I shook my head in confusion until I remembered talking to Graham's mom. "Charlie, it's a—I don't mean that with him. You know that."

"What if Keith heard you? He loves you! And I keep thinking that this new Deacon is who you really are and I have *stupidly* let myself fall in love with that side of you!" she cried.

"What?" I asked on a breath. That word . . . that fucking word. "No . . ."

"But it's just an act; you were just pretending. Because as soon as we're not around, bachelor Deacon is back, isn't he? The one who hates kids and has family as the *last* thing on his list."

"That's not true, that's—"

She laughed sadly and gestured toward me. "But I can't be mad at you because this is my fault, right? Because I hoped for something that you told me you could never give me. I hoped for something that you obviously never wanted. But I'm not the only one who loves you, and one of these days Keith will catch on to what you're saying. And since he's the *first* thing on my list, I need to make sure that day doesn't come."

My chest felt uncomfortably tight, my arms felt heavy as they hung at my sides, but I couldn't make them move as the weight of Charlie's words bore down on me. It felt like I was going through the worst kind of breakup imaginable, but with a girl and her son who weren't mine, though they had easily rooted themselves in my life.

I wasn't ready for this.

I wasn't ready to lose them.

"What are you saying, Charlie?"

She shook her head and took a step back, but paused and gave me a sad smile. "It's not like I expected you to *want* a family with us. But with the way you are with him? With the way you act like he makes your world better the same way you make his?" she choked out, and had to clear her throat. "You can't blame *me* for wanting it. You can't blame me for giving you my heart and praying that you wanted to keep it."

"Charlie—"

"I'm walking, Deacon," she said tightly, her voice rough with emotion, her cheeks stained with tears. "Let me walk."

With that, she turned and walked around the back of her car, and I watched her drive away as her words kept me nailed me to the ground.

Charlie

July 4, 2016

I finished drying off my body once I stepped out of the shower a couple hours later, and reached up to undo the messy knot on top of my head just before I heard something that made me pause.

I glanced at the doorway leading to my bedroom, and listened for a few seconds until I heard the loud boom of fireworks over the lake.

The breath I had been holding in was quickly forced from my lungs, and I reached up for my hair again when another noise filtered in from the front of my house that I was certain wasn't fireworks.

I let my towel fall to the bathroom floor and tried to remain as quiet as possible as I walked into my bedroom and pulled on a clean shirt and pair of sleeping shorts, then grabbed my phone off the nightstand and pulled up Deacon's number as I crept out of the bedroom and down the hall.

It didn't matter what had happened between Deacon and me at the LaRues' house. It would take the sheriffs much longer to get here than it would Deacon, and I knew he cared about us enough that he would at least hurry.

Besides, he was the most intimidating-looking man I knew.

I paused near the end of the hall to listen to the noises in my kitchen, long enough to be sure that Keith hadn't woken up and wasn't the one making the noise, then tapped on Deacon's name, and tried to figure out a way to get to Keith without being seen.

Seconds later, a phone began ringing in my kitchen before it abruptly cut off when Deacon answered my call.

"Charlie Girl."

My shoulders sagged, and I forgot about trying to remain silent as I stepped out into the living room, bringing me face-to-face with my *intruder*.

"What the hell are you doing?" I demanded through gritted teeth.

His eyes never left me as he ended the call and set his phone on the counter, then took two large steps toward me. "How's Keith?"

"I asked you a question, Deacon. What are you doing, and why are you in my house?"

"Tell me how Keith is."

I lifted my arm out in front of me, gesturing toward the other side of the house that held Keith's room, then let it slap down on my thigh. "He's asleep. He got sick a couple more times. Now what are you doing in my house?"

He glanced back at my kitchen island, as if the answer should be obvious.

I looked at what it was now covered with—medicines and sports drinks and the types of foods meant for sick stomachs, none of which I had bought. "You got all this?"

He ignored my question, and instead said, "If you don't want me in here, you shouldn't have made sure that I was one of the people who had a spare key."

"I told you I was walking. That should have been a sign not to come here tonight, and especially not come in uninvited!"

"You don't get to do what you did tonight," he said in a low tone, and closed the distance between us a little more. "If you're gonna walk from me, then you better do it for a damn good reason. But you can't just take Keith from me because of a knee-jerk response I had. You can't just take *you* from me because you've decided that I don't want you." He gestured around us, and said, "That I don't want all of this."

I shook my head quickly. I didn't want to listen to what he was going to tell me. I didn't want to believe his lies. "I heard you tonight, Deacon!"

"Yeah, you heard something I've said most of my life. It's gonna be hard not to automatically come back with that. But I also *panicked* tonight when Keith got sick, and I just had to stand there and watch and wait because I didn't know what to do, and you wouldn't let me help you. Do you see this?" he asked, and threw his hand behind him toward the island. "You left and I immediately began searching what Keith needed and calling my grandma for help, and then I stood in a store for nearly an hour staring at boxes and reading them trying to figure out if it would help him or not because after all that, I'm still fucking clueless. That should tell you what I want, Charlie. I don't know what the hell I'm doing, but I want to try. I want to learn. I want to take care of him, and I want you to let me help you. I want you to let me take care of *you*." His last statement was full of multiple meanings, his eyes pled with me to hear every one of them.

Heard, Deacon. Lies received.

"Just last week you said—"

"A lot can happen in a week, Charlie!" He laughed, but there was no humor behind it. "A lot can happen in a day, or a few hours, or even a couple minutes if you think everything is being taken from you." His chest moved exaggeratedly as he stared at me.

As much as I wanted to continue denying his words, pushing them from my mind, I couldn't. Not with that look, not with those words.

Because I knew both too well.

The tortured look on his face and in his light brown eyes screamed exactly that—that he'd felt like everything was being ripped from him. Like it still was . . .

He took a cautious step toward me, and then another.

"I won't tell you that I'm in love with you, because I'm still not sure that I'll ever know what that word means. But I know that I can't lose you. I know that my life feels wrong if you and your son aren't in it. I know that I wanted to tear my damn heart out watching you walk away from me."

He took the last step and cradled my face in his large hands, and tilted my head back so he could look directly into my eyes.

"Do you understand me, Charlie girl? I want your heart. I want it all." Deacon's mouth fell onto mine in a burning kiss that I knew I wanted to experience again and again. His arms curled around my body, his large hands searching and gripping and teasing until I was bowing into him.

His tongue tortured mine in a slow, declaring dance that didn't match the rhythm of our hands or my pounding heart as his fingers trailed just inside the band of my shorts.

And then everything stilled.

His hands, his mouth, my heart . . .

Seconds passed before two of his fingers twitched against my bare hip, and I shuddered against him when his hands slowly moved lower, searching for underwear that he wouldn't find.

A low rumble sounded in his chest before Deacon took my bottom lip between his teeth and tugged gently. "What are you doing to me?" he whispered mostly to himself, and started to pull me closer, but I skipped out of his hold and stepped back toward the hallway leading to my bedroom.

I didn't know what I was doing to him, but I knew what he was doing to me . . . what he'd done.

I'd thought I would never be able to trust anyone with my heart again, and though I had tried to keep it from Deacon Carver, it had been impossible. Even during the confusing times, even during the times when he'd broken a little piece of my heart, all I saw when I closed my eyes was him and what we could be. What we *would* be, because I knew he loved me too, and there was no longer a point in fighting it.

Deacon's eyes darkened as he watched me back away, and suddenly he was stalking toward me. His long strides didn't falter as he lifted me into his arms and walked us toward my bedroom.

His mouth never left mine. His hands gripped my body so tightly it was as if he wanted to memorize the feel of me beneath his hands, as if he wanted to make sure I was there.

The air in my lungs rushed out when my back hit the bed and Deacon's body settled on top of mine. And just as he had been doing before, I dug my fingers into his back and shoulders. I felt like I had to hold on to something real; like I had to feel his body to know I wasn't imagining this.

His mouth left a trail of hot kisses down my throat as he slowly lifted my shirt up my stomach, but both his touch and his mouth stopped when the bottom of the material teased my nipples.

"Remember what I said the other night." His deep voice rumbled against my skin. It was more of a request than a question. "Say *wait* at the last second, and I'll wait. Charlie Girl," he demanded after a short pause.

"I know," I said quickly, then sucked in a sharp gasp when his head suddenly dipped and he pulled one of my exposed breasts into his mouth.

His tongue rolled around my nipple and his teeth grazed the sensitive skin there, sending little shock waves straight to my core. Over and over again until I was gripping his hair and whimpering his name and moving restlessly beneath him, needing more.

I lifted my hips from the bed when he pulled at my shorts, and exhaled shakily when he moved in a line down my stomach and spread my thighs.

"Deacon." I swallowed thickly, and tried to ignore the way my heart was racing and chest was heaving with each ragged breath.

Because I wanted this. My body was screaming for me to let him to continue. But this . . .

I didn't know how to let him do this.

Brown eyes met mine, his face just above my hips. "Say the word." But even though his tone held so much promise, as he spoke he pushed my legs until my knees were bent and feet were planted on the bed. "Say the word, and I'll hold you for the rest of the night."

My head shook quickly as I fought with what I wanted and what I was too ashamed to allow to happen. "No, that's not—I can't—I don't—I've never," I said quickly, stumbling over the words. "He never . . ." I trailed off when Deacon's brows arched up, and then a determined and possessive look slowly covered that handsome, handsome face.

A wicked grin tugged at his mouth as he pushed himself farther back, and then lowered himself until I could feel his breath against me when he said, "Wrong word."

My back arched away from the bed and my hands fisted in the comforter when his tongue moved from my entrance to my clit. My skin covered with goose bumps as his tongue continued to torture me in a way I'd never imagined possible, and the warmth in my belly suddenly felt white-hot.

One of my hands shot to his head, my fingers wove into his hair and gripped when he pressed two fingers inside me. "Oh God!" I said breathlessly. "Deacon!"

I felt him smile against me before he resumed the sweet suffering.

It was too much. The soft and the hard and the feel of his smiles and silent laughters when I would gasp out a plea or curse from it all.

Something low in my stomach tightened, and that warmth burned hotter and hotter until that too felt like it was too much. My breathing hitched and my toes curled, trying to find some purchase in the comforter. My chest moved raggedly with my uneven breaths until it halted as my breathing stopped altogether . . .

And then came out with a rush when Deacon's mouth and hand disappeared.

I felt his loss on more than a physical level. It felt like my body was screaming at him to come back and continue, when I couldn't speak at all.

I threw one of my hands over my face when his wicked grin came into view as he moved over me. I needed to block that heated stare from seeing exactly how much I'd enjoyed that, when I was still completely mortified by it and embarrassed by the way my body *craved* more. I didn't want to know that my inexperience was amusing to him when I knew all too well about his experience.

The sound of clothes being removed and hitting the floor was the only thing that joined my uneven breathing for a while before I felt his hands gently moving my shirt that he'd left rolled up on my chest earlier.

"Beautiful. You're so damn beautiful, Charlie." Deacon sounded like a blind man seeing the sun for the first time. My name left his lips like a prayer.

None of the teasing I'd expected. No condescending tone.

None of the old Deacon I kept worrying would show up again.

Relief flooded me at his words, and my lips twitched into a smile. I kept my eyes shut when he slid the shirt over my arms and head, and let it fall to the floor as well.

He settled himself between my legs, a soft whimper moved up my throat when he pressed his length against me. "You walking?" he murmured as his mouth brushed across mine in the softest, sweetest kiss.

I curled my hands around his face when he rested his forehead on mine, and shook my head. "No."

No, I was seeing everything Deacon couldn't admit because he didn't know how. I was enjoying living in this moment and being loved by a man like Deacon Carver while loving him the best way I knew how . . . with my eyes shut.

A low growl built in his chest when I curled my legs around his waist and lifted my hips so the tip of him slid against my entrance. "Christ, Charlie."

He pushed in the slightest bit, and reached between our bodies to brush his fingers against where I was aching and craving him, but stopped when I attempted to bite back a moan.

"Tell me if you're not ready," he pled gently. "Tell me, or I'm making you mine, and you're done walking away from me."

"Are you waiting for me to change my mind or trying to give me time to remember my promise to myself?" I whispered, and slowly opened my eyes and found his directly above me. I continued to cradle his face for a brief moment, then let my hands slide to his neck and across his shoulders. "If you have no intention of giving me your heart, then don't do this to mine. But my heart was yours even when you weren't ready for it, so take it or let me—"

Deacon's mouth crashed down onto mine, swallowing my shocked cry when he forced his thick length inside me.

Like no time had passed at all, that tight feeling in my stomach was back, and the heat felt like it might consume me as my body adjusted to his.

But, oh God, when he moved . . .

I never knew it could be like that. I never knew it could feel like it was not enough and too much, and like he was holding back—leaving me seconds from begging for more—while high-pitched moans kept escaping me from the intensity of it all, all at once.

Sex with Ben had been fast and to the point, and I'd thought at the time that it had been everything I could ever want. But he had never touched me. He'd never left my body feeling like it might burst if he didn't continue touching me, and like it might fall apart if he didn't stop.

This was perfection.

Deacon's movements slowed, the unhurried roll of his hips brought him deeper and deeper inside.

That heat swirled and built until my body felt like it was strung so tightly I was sure I was going to shatter.

My breathing grew ragged and uneven, and one by one I pressed my fingers firmly against his shoulders and back, somehow knowing that I was going to need to hold on.

A short, broken huff was forced from my chest when he pushed in harder, and my grip tightened, eyes fluttered shut, and head fell back onto the bed. "Deacon," I breathed, my voice barely making a sound. "Deac—" My arms and legs locked up and my fingers dug into his skin just as my body began vibrating.

"That's it," he breathed against my neck, and slid himself into me again and again. "That's it, Charlie, let go."

Before I could grasp his demand, he pulled all the way out then slammed back into me, and my body felt like it went up in flames.

A warm shiver shot down my spine and that white-hot heat shot through my veins. The vibrating turned into trembling and then shaking as warm shivers continued to torment my body.

Deacon hissed and bit down on my collarbone to muffle his sudden curse. His body felt rigid against mine for only a moment before his hips moved harder and faster than before, then harder still.

Each movement from him prolonged what was happening inside me, and I both loved and hated it. I never wanted it to end, but I felt out of control and terrified by that.

A shudder rolled through Deacon's back, and he groaned against my neck as his hips jerked against mine when he found his release inside me. His back shook from his exaggerated breaths, the muscles there rippled beneath the tips of my fingers as we both tried to find our way back to ourselves.

He lifted his head, and his eyes met and searched mine as he slowly rolled onto his side, taking me with him. "You okay?"

Exhausted, wanted him again, and never felt more alive, but "okay" would do. I nodded once, but wasn't able to voice the response he needed. The way Deacon was looking at me was all I could focus on. "Why are you looking at me like that?"

It was as though he was worried and proud, felt possessive and protective.

Deacon brushed away a chunk of hair that had fallen out of my bun, and cupped my cheek in his palm. "Never going to want to give this up, Charlie Girl. He was insane to."

I smiled weakly as my chest warmed at his words. "I gave you my heart, you don't have to."

But I knew what I would have to give up in order to keep this.

Stranger.

For the first time in too long, I was acutely aware that the man holding me close to his body with his lips pressed firmly to mine was not the same man I texted every night.

It had been too easy to visualize Stranger as Deacon while talking to him. To swoon over his words and fall for him even though I knew I couldn't. Even though I knew that it would be entirely stupid to allow myself to. Then again, I hadn't had much of a choice in the matter when Stranger had so clearly known the way to my heart without even trying.

Some odd mixture of guilt and denial and fear filled me as I acknowledged the extent of my conversations with Stranger. How they'd made me feel, and how I'd come to crave them even as I'd told myself that they were innocent. Even as I'd told myself that he was a fictional character in one of my books.

Because somewhere out there, he *was* real. Because no matter what I told myself, the conversations weren't innocent if the thought of Deacon ever seeing them had ice sliding through my veins. Because even though I'd envisioned them to be the same person, I had to accept that Deacon and Stranger were two separate men, now that I was about to lose one of them.

I looked up into light brown eyes when Deacon pulled back, and made up my mind. The song was finished; it had been for a few days. I would send it to Stranger, and then I would tell him good-bye.

Why did the thought of never speaking to him again hurt so much, when I was staring at what I wanted?

Chapter Eighteen

Deacon

July 4, 2016

NEVER GOING TO *want to give this up.*

I didn't know where the words had come from when they had slid off my tongue before, but the thought continued to float through my mind again and again as I lay there with my arms tightly wrapped around Charlie's body, and my head resting on her stomach.

Charlie's fingers gently moved up and down my back, trailing over the raised lines from her nails, and every now and then one of her fingers would pass over where she'd broken the skin just as she'd fallen apart beneath me.

Her hesitations and reactions tonight hadn't been something I'd expected. Considering her past with Ben, I'd never thought Charlie would be as innocent as she was. But, Christ, it had made my blood pound knowing no one had touched her that way. Knowing I was the first to take care of her the way she should be. Knowing no one else had made her feel the way she had tonight.

Ben was a damn idiot for not treating her like she was everything, but I wouldn't complain, because I knew I would remember the way Charlie had responded to my touch, and the look on her face, for the rest of my life.

I'd remember everything about tonight for the rest of my life.

I blew out a slow, steadying breath against her stomach, then kissed the skin there as I thought about my wallet and what I had left in there. What I hadn't even considered grabbing because I'd wanted Charlie, had wanted to feel her come undone while I was buried deep inside her, so damn bad.

Then again, I had a feeling just the fact that it was Charlie would have had me forgetting everything else but her, because she was the only one who could.

"I'm sorry," she whispered as she traced over her mark on me. "I didn't mean to."

My mouth curved into a smile, and I lifted my head to look at her. "Don't," I said simply. If she only knew how fucking hot it had been. "Besides," I said in a low tone as I pushed myself higher up on her body. "I'll return the favor." It was a promise emphasized when I dipped my head to bite the underside of her breast.

Charlie let out a soft gasp, and her fingers tightened on my back. She cradled my body between her thighs, and curled one of her legs slowly around one of my own—and already, that foil packet in my wallet was forgotten.

Never before, but Charlie Girl wasn't like any of the others.

I rolled my hips against hers, and covered her mouth with my own, swallowing the next quick gasp that left her at the contact.

"Wait," she said halfheartedly, but pulled me closer to her warmth. She shuddered when I rocked against her again, and bit down on her bottom lip as her head dropped back when I did it again. "Oh God," she whispered.

"You gonna walk now?" I asked, my tone teasing, and kissed her soundly.

Her head shook faintly. "No. No, wait," she said more firmly. "Wait, just let me—before I get too consumed in you, let me go check on Keith."

"Shit," I hissed, and pushed away from her. "I forgot. I'm sorry, I forgot."

Her face, that just seconds before had shown her need and her pleasure, was now full of amusement as she watched me hurry around her room gathering clothes. "Forgot what, exactly?"

I paused once I had my boxer briefs on, and hesitated for only a second before deciding to tell her the truth. "Forgot he was here, forgot he was sick. Forgot everything . . ."

Red stained her cheeks as she shrugged into her shirt,

but she remained silent as she climbed off the bed and pulled on the shorts I had tossed at her. She walked slowly up to me to kiss my bare chest, her blue eyes flashed up to mine for a brief second when she said, "Glad I wasn't the only one. Give me just a minute, I'll be back."

I watched her walk out of the room, then turned to grab my jeans. After I finished buttoning them up, I bent to pick up my shirt, but froze when something on her nightstand next to a small stack of books caught my eye.

No.

I stayed there, hunched over and staring at the offending object for what felt like years as I tried to make myself see something else. Something other than the brown, slightly worn, soft leather journal that had entered my life and changed everything just over a month ago.

After long moments, I finally forced myself to straighten, and walked over to the nightstand. I picked up the pen that sat on top, and ran my hand over the journal.

Not her. Not her, not her, not her. Not this. It can't be the same.

My Charlie reads books, she doesn't write songs.

Words, to me, had been an escape from the Deacon everyone knew. She'd been a way for me to be myself when no one else had allowed me to be, and then I hadn't been able to leave her.

I opened the cover, and my eyes shut when I saw the writing. "Fuck."

I flipped faster through the book until I got to the pages where we'd written back and forth to each other, then slammed the journal shut and backed away from the nightstand.

"This isn't happening. This isn't fucking happening," I hissed.

It didn't matter that I'd visualized Charlie as Words, she couldn't be her.

Because before I had been terrified about what Charlie would say if she'd ever found out about Words, but now I didn't know what to do about the fact that while I'd been trying to win Charlie over during the day, she'd spent her nights freely talking to a stranger in a way I always had to *beg* her to talk to me.

I snatched my shirt off the floor and shrugged into it and my shoes as I hurried out of Charlie's room and down the hall. I entered the living room just as she did from the other side of the house, and her eyebrows pulled together when she saw me completely dressed.

Fear and hurt flashed through her eyes before she could try to hide it, but her shoulders still sagged as she studied me. When she spoke, her voice shook. "You're leaving."

It wasn't a question, and it sounded as if she'd expected this all along.

I wanted to fall to my knees in front of her and wrap my arms around her. I wanted to tell her that not everyone would do what Ben had done to her; that despite my past, the guy she had given her heart to was the real Deacon. The Deacon that wanted nothing more than to spend the rest of the night, and every other night, in the same bed as her.

But all I could think about were my countless conversations with Words—things Charlie had thought she was saying to another man—and my need to prove that this wasn't real somehow. That maybe she'd just found the journal because she worked at Mama's.

It took me a second to realize I was nodding before I could shake my head. "No. Not like that," I said quickly.

Her face was now guarded as her head slowly bowed, her stance rigid as she curled her arm around her waist.

No. No, don't hide from me, Charlie Girl, I thought as my stomach churned and chest ached.

I just needed to get my other phone and check something before I lost my damn mind.

I finally blurted out the only other thing I could think of in that moment. "Condoms." I swallowed past my unease, and pointed at the door.

Charlie's blue eyes darted to the door before locking on me. "You're going to get condoms," she said in the same tone.

I could feel the one in my wallet as though it weighed ten pounds. For the first time since I found the journal, I took a steadying breath, and met her gaze straight on as I told her the only truth I could right now. "Like I said, you make me forget everything, and I know I'd forget again the next time I get close enough to have you. I need to protect you, or else I'll be no better than he was."

Her guarded expression cracked, and her face finally softened. "Okay."

"Okay?"

She dipped her head in a nod. "Yeah. Just let yourself in when you get back."

Instead of leaving, I took long, quick steps toward her, and brought my mouth down onto hers as I pulled her close.

She melted against me, and I forced myself not to say everything I was thinking.

Please forgive me.

Please don't be her.

Please understand. . .

"Come back soon," Charlie whispered against my lips, and without looking at her, I turned and strode for the door.

Despite the twitching in my hands to grab Candy from my center console, where I stashed it most days now, I waited until I was out of Charlie's driveway and off her street. Then continued to drive until I was near one of the docks at the lake.

I put my car in park and just stared out at the lake for long seconds until I couldn't stand it any longer, then dug in the console until I found the phone. It felt like I was moving through water as I went to the contacts and opened up Words's, then pulled out my other phone, and did the same to pull up Charlie's.

I'd just glanced at Words's number, so I already knew. But I refused to believe it until I was holding my phones side by side.

My head dropped back against the headrest as dread filled me, and I barked out a curse as I flung Candy across the car. It hit the passenger door with a loud smack and fell to the floor seconds before it chimed.

Then chimed again.

I slowly looked down to where it lay. My chest felt tight and heavy as I tried to tell myself that it wasn't her.

It couldn't be her. It had to be someone else.

I leaned over to grab the phone off the floor, and tapped on the screen until the messages were pulled up.

Words.

A brief flash of disbelief and jealousy flared in my chest before I told myself that she might be doing exactly what I would've.

I'd been trying to walk away from Words for days, and hadn't been able to. But I knew without a doubt that if I hadn't found out who Words was, I would have walked away from her without a second thought after what had happened between Charlie and me tonight.

I opened the message, and that jealousy and disbelief grew and grew as anger simmered in my veins.

Words: *Hey, Stranger. Thought you might want to see this.*

Below was a picture of a page in her journal. The very one I'd just been holding.

> You can't believe it's daylight
> We stayed up again all night
> Talking just cause you like the way I make the words sound
> I triple-double dare you
> Fess up and make the first move
> You need me like I need you
> That's why you come around here
> Cause you know I've always been the one

With my heart tied behind my back
You can't help it when I look at you like that
Don't deny it cause we both know
I could love you with my eyes closed
I could love you with my eyes closed

Who listens to your sad songs
The shoulder that you cry on
Out on that ledge you walk on
When you're sinking
Who keeps your secrets locked up
When there's no one you can trust
I know it's much more than just wishful thinking
Just say the words and you know I'll be there

With my heart tied behind my back
You can't help it when I look at you like that
Don't deny it cause we both know
I could love you with my eyes closed
I could love you with my eyes closed

I clenched the phone so tightly in my hand, I was sure I would break it.

I got it now . . . who she'd started writing about. Ben. Because there'd never been anyone else for Charlie than him until I'd finally seen what I should have long ago.

But I also knew she'd changed the song to start writing about me. Well, *Stranger*, for her.

And right now all I could see was that part where she talked about her heart and loving him.

Was it possible to be jealous of yourself?

Was it possible to be mad that your girl was in love with you?

When she didn't realize that it was you, and thought it was another man entirely, the answer was yes.

I shoved my car into gear and took off away from the lake without thinking about what I was about to do.

I was back at Charlie's faster than I should have been, and though I knew I needed to calm myself down, each step closer to her door had my anger growing hotter.

The door was unlocked and I flung it open easily, and I only spared a second to glance in the direction of Keith's room to make sure I didn't see or hear him before storming into Charlie's room.

The smile that had been lighting up her face immediately fell when she noticed my anger, and though she called my name, I didn't respond.

My eyes scanned her room for the journal that was no longer on the nightstand. As soon as they landed on it, I walked over and snatched it up from where it sat next to her on the bed, and didn't miss the way she reached for it, trying to stop me, as though she was afraid of me having it.

"Deacon, give that to me!" she said quickly, her tone full of worry.

"You and your words," I sneered.

Her head snapped up. "What did you just say?" she asked breathlessly.

I slammed Candy on top of it and thrust both at her. "An hour," I growled when she took them from me. "Not even. I was inside you not even an hour ago, and you're already sending this shit?"

"What is this?" she asked in a shaky voice. "Whose phone is this?"

I leaned forward and planted my hands on the bed so my face was directly in front of hers. "You gave me your heart, Charlie Girl, yeah? Or did you give it to Stranger? Or maybe someone else that I don't know about."

Dread filled her eyes. "How . . . how do you know—"

"I made you mine. I'm pretty sure I wanted to continue making *only you* mine for the rest of my goddamn life, and it's *you* who can't choose just one person?"

"No." Her head shook stubbornly. "No, you don't know what you're talking about!" She held the phone up, and asked again, "Whose phone is this, Deacon?"

I pushed away from the bed and ran my hand through my hair as I took a step away from her. A frustrated huff burst from my chest that she was refusing to see what was happening. "Mine!" I snapped when I faced her again. "It's mine, Charlie. I'm Stranger, you're Words. Don't you fucking get it?"

"No, this isn't your phone. *That* isn't—I have your num—you don't talk to me the way—I thought he was—" She quickly cut off her frantic rambling, and leaned away from me when I bent close to her again.

"Thought he was who?" I demanded. When she only shook her head, I yelled, "Who, Charlie, who the fuck did you think you were falling in love with?"

"You!" she cried, and her blue eyes welled with tears. "I fell in love with *you*, but you can't be him—"

"You sure about that?"

"—you can't be Stranger!"

"Then tell me who is!"

"I thought it was Graham!"

I stumbled away from her and the bed as if her words had been a physical blow to my chest.

Her confession mixed with my demand, both lingered in the space between us and louder than I could handle in the silence that now filled her room.

I staggered a step away from her, and then another, before I turned toward the door. Just as fast, I turned back around. "You thought you've been talking to my best friend, and this entire time, all I've been able to see was you?"

"No, that's not it. That's not what I meant. I always pictured you, but it was the things—"

"Save it, Charlie," I whispered, my tone bordered on a plea.

"Will you let me talk?"

I lifted my arms to my sides, then let them fall. "Why? So you can drive that knife into my chest a little more?" I laughed softly, but there was no humor behind it. "You know, I couldn't figure out why it was so hard to even consider walking away from Words, but I get it. I fucking get it now because I never would've been able to walk away from you." *Before . . .* I mentally added.

"You knew . . ." She murmured when I started to back up again, her tone now filled with suspicion. "How long have you known, and how long would you have let it go on if we hadn't had sex tonight?"

"Tonight." I nodded toward the journal, still in her hands. "I saw it when you went to go check on Keith. Don't try to turn this around to something I did when I've been trying to walk away from Words for nearly a week. I knew when I came after you tonight that walking from her was exactly what I was going to do. And what did *you* do?" My lip curled as I stared her down. "You told who you thought was another guy that you loved him as soon as I left your damn bed."

"No!" she whispered, horrified. "No, that's not true. That's not who the song was about!"

"Bullshit, Charlie!" I roared. The loud boom of my voice made her jump, and tears fell from her eyes.

"I'm telling you the truth!"

I pointed at the phone, and yelled, "Don't forget, I've been present for every fucking conversation."

"The chorus was about you, Deacon! I was going to tell him that I was done tonight once I sent him the rest of the song!"

I sneered a laugh. "Oh bullshit. Again, Charlie, save it. I'm done."

"Is this what you've been waiting for?" She asked to my back, and I heard the bed shift as she got off it and her footsteps as she followed me. "To get me in bed, and then use this as your reason to leave me? Use this as a reason to do what you do best: find someone else to fill your bed?"

I paused, and stared straight ahead as I spoke through gritted teeth. "I've spent the past month and a half doing everything to get you to trust me and see the real me because I wanted you more than I've ever wanted anything, but, yeah, you're right, Charlie. Fucking you then leaving you has been my plan all along." The mocking in my tone was thick and unmistakable.

"You just wanted me because I didn't willingly throw myself at you."

"How'd you know?" I pressed as I slowly turned, and grinned lazily to give her what she so clearly needed to see from me. I ignored the hurt and the anger and the betrayal on her face, and stepped close. "Too bad for you I won't stick around. Maybe you can trick another bastard into getting you pregnant before he smartens up and leaves you too."

I caught her wrist in my hand before her palm could connect with my face, and forced myself to stare into her tear-filled eyes as her chest hitched with a silent sob.

"You're such an asshole," she choked out.

I leaned close until my lips were at her ear, and whispered, "And you're the biggest tease of them all, Charlie Girl."

I released her, and stepped slowly away. My expression remained hard and taunting until I hit the doorway, and then I cracked. I let her see everything I was feeling, everything she'd done to me. Just before I left, I said, "Just in case you're not used to seeing someone else doing it: this is what walking away looks like."

Chapter Nineteen

Charlie

July 22, 2016

I DIDN'T SEE him.

I didn't hear from him.

No one spoke about him.

He didn't come into Mama's.

He was gone, completely removed from our lives in a way that was impressive considering the size of our town and how often I had seen him before all of this had begun.

In his absence I felt a loss unlike anything I'd thought I would feel again.

Not only had I lost the first man I had fallen in love with since Ben, but I'd also lost the only man I'd ever been able to talk to without judgment or reservation.

It made me want to rip my heart back from Deacon's grip. It made me want to hide it away from every man in the world. It made me want to hate him for what he had done to me, for what he had done to my son.

I'd found Keith sobbing in his room after Deacon stormed out of the house two and a half weeks ago, and he'd been quiet and distant ever since. He didn't want to talk superheroes, he didn't want to talk about ladybugs or Darth Vader, he didn't want to talk about anything, really.

I wanted to hate myself . . .

Because if it weren't for both Deacon *and* me, my son wouldn't still be moping like he'd lost his best friend.

I jerked when I felt someone kiss my cheek, and focused my eyes on Grey pulling at the book in my hands.

They'd come over for breakfast, but had only watched me while we ate, waiting for me to tell them something I wouldn't. So I'd cuddled up with Keith on the couch after, and grabbed my book that sat on the coffee table in an attempt to do something other than sit in the uncomfortable silence, but I didn't know how long ago that was.

I'd forgotten they were there.

"You haven't turned the page the entire time you've been sitting here, Charlie. Are you ready to talk yet?"

I released my grip on the book and sighed. "No."

All Jagger or Grey knew was that I'd yelled at Deacon at the LaRues' Fourth of July party, and that he'd left not long after I had.

They didn't know how he'd come over to take care of Keith. They didn't know the beautiful way we'd come together that night, or how we'd fallen apart not long after.

I didn't know how to tell them. I didn't know how to tell anyone when I couldn't even figure out how it had all crumbled beneath my feet.

I had envisioned Stranger as Deacon, but had been positive that they were two separate people. So much so, that it was still so difficult to let myself believe that they were one and the same, even though all the evidence had been thrown in my face that night.

Grey gripped my hand in hers; her eyes darted up behind me to where I could feel Jagger's presence. "We're going to take Keith home with us so you can have today to yourself to do whatever you need to. Sleep, run errands . . ." She drifted off, then hesitantly said, "Go see Dea—"

"Don't," I pled. "Please don't."

Irrational, betraying heart.

She paused for a second, then dipped her head in a nod. "Okay. Call us when you're ready for Keith to come back, or just come pick him up."

I stood with her, and wrapped Keith up in my arms as we all walked toward my front door. I whispered my love for him, then let him follow Grey and Aly out the door, purposefully avoiding Jagger's eyes.

"Why won't you tell us what happened?" he finally asked when he realized I wasn't going to look at him.

"Because there's nothing to tell."

"Charlie . . ." He sighed. "Charlie, we're worried about you. I'm worried about you."

"Why?" My eyes flashed to his. "You got what you wanted."

I turned and walked toward my room without giving Jagger a chance to respond, leaving him standing at my door, knowing he would eventually leave.

I HATE THIS place, I thought to myself two hours later.

I would never understand why Grey and Jagger loved going there. Keith, I knew, was too young to fully understand what that place meant, and I wondered if he would still love going there as the years went on.

But even though Keith wasn't with me, and despite the way seeing them made me feel, I'd brought fresh flowers for Ben because I knew my son would have demanded them.

After I replaced the flowers that Keith and I had brought during our last trip to the cemetery, I sat down in front of Ben's headstone, and just stared at it as if I were staring Ben down himself.

Minutes came and went before I broke the silence in the one-sided stare-down.

"I never figured out why Grey always told me to come talk to you. She thought it would help, I thought it sounded like reopening old wounds. Wounds I didn't want to feel or see or face. But I think I might understand now. Maybe, I don't know . . ." I trailed off, and let my eyes wander around the other graves.

"Or maybe I just know now why it sounded like absolute torture to try before. Because before, I was still waiting for you to come back and love me when you never would. Before, I was upset with you and mad at you, but still hopelessly in love with you. Before . . . before, I was too blind to see that you never deserved me or the way I loved you.

"I messed up, Ben. Dea—he and I were probably doomed from the start. We don't . . . we don't fit, his life and mine." My voice wavered for the first time, and I tried to swallow back the emotions that threatened to come pouring out. "But even if we could have worked, I wouldn't let us. I kept waiting for him to mess up. I kept waiting for him to turn back into the guy I'd grown up with—because the guy I grew up with? That guy would do exactly what *you* did to me."

I clenched my teeth against my trembling jaw, and gritted out, "I have let you ruin so many things in my life. I let you ruin my heart, and let you continue to long after you were gone. I let you ruin any possible relationship I could've had, because all I wanted was you. I let you ruin the best thing that has ever happened to me, or our son, because of what you did to me. I've let you ruin me because I loved you, and you never deserved any of it."

Slowly, I stood from my spot and brushed off my pants as I blinked back tears and cleared my throat. "You're missed. You are *so* missed. Keith looks just like you, and it breaks my heart and fills it all at the same time to look at him and see you. Thank you for him, Ben. A million times, thank you. I will cherish those nights with you for so many reasons, but I hate that I've wasted my life loving someone who never loved me."

I took a few steps back, then paused. "For so many years I've wondered how you could give me everything, only to rip it away just days later when I was so sure you wanted it too. I'm done wondering now. Wondering ruined the short time I had with *him*. I won't let it ruin anything in my life ever again."

Chapter Twenty

———————————————

Deacon

July 31, 2016

I'D SLEEPWALKED THROUGH the past month.

I couldn't remember when I'd worked or when I'd driven. When I'd actually slept in my bed or eaten, or when I'd lain down exactly where I was at that moment. I couldn't remember anything other than Charlie.

I was constantly consumed with thoughts of her.

I wanted to be consumed by her again.

I wanted to go back and take away every conversation with Words so I could have prevented losing Charlie. But at the same time, I'd gotten to know Charlie, and she'd gotten to know me, better than anyone else ever had because of those conversations, so I knew I would never regret them.

I would just always regret losing her; losing Keith.

I stilled when I felt a small body settle in next to mine, and slowly opened my eyes to stare at the ceiling of the living room before looking over at my side.

A huff left me when I saw long, flaming red hair spilling over my chest and shoulder.

"What are you doing?"

"Graham asked me to come since you didn't show up at Sunday brunch again," she responded simply, then flopped one of her arms over my chest to try to hug me as tightly as possible.

I squeezed her forearm. "Thanks, Grey."

"Exactly what you needed?"

"Exactly."

She rolled onto her back again so she was facing the ceiling as well, and let the silence creep between us for a few moments. "Charlie won't talk to us about what happened."

The guys and Harlow said her name constantly, trying to get me to tell them what happened, trying to get me to go back to her and fix it . . . but hearing her name always made me feel as though I'd gotten the wind knocked out of me. I rubbed at my chest and grumbled, "I'm not gonna talk to you about it either. Graham shouldn't have called you."

I'd spent two weeks sleeping above the garage at work before I'd finally came home and had it out with Graham.

He'd been clueless about Stranger and Charlie's

thoughts that it might be him. Not that I'd thought he'd ever known—I'd just been pissed off at the thought of her wanting him. But all of it had been made more apparent when in the middle of our fight, Kate came running out of Graham's room in nothing but his shirt.

Kate, who we'd all gone to school, and grown up, with.

Kate, who none of us had ever touched because she'd wanted nothing to do with guys like us.

Kate, the *mystery girl* Graham had apparently been in love with for years and was now finally dating.

Love . . . that fucking word.

Grey sighed. "Why did I have a feeling you would say something like that? And why are you both being so stubborn? You love each other, go fix—"

"No," I said roughly. "No, I don't."

She twisted so she could look up at me, her face pinched in confusion. "What do you mean you don't? I've seen you with her, Deacon. I've seen the way you talk to her and treat her. I've seen the way you loo—"

"I don't love her, Grey. Simple as that."

Disappointment radiated off of her. "Then why do you look just as bad as she does?"

I shrugged. "I don't know, but she knew. She knew I didn't believe in love."

"And so that's stopping you from being with her? The fact that you think you don't believe in love is what's causing the two of you to look like this for almost a month?"

A sharp, miserable sounding laugh burst from my chest, but I didn't respond.

Grey just nodded, and sat up. "I have something for you."

My eyes narrowed and darted to her, then over to where she was looking. If it weren't for the baby in Jagger's arms, I would have tensed in preparation for the ass-kicking I'd been waiting for all month.

But when Jagger passed Aly off to Grey, I did exactly that. I scrambled up and curled my hands into fists.

I knew I'd said some shitty things to his sister, but she'd broken my fucking heart. I wasn't about to let him get in any free hits.

"Here, Deacon."

I shot a look to Grey, and flinched away from her when I noticed she was holding their baby out to me. "Don't."

"Here, take her," she urged, and took another step closer to me.

I stumbled a couple steps away from Aly and Grey and Jagger, and shot Grey a dark look. "Dude, keep it away. I've been traumatized enough for a lifetime by one baby, and that was over eight years ago."

Grey smiled sweetly, deceivingly, and tried to come closer. "She's just a baby, Deacon."

"Yeah, and it also crawls now. You know what else crawls? Bugs." I twisted away when they got close, flinched when the baby grabbed for my shirt, and then froze when a small voice rang out in the living room.

"Deaton!"

I turned toward his voice, and something in my chest lurched when I saw his messy black hair—and blue eyes just like his mom's.

Forgetting all about the baby and Grey, and Jagger's

murderous stare, I dropped to my knees as Keith ran toward me from Graham's side, and caught him when he launched himself at me.

"Deaton! Deaton! Where was you, I miss you."

Fuck. "I missed you too, kid," I said, my voice thick with emotion. "I missed you, too." I held him away from me so I could look at him, and had to clear my throat before I could ask, "Who are you today?"

Keith's face fell, and his eyes dropped to the floor. "Keith."

If he hadn't looked so upset over that, I wouldn't have pushed. "Not Captain America? I thought you were gonna knock me over just then."

He shook his head stubbornly, then looked at me hesitantly. "You and Mommy was mad and talked mad at each other, and then all the ladybugs came and took my supapowers away forever 'cause you left me. I thoughted you went to the grassy place."

It felt like the ground rocked beneath me. The ache in my chest from missing him grew into something so much more as I tried to put myself in his shoes. I'd spent nearly a month missing them, and he'd spent nearly a month thinking I'd died.

I felt like I'd abandoned him, like I'd failed him.

"Keith, no. I'm here . . ." I trailed off, and my head shook slowly. "I'm here, and they didn't take your superpowers away. You still have them. I didn't leave you." I pulled him close and gripped him tightly when my eyes began burning. "Swear to God I won't leave you, kid. I love you."

Chapter Twenty-One

Charlie

July 31, 2016

I WAS THAT girl.

On the rare occasion that I was in the house by myself, I was that girl who lay on her couch watching sappy love movies and eating chocolate because of a bad breakup.

Except we hadn't technically broken up because we'd never actually been together.

And instead of a sappy love movie, I was watching *Beauty and the Beast*, and still wondering how my life hadn't turned out the way I wanted it to.

And my hands weren't covered in melted chocolate, or holding a spoon that dipped in the tub of ice cream over and over again; they were holding the book I was simultaneously reading.

That. Those two things. I blamed them for why my life was the way it was.

Once upon a time and *happily ever after* . . . words I grew up hearing from Disney and children's stories, and words I'd always believed in. As I grew up and my reading material grew with me, my standards for my Prince Charming morphed, but never lessened. I was so sure I would find my Prince Charming, even if he wasn't as *princely* as I'd dreamed when I was a little girl.

I glanced down to the book in my hands . . .

As I said, my reading material had grown with me.

I'd always thought every event in our lives—major or otherwise—was just another part of our story that made us who we were meant to be for our Prince Charming. I knew my story would never be found forever engraved on the pages of a novel—only woven within the songs in my notebook—but still I waited for my love story to put all other love stories to shame. For my happily ever after . . .

Only to find out that none of it was real.

"He's not really changing for you or falling in love with you, he's lying to you to get what he wants. He just wants the curse to be broken," I mumbled, and looked back at my book. I froze when I realized what I'd just done.

Oh no, I'm also that girl.

The one who tries to stop a fictional character from making a mistake with another, even though there is no mistake to be made. I was trying to stop my favorite

Disney couple from being together. That would be pathetic any day. After almost a month? It was depressing.

At least I wasn't in three-day-old pajamas, and I had still gone to work that day, as I had every scheduled day that month. Because I refused to let Deacon Carver see how he had broken me with his words and when he'd walked away.

Not that he'd seen me, but this town talked.

"That's right, Belle. Run home."

My head snapped up when someone knocked on the door, and I quickly searched for my phone so I could check the time.

Grey and Jagger had taken Keith today instead of having me take him to the babysitter's, but they'd said they had something planned and wouldn't be back for another couple hours.

My arms tingled as goose bumps covered my skin, and my heart steadily beat faster and faster as I slowly stood from the couch and walked toward the door.

No one else ever came over here, and I knew it was stupid to dream it could be him, but I wasn't able to stop it.

Irrational, betraying heart.

I'd spent so much time during the past month agonizing over my heartache, and even more time thinking of where I had gone wrong. How I'd kept expecting Deacon to revert back to his old self. And, most important, how I'd continued a relationship—for lack of better word—with Stranger even though I'd known deep down that it was wrong, once Deacon and I had taken a turn in ours. But no matter how much blame I put on myself for our downfall, Deacon had betrayed me just the same. Because as Deacon had said, he was there for every conversation, as was I . . .

Stranger had known the way to my heart, and had very clearly needed Words the way I'd needed him.

Stranger had told me he didn't know if he'd be able to walk away from me, from our conversations, and I'd known what he was saying was true.

And while Deacon was subconsciously falling in love with me, Stranger had fallen for Words.

Stranger had taught me how to trust someone with my heart by taking the small pieces of it and putting it back together, one conversation at a time. Our conversations and his words left their mark; I would never deny that. But he and I knew that what he was doing was preparing me for someone else. And once my heart had been made whole again . . . I gave it freely to Deacon.

Deacon had told me that he wanted a life with my son and me. He'd made me believe he was giving me his heart in return.

He'd made me believe it was only me for him, when in reality—or depending on how you looked at the situation—I wasn't.

I never had been.

Another knock sounded, and I held my breath as I reached out for the knob.

I opened the door, and the breath I'd been holding rushed out as disappointment flooded me.

Irrational, betraying heart.

"Graham. Hi."

"Hey, how are you?"

"Uh . . ." I had just realized how devastatingly depressed I was a few minutes before, and had foolishly hoped I would open the door to someone else. But Graham was Deacon's best friend, and I couldn't allow him to see my pain. "I'm great. You?"

"Good, good." He looked pointedly at me. "Can I come in?"

"Oh, right." I quickly backed away, and opened the door wider. "I'm sorry."

Graham stepped inside my house, and smirked when he saw what was playing on the TV. After turning around in a circle in the living room, he faced me, and just stared.

"What are you doing here?" I finally asked.

"What, can't I just come visit?" Something in my expression must have answered him for me, since Graham hadn't been to the house since he'd helped me move in. He sucked in a quick breath through his teeth, then released it. "Yeah, all right. Uh, I'm here to get Deacon's phone."

It felt as if my entire body fell through the floor at the mention of his name. It was the first time I'd heard it said out loud since the night he'd walked away. I swayed on my feet before I was able to steady myself, and shook my head to clear it. "You what?"

"Deacon wants his phone," he responded. "He asked me to come get it." At least he had the decency to look embarrassed.

I turned my head slowly toward my bedroom when I heard something come from that direction, but my eyes stayed on Graham as long as they could before dragging to look blankly down the empty hall.

"Hey, and no hard feelings, right?" he said on a rush.

"What?" I breathed, my voice sounded pained.

"About Kate."

I looked back at Graham, my brow drawn together. "Kate? Kate . . . that you grew up with, Kate?" When Graham nodded, I asked, "What about her?"

Graham stuffed his hands in his pockets and lifted his shoulders to his ears. "We're dating now."

I think I looked shocked. I felt it, but I was still reeling from hearing Deacon's name, and the fact that he'd sent Graham to come pick up something he'd left at my house weeks ago.

I hadn't expected Graham to date anyone, ever. Then again, I hadn't expected Deacon to, either. "That's great. Why would there be hard feelings?"

"Well, considering I almost got my ass handed to me because you thought I was some stranger, or something." He placed a hand on his chest, and ignored the way my cheeks reddened. "I'm flattered, Charlie, really. But, I've been waiting for Kate to give me the time of day my entire life. I'm sorry if you wanted me to be some guy on a phone, but—"

"Wait, what? No." I cut him off, and made a face. "Graham, I didn't *want* you to be the guy I was talking to; I just *thought* you were him. Every time I saw you, you ended up saying something that was nearly identical to what Stranger had said."

"Huh, well this is embarrassing." He brought his hands together with a clap. "How about that phone?"

Right. The phone. Deacon's phone, which had randomly gone off with messages over the first week from girls I didn't know who wanted a night with him. I guess he would miss that phone.

I gestured down the hall, and started walking that way. "Yeah, it's in my room."

Graham's mouth suddenly pulled into a wry grin. "Perfect."

I faltered at his look and tone, and said uneasily, "I'll bring it to you."

He held up his hands. "I'll wait here."

I hurried down the hall and into my room, and tried to hold back the angry tears that welled in my eyes as I searched through my nightstand for his phone. The fact that he wanted this phone back, the fact that he had been avoiding me for the better part of a month, the fact that he was gone . . .

It hurt, it made me angry, it made me want to beg him not to be that guy.

I gripped the phone in my hand and pulled it out of the drawer, but had taken only a step away when I noticed my notebook lying open on my bed. The same notebook that was supposed to be inside the drawer I'd just been searching through.

I reached for the notebook, but paused halfway there. My heart skipped, then painfully took off when I saw the page it was on.

It was lists of names of guys I knew in Thatch. Guys

I worked with at Mama's. Guys that I knew for sure had come into Mama's the days the notebook had been passed back and forth between Stranger and me. Guys that could have possibly been Stranger.

Nearly all of them were crossed out. Deacon's included.

Graham's name was circled a few times with question marks following it.

On the very top of the page was a note in a messy scrawl I had memorized, and knew as well as my own. A note that hadn't been there before.

> WORDS . . . I TOLD YOU I DIDN'T KNOW IF
> I'D EVER BE ABLE TO WALK AWAY FROM
> YOU. TURNS OUT I WAS ONLY ABLE TO
> AFTER YOU BROKE MY HEART AND I
> TORE OUT THE PIECES TO LEAVE WITH YOU.
> HARDEST FUCKING THING I'VE EVER DONE.
> SECOND HARDEST WAS STAYING AWAY . . .

A shiver moved slowly down my spine when I heard my bedroom door softly click shut, but I didn't take my eyes off the note when I felt him move toward me.

"You aren't supposed to sweep me off my feet, Stranger," I whispered.

"Third hardest," he began in a low, rumbling voice, and stepped up behind me. "Not being able to stop myself from telling Keith that I love him after seeing him for the first time in four weeks—"

My chest hitched with a silent sob. One of my hands

covered my mouth while the other pressed firmly against the bed to help me stay standing.

"—and realizing that I might not ever get the chance to tell you that I love you."

Deacon's large hands slid around my waist and shoulder to turn me, and my first glimpse of him after all this time made me want to crumble into tears and scream at him and kiss him and apologize and a dozen other things.

"I couldn't figure out why it felt impossible to walk away from those conversations. But it's because it was you. Always you, Charlie. Only you."

All I managed to get out was a weak "Deac—" before my voice gave out, and he pulled me into his arms, his mouth crashed down onto mine.

"We can't. I can't," I said against the kiss, and pressed against his chest.

He pulled back just enough to look into my eyes. Fear swam through his light brown ones as they bounced back and forth, taking in mine. "Don't say that."

"How do we trust each other after this? How do we get past this?"

"One day at a time," he said with all the confidence in the world. "We both fucked up by not walking away from those conversations long ago. I hurt you that night I walked away, I know." He pressed his forehead against mine, and asked, "Charlie Girl, did you give me your heart?"

The tremor in his voice, as if he was afraid of what my answer would be, made my chest ache. "Yes, but—"

"Do you regret it?"

I stared into his eyes for long moments, then slowly

shook my head. No matter how much I wanted to, I couldn't. "You caused so much chaos in my shattered heart for years, and I always shied away from it, and then hated you for it when I moved back. But you—*Stranger*—put my heart back together so I could give it to you. It was always meant to be yours."

His eyes seemed to burn, and his hands moved to curve around the slope of my neck and tilt my head back until our lips brushed. "An hour ago, I was still so sure that I didn't know what love was. That it didn't exist. Then Keith . . . that kid . . ." He trailed off and his chest moved with his silent laugh before the amusement suddenly left his face. Almost absentmindedly, he shook his head. His thumbs brushed along my jaw. "Things can change in just a couple minutes when you think you're losing everything . . . yeah?" he asked, bringing up our conversation from our last night together.

I nodded slowly.

"Funny what suddenly becomes clear in an instant when even half of what you've lost comes running back to you."

I didn't know where he'd seen Keith, but I was thanking God for that reunion.

"We have a lot to get through. We have a lot of trust we have to build back up, but I won't give up until we do. Because I want my days to consist of superheroes and powers, and ladybugs and Darth Vader, even though the last two have nothing to do with Marvel comics."

A muted laugh escaped my lips as I attempted to contain my smile.

He backed me up until my legs hit the bed, and laid me down as he crawled on top of me. "I want my mornings to begin with you in my arms, and my nights to end with me inside you." His mouth brushed against the base of my neck, then my jaw and both of my cheeks. "I can't promise I won't hurt you again. I can't promise I won't fuck up. I can't promise I won't say something wrong. But I promise I'll take care of your heart for the rest of my life, Charlie Girl. You've shown me what it means to love someone, and I swear to Christ I love you."

"I love you too," I choked out past the tightness in my throat.

He dipped his head, but stopped just above my mouth. "Is this the part of the story where the hero kisses the girl?"

A soggy laugh burst from my chest, and I nodded even as I said accusingly, "I thought you weren't a hero."

"Superheroes get the girls too."

His mouth captured mine with the kind of force I'd come to expect and crave from Deacon, and my body melted beneath his when he gently prodded my lips with his tongue.

Always asking, always devouring when I gave.

Always perfect.

Deacon tensed when shouting came from the front of the house, and seconds later, the door to the bedroom burst open.

We barely had time to stop kissing before the sound of light feet met with the scream, "Superman!" and then there was nothing at all.

Crap.

Deacon let out a low *oof*, and I grunted with the weight of Keith landing sideways on top of him.

We both looked over at the cheesy grin lighting up my son's face as he watched us. "Are you pissing Mommy?"

"Oh gosh. Bud, it's *kissing*. He was *kissing* Mommy."

Keith sighed dramatically. "That's what I said!"

Deacon's smile matched Keith's. "I was."

My eyes stopped mid-roll when I realized what had just happened. I pulled in a soft gasp. "Baby, who are you?"

Blue, blue eyes found me, smiling just as much as the rest of his face. "Mommy, don't be silly. I'm Superman!"

My chest felt heavy with every emotion, the most prominent of which was all the love for my little man. "You are?" I asked as I wiggled out from underneath Deacon, my voice thick with my surprise and excitement.

"Who else would I be?" Keith started to ask just before I pulled him into the tightest hug.

"Whoever you want to be," I whispered against his head as I peppered it with kisses.

I glanced up at Deacon as my mouth split into the widest smile. Holding Keith tighter to my chest, I covered his free ear, and whispered to Deacon, "He's only been Keith since you left. Wouldn't even talk about it. Any of it."

Pain and acceptance flashed across Deacon's features. He nodded once, then ran his hands over his face and through his hair. Pinning me with his stare, he mouthed, "I'm so sorry."

"Don't apologize. Can't you see how happy I am?" I released Keith, and said, "Hey, buddy, are Aunt Grey and Uncle J still here?"

Keith nodded enthusiastically. "We brought dinner!"

"Okay, why don't you go back out there, and we'll follow you right out."

Deacon waited until Keith was running away screaming to say, "I never should've walked, Charlie."

"We both shouldn't have done or said what we did." I traced his handsome face, and let the tips of my fingers linger on his lips. "Deacon, I don't want Graham. I've never wanted Graham."

"I know." He nodded toward the door. "I heard you."

That didn't surprise me. As soon as I'd heard him walking up behind me in the room, I'd known he had to have heard everything.

"And the song . . . you have to understand what happened with the song on that last night." I grabbed the notebook where it rested beside me, and flipped quickly to the finished song. "Look at the chorus. Read it." I waited for a few seconds, before I asked, "Do you see it? 'When I *look* at you like that' . . . Deacon, when had I ever knowingly looked at Stranger before I finished the song? The chorus was about you. I was only falling in love with you."

His eyes met mine and flashed with understanding and awe. "Charlie Girl," he murmured, his voice weighed down.

"And that last message . . ." I trailed off and shook my head. "I don't know if you'll ever believe me, but I was going to tell Stranger good-bye that night. I thought he deserved to see the full song. Once he—once *you* responded, I was going to explain the chorus and tell him that I was done. But there was no response, and then you were back in my room."

There was a short hesitation before Deacon sighed. As he spoke, he moved to sit on the bed and pulled me into his arms. "All I saw that night was that you messaged him and I saw the words *heart* and *love*, and I lost it. I didn't even fully grasp the other words; I didn't understand that it didn't fit for someone you'd never seen. But it makes sense now."

My eyes landed on the phone resting forgotten at the foot of my bed. "That phone . . ."

Another long sigh. "I never thought I would hate that I had that phone."

"It went off a lot that first week before it finally died."

Deacon's forehead landed on my shoulder, and for a moment, he didn't speak. "I had it for the girls I slept with. I didn't want them to have my real number. I gave it to Words because I was trying to figure out if she was one of them . . . if she was someone I should stop talking to immediately. Didn't know the number when you messaged me, obviously. Didn't even recognize yours when Grey sent it to me."

"Oh."

"Yeah."

My stomach churned and chest ached, but I tried to push those feelings away. I knew this was from a different Deacon. A lifetime ago.

"After that day I forgot to pick you up from work, I have only used that phone to talk to Words. No one else. Graham knew I was still using it, and he and Knox about lost their minds because they knew I was seeing you. But I didn't tell them about Words until after the Fourth." He nodded in the direction of my door. "Graham's waiting to set the phone on fire."

"I'll help."

Deacon's fingers curled around my jaw to turn my head to face his. He was smiling sadly. "I'm so damn sorry."

"One day at a time?" I asked hesitantly.

"One day at a time," he agreed, and pressed his mouth to mine. "*Only* you, Charlie Girl."

My body warmed with his words and his kiss, but it ended soon after when we heard Keith yelling in the front of the house.

After another lingering kiss, I pushed against his chest. "Come on, let's go destroy this phone and eat with everyone before Keith comes storming in again."

"That's why Jagger tried to keep us apart," he mumbled as he helped me off the bed. When I looked back at him with a confused expression, he clarified, "Graham told him about the phone. Everyone thought I was sleeping around on you."

"Oh." My eyes shut, and I released a slow breath as we walked toward the door leading to the hallway. "That's something else we'll have to deal with later."

"What, your brother?"

I arched a brow when I looked back up into those light brown eyes. "Yeah. He's not going to believe you as easily as I did."

"I don't know about that."

"What do you mean?"

He shrugged. "I told him earlier that I was spending the rest of my life with you and your son."

I faltered, then stopped. "You what? What did he say?"

A mischievous smirk flashed across Deacon's face as he bent to kiss me. "You found me in your room, didn't you? He wouldn't have helped me through the window if he wasn't okay with me marrying you someday."

I stared openmouthed at him for long seconds after he pulled away, and that smirk on his face grew.

"You and your words, Charlie Girl."

Epilogue

Deacon

A year and a half later . . .

"HEY THERE, LITTLE stranger," I whispered, and settled into the recliner next to Charlie Girl's bed. "Looks like it's just you and me now."

Wide, dark eyes stared up at me. Eyelids heavy and blinking slowly.

"Your brother's gonna come see you soon. He's going to give you a superhero name. But don't worry, you have a few years to grow into the name, and we'll keep the ladybugs away from you until then."

"Pink looks good on you, Deac."

My eyes flashed up for only a second, to see Knox and

Harlow standing in the doorway, before I was staring at my daughter again.

"Considering you were still running away from Jagger and Grey's kids just two days ago, I didn't expect to walk in and find you like this," Knox teased as they stepped into the room.

"Shut up, man," I said halfheartedly.

This was different. I didn't know if I was ever going to be able to put her down.

I glanced up at Harlow, and something in my chest pulled uneasily when I noticed her watery eyes.

For her . . . for the people I thought of as my family, I would figure out a way.

It turned out that Harlow wasn't able to have kids from the intense physical abuse that her first husband had put her through, but she and Knox were just waiting for the call from the adoption agency saying that they were chosen for a baby.

Harlow always acted as if it didn't affect her, but we all knew differently. And when Graham's fiancée found out she was pregnant just after Grey had her second baby, followed quickly by Charlie, it wasn't hard to miss the pain that Harlow tried to hide.

"You want to hold her?"

The tears that had been filling Harlow's eyes immediately fell down her cheeks, and her jaw trembled as she nodded. "Please."

I reluctantly let my world go, and met Knox's thankful look.

Today was already emotional enough. I'd cried as soon

as they'd put my daughter in my arms. I didn't need to cry watching my warrior break down, or one of my best friends looking like he was on the verge of joining her.

I cleared my throat, and asked, "Kate?"

Knox swallowed thickly, and shrugged. "Caught Jagger and Grey headed over to the room. We were going to head over there next."

"Do you know what time she had him?"

He laughed softly, trying not to wake Charlie. "No, man. But I got the money ready."

"You're all ridiculous," Charlie murmured, and I looked quickly over at my wife to see her cracking her eyes at us. She sent me a mock glare, then looked to Harlow and Knox. "He was asking if I could hold off on pushing."

Knox laughed.

Harlow gave me a less-than-amused look through her tears. "Deacon."

"What?" I smiled wryly at Charlie, and wrapped my hand around one of hers. "I thought we'd had it in the bag. I didn't expect you to go into labor while we were waiting for Kate to have her baby."

"Terrible," Charlie murmured.

"Not my fault. He's the one who made the bet."

"And I'm coming to collect!" Graham said breathlessly. "I have about five seconds before I need to run back to our room. Time," he demanded.

Charlie answered him before I could. "Two fifty-four P.M."

"Damn it!" Graham groaned, and let his head fall back. "Couldn't you have pushed faster?"

Knox dug into his pocket and pulled out two wads of cash. "Two thousand to—"

I started to refuse Graham's half, my head already shaking, but Charlie and Harlow suddenly hissed, "Two thousand!"

Charlie glared at me. "You bet two thousand dollars?"

"I bet a thousand. And, technically, it was before we started dating." Her glare deepened. "I'm not gonna take his money, Charlie Girl. I'm just taking my half back."

"I would've taken all of it," Graham said unapologetically.

I snatched my half from Knox, and pointed it at Graham. "Exactly why I wanted my baby to come after yours."

Graham grinned like a bastard and stepped over to Charlie to kiss her head, then did the same to Harlow. "Charlie. Warrior." He peered over Harlow's shoulder at my daughter, and whispered, "Hi, sort-of niece. I'm gonna come back later with your sort-of cousin so you can meet him and I can hold you." He smiled at Charlie again, and said, "She's gorgeous." With the wadded-up money, he pointed at me. "Deac . . . *dad* looks good on you."

It was my turn to grin like a bastard. "You too. Then again, it's looked good on me for about a year and a half now." I slipped my money into my pocket, and shrugged when Graham's face fell as he finally realized his mistake. "Not my fault you didn't think to apply the bet to kids already born."

Graham laughed humorlessly. "Again . . . damn it."

The girls shared a look and rolled their eyes before Harlow went back to cooing at my new girl.

"So now that she's here, what'd you name her?" Knox asked as he stood behind Harlow, looking down at the baby.

I looked at Charlie, and she smiled through her exhaustion. "It wasn't my idea," she finally said when I didn't volunteer anything.

"Charlie Girl, you can't break the tradition."

"That my mom started," she argued gently.

It was an argument we'd had a hundred times. She hadn't won, obviously.

"This is Brianna," she told them with a soft smile. "Named after Brian Jones, one of the original members of the Rolling Stones."

"Hate to say it," Harlow began, "but I agree with Deacon. No way you could've broken that tradition. She'll fit in perfectly."

"Dad!"

My smirk grew into an unrestrained smile when I looked at Grey standing in the doorway with Keith. I stood to go to them, and tuned out Harlow and Knox saying their good-byes as he smashed into my legs. "Hey, bud."

"My parents just got here with him and Aly," Grey said quietly. "Are you ready for him?"

"Oh yeah." I pressed a hard kiss to her head, then nodded toward the hall. "Go back to Graham and Kate. I'll make my way there later." Once Grey was walking away, I took Keith over to the sink so he could wash his hands, and reminded him softly about being gentle and quiet with his new sister.

Things we'd been going over for months, and things I was sure I would be going over again in about a minute. He was shaking, he was so excited.

"All right, you ready to meet her?"

"Dad! Come on! Let's go!"

I smiled at Knox and Harlow as they slipped out of the door, and then just stood there, frozen as I watched my wife holding our new daughter, singing softly to her.

I didn't need to be able to hear the words to know what she was singing, because it was a song I knew well. It was ours.

There were those damn emotions again.

And there was that word. Love.

Yeah . . . used it all the time now.

I cleared my throat and kept my hands on Keith's shoulders to keep him from jumping onto the bed like I knew he wanted to as we walked closer, and then I helped him climb up next to Charlie and Brianna.

"Hi, Storm!" Keith whispered as he leaned over to get a look at his new sister.

My brow pinched, and I looked up at Charlie just in time to see her force back a laugh.

"Storm? Is that who she is?" I asked as I sat down by Charlie's feet.

Keith looked like he was studying Brianna really hard for a minute, then he nodded. "Yeah, don't you think so?" Without waiting for my reply, he dove right into a hushed, one-sided conversation about ladybugs and how they could steal your powers from you if you weren't careful. "But I know how to keep them away," he whispered, as if he were telling her a secret.

"I was wrong," I said low enough that I wouldn't interrupt Keith, and looked into Charlie's eyes as she let her soft voice trail off. "I would lose sleep for the rest of my life to listen to *this*. To look at *this*. The three of you together. Our son talking to our daughter. You singing our song. All of it."

Charlie's face softened; her head shook slowly as her mouth curved up into a smile. "There you go sweeping me off my feet again, Stranger."

LISTEN TO CHARLIE & Deacon's song—"With My Eyes Closed," by Chelsea Stepp—on my website: http://www.mollysmcadams.com/show-me-how

Check out Chelsea's website: http://www.chelseastepp.com

Acknowledgments

THE BIGGEST THANK-YOU to **Chelsea Stepp** for allowing me to use her lyrics! I love her, and I absolutely *love* this song. As if that wasn't already obvious. Go check her out on iTunes, Spotify, or Google Play!

As always, thank you to my **husband** for helping me with so many things while I dive into my characters' lives. I love you so, so much!

Amy, thank you for being there every step of the way for this story! I honestly don't know if I wouldn't have been able to finish it if it weren't for you. Love you!

My Sef, thank you for always being there for me through everything, and thank you for not only introducing me to Chelsea Stepp, but for the amazing conversation that led to so many great things in this story! I love you!

Kevan, thank you for everything you do for me! You're such a rock star, I don't know what I would do without you.

Tessa, I just adore you. But I'm pretty sure after nearly four years you know that by now. A huge thank you for helping me trash that one story we do not speak of so that this one was possible!

Don't miss Molly's next novel!

I SEE YOU

Coming November 2016!
Read on for a sneak peek . . .

Part I

That Night . . .

MY EYES FOUND his again, as they had often in the two hours I had been here, and I curled my fingers against the back of his neck. Urging, pleading for him to take me away from the crowd of people. Somewhere I could study him and listen to him speak, and not worry about what his touches and teasing mouth were about to make me do.

His full lips made a pass across the line of my jaw until they were at my ear, and his arms tightened around me as he said, "Let's go."

Turning me so he could pull me close to his side, he led us through the packed house and up two flights of stairs. His eyes kept darting down to mine as we walked, but he didn't say a word as we made our way to a locked door and he took out a key. I hadn't taken him for a frat guy, but I wasn't going to question him.

Because I didn't want to know. I wanted tonight with him . . . I didn't want his life.

Or, at least, that was what I was trying to remind myself.

The energy and awareness that swirled between us made it hard to remember what this night was for. Made it hard to remember that it could only be *one* night.

I'd seen him immediately upon entering the house earlier with three of my closest friends. We came up to Duke because we'd heard about this house's parties, and we were looking for a night to be the girls we usually weren't before our senior years began.

For one night, we didn't want to be the good girls everyone knew us to be. For one night, we wanted to let loose, and not have to worry about the consequences tomorrow. Everything we'd avoided the past three years, which was why a party at Duke was so perfect. And I'd found the guy I wanted to remember for years to come.

His presence had filled the room packed with people even though he'd been in the far corner when we walked in, watching the crowd silently by himself. He didn't seem to be looking for anyone—just watching. Studying. Everything about him screamed trouble. The way he stood: tall with hard, lean muscles, and sure of himself. The look on his face, a calm so unnerving, it was like the calm before the storm. All of it paired with dark, sinful eyes that kept finding me until I finally found myself pressed close to him as we danced to the music that poured through the house.

A gasp tore from my chest when we entered the room and the guy quickly pushed me up against the now-closed door. But all coherent thoughts left me when my back settled against the door and I looked up into dark eyes.

He placed his hands on either side of my head and leaned forward until his mouth was at my ear. "Tell me what you want."

My lips parted with a quick exhale even though I tried to keep my composure. But his voice . . . his voice. It fit. The image, the eyes . . . it all fit. Now that we weren't in the middle of a sea of loud people and music that made it nearly impossible to hear anything, I could appreciate the sound of it. It was deep and hoarse. And in those few words, I knew that the sound of his voice would haunt my mind for years to come.

1

One Year Ago

Aurora

"RORIE!" TAYLOR YELLED over the loud music pulsing through the house—the sound still unable to mask the whine in my best friend's tone. "I'm starving and we've been looking for this mystery guy forever. This would have been so much easier if we'd known who to ask for."

My stomach instantly morphed into a tornado of fluttering wings. I didn't know his real name. God, I didn't even know his name, and that didn't bother me. That made the memory of him more intense—it made my heart beat harder and caused me to feel dizzy for a second as I replayed every second with him.

His lips on my skin. His husky voice in my ear. His intoxicating cologne clouding my mind. His strong hands learning every inch of me, branding me.

My face fell. Not knowing his name *hadn't* bothered me until this afternoon, when I'd decided that I needed to see him again. I hadn't gone more than a few minutes all week without thinking about him, and that had made my decision to come back up to Durham to try to find him. But all I had were memories and an alias.

He let out a long breath and his eyes drifted to the side. "Jay." *After a moment's hesitation, those dark pools of obsidian found me again.* "Just remember me as Jay."

I had known then that it was a random name to appease me, but hadn't cared. Because I had kind of done the same, and it fit to give each other aliases on a night where we both knew I was trying to be someone I normally wasn't.

"I told you not to come!" I yelled over the music, but Taylor was already turning to raid the table we were near.

I looked around us, hoping to get a glimpse of the only reason we were here. We'd already been here for two hours, and there'd been no sign of him yet. My chest had tightened a few times when I saw closely shaved heads—like the one I'd run the tips of my fingers over—but then the guy would turn and my heart would sink.

An excessively large Jolly Rancher was shoved directly in front of my face, less than an inch from the bridge of my nose, and my eyes crossed as I looked it over before glancing to where Taylor was glaring at me and sucking on her own piece of candy.

"Where did you get that?"

She pointed at the table behind her that was littered with liquors and cups and candies, and mouthed the word *starving*, but didn't attempt to actually respond over the music.

I forced myself not to roll my eyes as I made one more quick sweep of the area around us, then sighed in defeat as I grabbed the candy. I unwrapped the Jolly Rancher and popped it in my mouth, and turned just as someone barreled into me from behind.

I gasped at the force of the hit, causing the large candy to fly backward and lodge in my throat. Panic instantly set in when I couldn't get it to move.

"Ror—oh my God! She's choking!" Taylor screamed, and her hands fluttered all around me.

I was immediately grabbed from behind, and large, hairy arms crossed over my chest seconds before I was heaved into the air over and over again.

"That's not how you do it! What are you doing?" Taylor screamed, and started punching the guy doing some unknown form of the Heimlich maneuver on me as one of my stilettos flew off my foot.

Taylor's screaming, the partygoers' shocked and worried faces, and my inability to pull in air was taking my panic to another level. I tried to slap the man holding me, but my arms were pinned down to my sides.

Just as the edges of my vision started darkening, my feet hit the ground once again on the guy's downward drive, and the candy went shooting out onto the hardwood floor.

I started gasping wildly, but no one seemed to notice.

"You're going to kill her, you idiot, stop it! Stop!" Taylor continued to scream, her hands still hitting the massive man holding me.

"Stop," I whispered hoarsely. "Stop! *Stop!*"

"It's out, man, stop!" a deep voice yelled from somewhere in front of me.

"Stop!" I yelled one last time as my legs hit the floor. Before I knew it, I was going up in the air again, and my second shoe went flying off.

"Rorie!" Taylor screamed as the guy behind me finally set me down, and forced me to lay on the floor. "Rorie, talk to me!"

I looked over at Taylor to find huge tears streaming down her face. "I'm okay!" I assured her, my voice still rough from having the Jolly Rancher lodged in my throat.

"Girl! Girl, are you okay?"

I jerked against the floor at the booming voice as a massive, mostly naked guy entered my vision. Tighty-whiteys, shoes, and a football helmet. Nothing else.

I nodded, unable to say anything as I tried to get the image of him out of my head even though he was still standing right there.

"I saved your life!" He stood up and lifted his arms in victory, and I covered my face to block things I didn't want to see. "I just saved her life!"

There were loud cheers throughout the house, and the music turned on suddenly, making me jump again. I wasn't sure when they'd turned it off, but knowing that my choking on unusually large candy had stopped a party had my panic subsiding and my mortification kicking in.

"You scared the shit out of me," Taylor sobbed.

"Excuse me, Cinderella?" a deep voice called next to my ear.

Cinderella? I removed my hand from my face to look at the guy who belonged to that voice, then quickly pushed myself up onto my elbows when I took in his face, so close to mine.

My cheeks burned with embarrassed heat, but I didn't know how to look away from him. Despite a large red mark on his forehead, his face was flawless and masculine, with a strong brow and nose, a smirk I knew would've made my knees weak had I been standing, and a lethal stare from green eyes so clear it was as if I could see through the iris.

My gaze had become so fixated on the way his lips moved that it took a few seconds too long to realize he'd said something. "I'm sorry, what?"

The smirk broadened for a brief moment, giving me a glimpse of straight, white teeth. He leaned over me until his lips were at my ear, and if I'd had the capability to breathe around him, I would've stopped then. "I said I think you lost this," he drawled, and I swooned.

Literally . . . *swooned.* As in: all the air left my body in one hard rush, I was unable to keep myself up on my elbows any longer, my head felt light and dizzy, the room spun, and I was pretty sure I'd just entered a romance novel. It really didn't matter that it was from the lingering effects of nearly choking to death, and then unknowingly holding my breath for too long.

"Whoa." He quickly put a hand under my head before it could smack on the hardwood floor.

"I'm fine," I said breathlessly, and internally berated myself for doing everything imaginable to look like an idiot tonight. I tried to sit up, but the guy was still hovering over me, making it impossible to go farther than I'd been.

"Are you sure you're okay?"

"Yes," I promised, and blew out a steadying breath when he sat back.

"Good. I can't have you passing out on me, Cinderella."

"Cin—" My head shook firmly as I corrected him. "No, my name is Rorie."

With another slow smirk, he gestured to the red mark on his forehead for barely a second, then reached behind him and produced my stiletto.

My embarrassment from earlier couldn't compare to the level it was at then as I put it all together. My shoe had flown into his face.

"Oh my God," I whispered so low, the words drifted away with the bass of the music. "I'm so sorry."

He laughed easily, as if he hadn't just taken a five-inch stiletto to the face, and glanced from my shoe to me. "My name is Declan," he provided. "I already know this shoe belongs to you. What I want to know now, *Cinderella,* is if I give this back to you, are you going to run away from me?"

Despite my humiliation, my lips spread into a smile as the name finally made sense. I reached for the shoe, but Declan held it away from me. His expression showed he was still waiting for an answer. With a raised eyebrow, I said, "I lost both shoes. I don't care what Disney said, a girl can't run away very easily with only one shoe."

His smirk stretched to match my smile, and he dipped his head close. "Then I'm keeping the other one that hit the back of my head."

2

Aurora

I RELEASED A heavy breath and a wide smile broke free as I took in the sight before me. This was it, what we'd been planning and waiting for . . . we were finally going to be together. Not that thirty minutes away could ever be considered long-distance; but with how crazy both our senior years had been, Declan and I hadn't gotten nearly enough time together in the ten months that we'd been dating. And the time we had spent together had often been filled with other friends or studying. Now? Now it was just us. We'd both graduated a month ago, had debated on where we wanted to live, and then searched for the perfect apartment.

Apartment: *found*. Move everything in: *just finished*. Live out my happy ever after with boyfriend . . .

"Welcome home," Declan murmured into my ear as he wrapped his arms around me and pulled me against his chest.

. . . definitely working on it.

"Mmm, I like the sound of that." I felt my body loosen, and my head rolled to the side when his lips moved in a line down the side of my neck. "I need a bath," I said halfheartedly as one of his hands moved under my shirt. "That was code for I'm sweaty and gross."

Declan moved out from behind me and pushed me up against one of the living room walls. "I really don't care," his deep voice rumbled before he captured my lips with his.

His fingers found the hem of my shirt and pulled up, forcing us to break apart for the split second that it took to get the shirt over my head, then his mouth resumed moving against mine.

My breaths came out in short bursts as he moved down my throat and over my chest, his hands gripping and sliding over my hips and bottom as he slowly pushed my yoga pants and underwear down to my thighs. His teeth raked across my nipple over my sports bra, eliciting a gasp that was quickly followed by a low moan when he suddenly pulled up the bra and returned to what he had just been doing as his hand slid between my thighs.

I tore the sports bra off the rest of the way and dropped

it to the floor near my shirt as I reached for him. Before I could get to his clothes, he slid his hands back down my thighs and lifted me up. I wrapped my legs around his waist and fused my mouth to his as he walked us down the hall and into the bedroom.

Declan tossed me onto the bed, and was already shrugging out of his shirt by the time I sat back up and reached for him. Grasping the waistband of his athletic shorts, I pulled him onto the bed with me as I lay back, and smiled playfully at the growl that built up in his chest when I grabbed his length.

I'd barely gotten his shorts off before he was pulling my yoga pants and underwear the rest of the way off and climbing back on top of me. His hands ran up my legs and stomach, then continued to my breasts for a teasing moment before they were gone and he was spreading my thighs.

His name was barely more than a whimper as his fingers teased me and his mouth focused on each breast. I ran my hands over his head and secured my fingers in his hair, my body restless as his lips slowly moved from my chest, down my stomach. My eyes fluttered shut when I felt his hot breath against me; a shaky moan climbed up my throat when he leaned forward to taste me.

Within minutes my body felt like it was suspended in air as he relentlessly teased and licked me. Heat pooled low in my stomach, every muscle tensed in preparation of what I knew I was only seconds from.

"I'm—" I cut off when an image flashed through my mind, too real to ignore for the second it was there. But just as quickly it was gone, and suddenly Declan was kneeling between my thighs and pushing inside me, and pushing me over the edge. "Oh God! Dec!"

My toes curled and body trembled as Declan moved roughly and quickly inside me. Another moan tumbled from my lips.

"Declan Veil, I suggest you get out here this instant!" a very distinct, very frustrated, feminine voice called out from the front of the apartment.

Declan slapped his hand over my mouth to quiet the moan, and we froze in horror for all of two seconds before we scrambled away from each other.

"Crap!" I hissed, and searched the floor for my pants after I got my underwear on. "Crap!"

"Declan!" she called out again.

"Yeah, hold on!" Declan yelled back quickly as he pulled on his shorts. His expression showed every bit of his frustration.

"What is your mother doing here?" I whispered harshly, and covered my bare chest as I looked around for my shirt.

"I gave her a key . . . for emergencies." Declan said the last two words loud enough that I knew his mom could hear. His shirt hit my arms, and I hurried to catch it before it dropped to the floor. "Just put it on; she'll come in here if we don't go out there."

I put the shirt on as we rushed out of our room, and didn't realize it was inside out and backward until we were in the hall. Heat flooded my cheeks, and I wanted to crawl into a corner and die when we walked into the living room, and saw Declan's mom, Linda, holding my shirt and sports bra. Folded.

"I believe you lost this," she said in her thick drawl. Her wide eyes glanced to Declan, and then she pointed to his shirt on my body. "And I believe *you* lost that, son."

"Mom," Declan said in greeting from where he stood a few feet away from her. "I wasn't expecting to see you today . . . also wasn't expecting you to just walk in."

"Now, is that any way to talk to the woman who spent thirty-seven hours birthing you?" Linda took in a steadying breath as her eyes bounced between the two of us. "I wanted to see what you did with your new place, as any mother would. So why doesn't someone get me a glass of sweet tea before you start showin' me around, and we're gonna pretend like the last few minutes didn't happen." But I could tell from the narrowing of her eyes that she wouldn't forget about what she'd walked in on, what she'd heard—just as we wouldn't.

"I'll get it," I murmured, and hurried into the kitchen to start brewing the tea.

I let loose a shaky breath once I was standing at the counter with my back to both of them, and thanked God for those few minutes to gather myself and clear my mind without Declan or Linda watching me.

Emotions flooded me, threatening to overwhelm me and making it nearly impossible to keep them from my face.

The humiliation of Linda hearing something she shouldn't have was nothing. Nothing compared to the betrayal that sat low and heavy, and burned white hot in my chest. Because for a second while Declan had devoured me, it had been there. . . .

The feel of buzzed hair beneath my fingertips.

Eyes so dark they looked black.

A wicked smirk.

Hard and soft.

Ten months after only one night with him, and *he* still managed to invade my mind. My hands shook as I pulled down a few glasses that I'd unpacked not long before, and guilt ate at me as I forced all thoughts of him away.

Present Day

"Rorie!"

I jerked away from the fingers snapping in my face and looked at my best friend. "Yeah?"

"You just completely zoned out . . . *again*." Taylor's tone was full of worry, and I hated hearing it. "Do you want to call it for today?"

I looked around at the mass amounts of construction paper, paint, glitter, and letter and number cutouts piled around the living room, and tried to bring myself out of the past and back to the present of prepping for my new kindergarten class. "No, no. Sorry, I must have been daydreaming."

"Or just dreaming," she countered teasingly.

"*Not.* Anyway, thank you for helping me with this. I'm so behind in getting everything ready for my class. I still can't believe school is starting a week from tomorrow."

She waved off my thanks. "That's what best friends are for. Besides, your life is just . . . it's just chaotic right now with everything, and Declan's mom . . ." She trailed off at the mention of Linda, and I groaned. "I'm surprised you have time for anything that doesn't include trying to stay sane."

My mouth curved up in a smile. "That's why I have books. I don't have to try to stay sane; they keep me that way."

Taylor straightened and pointed around the living room of my apartment. "Oh sweet girl, bless your heart," she drawled, imitating Linda. "You just can't go around decorating with your books instead of putting them on shelves."

I huffed a soft laugh and stopped working on the sign to defend myself. "I didn't have money for the shelves I wanted, and I liked the way they looked!"

"Oh sweet girl," Taylor continued, and then dropped her voice down to a whisper. "Did you know that this furniture doesn't match? Maybe you should let me pick out some new furniture for the apartment."

That time I laughed louder. Linda had always been exceedingly opinionated, whether it was about how much time Declan and I spent together, how fast we moved in with each other, the way I decorated, or the way I dressed . . . she had something to say about it. But that was just how Linda was. She had too many opinions about everyone's lives, and she had no problem saying them.

It had become irritating extremely fast, made more so because of the fact that I took every opinion to heart and usually sided with her since I had wanted my boyfriend's mother to like me.

"Only you, Taylor," I said with a laugh. "Only you could make me laugh right now."

"I'll never stop making you laugh. Speaking of Lovely Linda, don't you have—"

A timer went off in the kitchen, and I whipped my head around to look in that direction.

"—family dinner soon?" Taylor finished, and pointed toward the kitchen. "Good thing you remembered that."

"Oh crap!" I dropped the brush I was holding and scrambled to find my phone. "Crap, crap, crap. Linda's going to kill me," I said as I hurried to get up and ran to the kitchen. "Just leave it all here, I'll work on it when I get back."

"Why is she going to kill you? You remembered to bake her . . ." She trailed off, and eventually gave up trying to remember the name of the dish. "Whatever thing."

"Yes, but I'm covered in glitter and paint, and I don't have time to shower."

Like it was nothing at all, like this wasn't a family dinner and this wasn't *Linda* we were talking about, Taylor said, "Just tell her you were working a pole or something. I'm sure she'll understand."

My face fell as I stared at her from across the rooms. "When you say things like that, it makes me question why we're best friends."

"Don't hate me because you don't share my genius way of thinking." She shouldered her bag as she headed toward the front door. "Call me if you aren't hanging out with Declan and need help this week."

"Love you."

"Back!" she called out just before she left.

THIRTY MINUTES LATER I was walking through the doorway into the kitchen to meet up with Declan and his family, and my hands were shaking from holding the dessert that I had made so tightly.

My parents and I had always been casual, not superclose, but not distant, either. We were just . . . there. Declan's family was always in each other's lives and had Sunday night family dinners—something that was important to Declan, so it was important to me. Which had been the huge deciding factor in living here instead of Raleigh.

The family dinners, for the most part, had always gone as expected. With Linda in the kitchen for hours upon hours, cooking enough to feed an army . . .

This time, however, was different.

Because this time I had a dessert. A dessert Linda had given me the recipe for. A dessert that I'd made three days in a row before today, trying to perfect it.

She'd handed me the recipe when she'd randomly stopped by earlier that week, and said, "It's time you start learning how to take care of my son. This is an old family recipe, and is very important to the Veil family. If you want to be a part of that family, you best learn how to make this. I'll be expecting it on Sunday."

I'd learned.

And now I was guarding it as if it were the most precious thing in the world. As if the dish in my hands were worth millions of dollars, and if I dropped it my world would end. And with Linda expecting the dessert, it just might.

I accepted a hug from Declan's two older sisters, Holly and Lara, smiled at their husbands as they helped Linda set the food out in the massive kitchen, and murmured a quick hello when Declan's dad kissed my cheek on his way out of the kitchen to answer his phone.

"Where can I put this, Linda?" I asked as I checked the full counters.

Linda looked at my dessert-filled hands and raised an eyebrow. "Well, what is it, darling girl?"

"It's . . . it's the white chocolate bread pudding."

"Is that what that awful smell is?" she said with a laugh, and looked over at her daughters and their husbands. They didn't laugh with her. Her wide eyes fell to the dish in my hands again, and she sighed dramatically. "Well, just set it anywhere. Let's see it."

I swallowed past the thickness in my throat, and looked around for a moment before finding a space to set it down. I didn't breathe as she lifted the lid and eyed the dessert like it was going to jump out and eat her.

"Good God," she drawled, then walked away to grab a spoon. When she came back, she moved the spoon through the dessert as if she were dissecting it, and then finally took a bite. After a moment she made a gagging sound and hurried to a trash can.

My jaw was locked tight by the time she'd spit it out.

I'd never been an angry person, but Linda had been

pulling it out of me as she'd slowly shown me over the last weeks what it was like to truly despise someone . . . as she'd gone from my boyfriend's too-opinionated mom, to the woman who loathed me with every fiber of her being.

The thought of her stressed me out until I had a headache. Talking about her frustrated me to no end, and usually left me shaking. Being in her presence had me in a constant state of fake smiles, clenched teeth, and hot blood pounding through my veins.

I hated who she was turning me into, and I wanted to hate her. Instead I felt sorry for all the reasons that led to her feeling like she needed to do this to me.

"Rorie, what are we going to do with you? Bless your heart, you don't even know how to bake. Sweet girl, that looked alien." Linda tossed the used spoon on the counter and walked over to grab a casserole dish from the other side of the kitchen. "Well, it's a good thing I was prepared." She placed hers beside mine, and opened it with a wide smile directed at me, and then the other people in the kitchen.

Of course she had made the dessert, too. *Of course.* Because it couldn't be that easy with Linda, to just do what she asked. No, I had to go through some form of embarrassment or harassment first. I felt stupid for even trying, and wanted to go scream and vent to Declan. Instead, I simply nodded as I looked at the nearly identical dishes. The only difference was mine had taken a spoon to it.

"We'll just put this poor thing out of its misery," she mumbled as she grabbed my dish and walked over to the trash. "You know, Madeline can whip up an amazing bread pudding."

I rolled my eyes at the mention of Declan's beloved ex-girlfriend.

I'd heard her name in passing over the months when Declan and I first started dating, but I now couldn't go a day without being reminded about how perfect Linda thought she was.

"Mom," Holly, Declan's oldest sister, began. Her tone was full of frustration, but she didn't finish as we all watched the dessert slide out of the dish and into the trash.

Declan's dad, Kurt, walked back in then. "What are we all standing around for? Let's eat, I'm starved!"

In what looked like an accident, but I knew wasn't, Linda dropped the dish into the trash on top of the dessert, and clapped her hands as she stepped away. "Yes, let's! Food is ready and getting cold. Everyone grab a plate."

I glanced up and caught Declan's sisters watching me. Both wore matching worried expressions, and Holly mouthed that she was sorry. I smiled at them and tried to shake off the horrible feeling Linda always left me with.

Once everyone was serving themselves, I looked over at Declan's plate sitting there untouched. I wondered if I was thankful or upset that he hadn't been there to witness his mom's hatefulness before my thoughts drifted.

Where are you, Dec?

About the Author

MOLLY McADAMS grew up in California but now lives in the oh-so-amazing state of Texas with her husband, daughter, and fur babies. Her hobbies include hiking, snowboarding, traveling, and long walks on the beach . . . which roughly translates to being a homebody with her hubby and dishing out movie quotes.

Discover great authors, exclusive offers, and more at hc.com.